Alligators, Outlaws, & Tourists!

With a section of old photographs and short historical essays at the end, "The River Way Home" is full of action, humor, and conflicts that remain contemporary today. It's a classic tale of friendship and coming-of-age that will take you back to your childhood favorites.

Praise for "The River Way Home"

"An adventure of epic proportions sure to ignite the imaginations of readers old or young!" —Tometenderblogspot.com

"A remarkably well-told tale that brings the past to life. The characters are incredibly real and it is easy to join in their joys, sorrows, fear, and excitement ... so much more than just a simple tale." —Readersfavorite.com

"...reminiscent of similar adventures to please either gender---like Tom Sawyer, Huck Finn and the Ingalls Family. Rich in geographical detail, this well written and educational adventure is a great summer read for middle grades and older." — Book Preview Review

"For YA or anybody who likes an adventure. READ THIS BOOK. Great summer read, great characters and setting. Enjoyed it so!" — Lisa King

"... a nostalgic novel with an environmental message that illuminates the book without distracting in any way from the fun." — Blogcritics.org

"The ending arrives much too quickly." —Garywstout.com

The River Way Home

The Adventures of the Cowboy, the Indian,
& the Amazon Queen

Mary E. Dawson

AQ Press
Palm City, FL 34990
AQPress@comcast.net

Credits:
Cover background photos by Tom Claud
Dawson photo by Lynn Kreps, Avenue Entertainment, Stuart, FL
Cover design by Mary E. Dawson

ISBN-13: 978-0-9915184-1-8

Acknowledgements

This book would have been impossible without the people before me who recognized the unique history and character of Florida's last frontier and dedicated their time and talent to preserve its images and stories and share them with us.

For information and photos portraying Tantie and the early history of Okeechobee City, I relied heavily on *Tommy Markham's Genealogical & History Home Page*, maintained by Thomas A. Markham at www.TommyMarkham.com. For a firsthand account of Lake Okeechobee and its cat-fishing and boating industries, I discovered to my delight Lawrence E. Will's *Cracker History of Okeechobee* (1977) and *Okeechobee Catfishing* (1990).

For the written and pictorial history of eastern Martin County, I owe my deepest gratitude and admiration to that area's preeminent historian, Sandra Henderson Thurlow, especially her book *Stuart on the St. Lucie: A Pictorial History* (2001). Thanks also to Dr. W. Jay Thompson for sharing his insight into Stuart's historic African-American Community.

Special thanks to Tom Claud for having the unique vision and skill to capture the essential beauty of the Florida landscape on film and the generosity to let me use his photos for the covers of this book.

I also thank all the others who helped me develop the skills and courage required to complete and publish this story, especially Carol Anderson, Gayle Swift, Walter and Leona Bodie, Glenn Gardiner, and other members of the Palm City Word Weavers, a chapter of the Florida Writer's Association.

And then there's Kim Anaston-Karas who listened night after night as Queenie revealed herself and came to life in our imaginations.

To my own blue-eyed boy whose story was far too short.

To Abiaka who refused to surrender.

And to Martin County, where the voices of Florida's last

frontier still sing in the moonlight.

Table of Contents

Author's Note

With the exception of the outlaw, John Ashley, his henchman Kid Lowe, and Anna, the Seminole woman with the twin tame hogs, the characters in this tale are entirely fictional. However, people very much like them did live on the Florida frontier at the time—and some still do today, a hundred years later. Their true stories inspire this tale.

Every place described in this book existed in 1914. Some have since been destroyed, and others have changed so much they are hard to recognize. But a few remain very much the same today. You just need to know where to look for them.

Everything that happens in this story could have happened or did happen to someone. On a good day, some could still happen to you.

"There is no more Punta Rassa as you knew it," Toby Cypress said, his eyes reflecting sadness. *"It is all gone, Sol, just as Lake Okeechobee as we once knew it is gone, and the custard-apple forest is gone, and the bald cypress trees are gone. You are trying to capture the fog, and no one can do that..."*

Patrick D. Smith
A Land Remembered (1984)

"The land I was upon I loved, my body is made of its sands; the Great Spirit gave me legs to walk over it; hands to aid myself; eyes to see its ponds, rivers, forests, and game; then a head with which I think. The sun, which is warm and bright as my feelings are now, shines to warm us and bring forth our crops, and the moon brings back the spirits of our warriors, our fathers, wives, and children...

"The white men are as thick as the leaves in the hammock; they come upon us thicker every year. They may shoot us, drive our women and children night and day; they may chain our hands and feet, but the red man's heart will be always free...

"I am done; when we know each other's faces better I will say more.[1]

Coacoochee, a Seminole warrior, on the
banks of the Indian River in 1841

[1] Excerpted from *The Origin, Progress, and Conclusion of the Florida War* by John Titcomb Sprague, published by Appleton & Co., Philadelphia, in 1847.

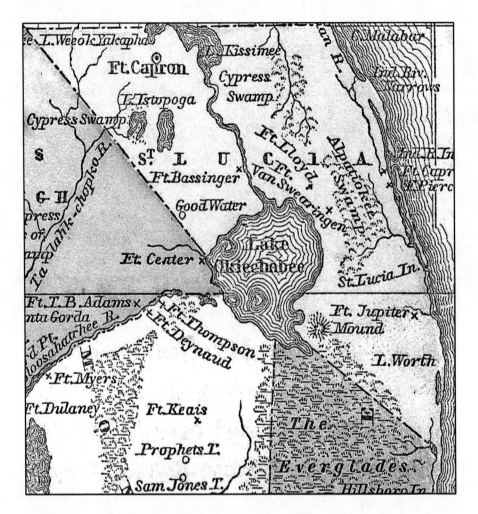

"Map of St. Lucia County, Florida," c. 1855, showing the lands immediately bordering Lake Okeechobee, including the Alpatiokee Swamp and the general location of two Seminole bands led by Sam Jones (Abiaka) and the Prophet. This map is remarkably close to scale, even though few white men had explored the interior of Florida and seen Lake Okeechobee before 1855. The forts established by the American Army during the Seminole Wars were the only white settlements in the interior. The inlet near the mouth of the St. Lucie River kept moving and disappearing over the years. In 1892, settlers in the Stuart area finally succeeded in opening a permanent inlet by using a dredge. Photo Credit: The Florida Center for Instructional Technology, University of South Florida, http://fcit.usf.edu

Prologue

"Turn your backs to the fire and shut your eyes. And keep them shut till I tell you to open them again."

The remaining few did what the old cowboy told them. Most of the news people had headed back to town right after the politicians, just before the blazing orange of the November sunset faded into the pitch black of the moonless night. Only a few of the guests had stuck it out to hear the last speaker of the evening—two reporters with no other story to cover, a small group of Boy Scouts working on camping badges, a few environmentalists, and a handful of locals who liked listening to old timers tell their tales.

"Shhhhhh," he quieted some of the boys. "Pay attention to your ears. Everything out here is trying to tell you something. You can pick up the language pretty easy if you listen close. That high singing sound? That's cicadas celebrating the fact winter hasn't quite got here yet. And that ... the low buzz underneath. That's frogs reminding us that it rained the other day." He waited. Many of the campers probably hadn't even noticed the two sounds until he pointed them out. It could take a while to isolate them.

"Hear that? That was the wind. Remember. You can *never* trust the wind. Right now, it's pretending to whisper secrets to the pine trees, but the wind's a trickster. What it's really doing is asking the fire to dance. And the fire is seriously considering the invitation. You can tell by the way it's starting to hiss and snap. Got to keep a close eye on the fire when the wind's around."

The cowboy was putting on a show. The kids from the high school audio-visual class had stayed to record this campfire story as part of a local history project. Earlier that day, he had signed control of one of the largest ranches in Florida over to the state. They were going to use it to help restore the Everglades. This was a big deal.

He was a tall, thin, white-haired man whose clear blue eyes hinted that he had been fair-haired and probably considered good looking when he was young. Like a typical Florida rancher, he wore a long-sleeved cotton shirt buttoned at the wrists and all the way up the front under his chin, straight-leg, high-rise jeans, a leather belt, and well broken-in cowboy boots. Since the sun had already set, his straw Stetson waited behind him on the hood of his truck. It, and other hats before it, had done their job over the years, leaving his face noticeably paler than his hands. Leathery and tan, they supported his claim that he'd spent most of his life working cattle in the sun out on the prairie. He spoke in one of those soft, old-time Florida southern drawls.

"Now see if you can feel the air. Not the wind … the air itself." He led them in a calm voice, mesmerizing like a hypnotist. "It's soft and warm tonight … like velvet on your skin. That's the water in it. When the moon comes up later, you might be able to see a rainbow."

"And, think with your nose. What can you smell? Everything out here has its own special perfume. Even the rattlesnakes…"

A few of the city folks squirmed where they sat Indian style on the ground. Two even started to stand up. "Whoa. Nothing to worry about." That got them every time. "Rattlesnakes are musky. You can smell them coming long before you hear them. And I checked before you got here." He chuckled and exaggerated a few theatrically loud sniffs. "Still clear."

He grinned to himself, and once his audience settled back down, he continued, "Now, my family's been taking care of this land for almost seventy years. This is our last day in charge, and I don't rightly know how I'm going to feel about that in the morning. So, on this my last night, I'd take it kindly if you'd let me tell you the story about how we first got involved with this place."

He paused, sucked in a deep breath, and gathered himself. "Sometimes it helps to know how things got started. Helps you make sense of where you are today." A hitch in his voice stopped him again for a moment.

"Today…" He started over. "This ranch is part of what they call the Allapattah Flats. Even though it's close enough to Stuart, Fort Pierce, *and* West Palm Beach you could all get here in under one hour, you are sitting on the best native pasture land left on the east coast of Florida. Back then … the first time my father walked it … this land didn't look like what you saw on your tour today at all. Back before the government dredged the drainage canals north and south of here, the Everglades ran all the way up to … to right over there."

He caught himself pointing toward the east even though their eyes were still closed. "To the east of here, he clarified. "The Everglades started not half a mile away. Most everything between the sand ridge you're sitting on and the coastal ridge sat under two to four feet of water almost all year long."

Now, the old cowboy strolled around the campfire so his voice came at the group from different angles. "My father was only thirteen years old at the time, but folks grew up early in those days. He went by the name of Billy, and his best friend was a Seminole Indian he came to call the Chief. The story I'm going to tell you starts when those two met an African-American girl they called the Queen, and the three of them got caught up in an adventure."

He warmed to his tale now. Getting them ready. "Use your mind's eye. Try to see it… It was not even a hundred years ago. People in places like New York City already lived stacked one on top the other in skyscrapers and rode underground subway trains to work in office buildings. Sure, Mr. Flagler's railroad had already reached Key West. But this part of Florida was still so empty and wild and full of strange and dangerous creatures that it reminded folks of darkest Africa. They even called it the Florida jungle."

He gave them a little time to think about that. "Now, so much has happened since then that you could fairly expect those days to be gone completely. Out here, though, some things never seem to change. You can still get the sense of it."

Hoo. Hoo... Hoo, hoo, hoo-ah.

He shook his head in wonder. The barred owl had called out from a little ways off. He couldn't have planned it better if he had tried. A few of the campers gasped, not from fear, but at the magic of it all. He smiled to himself. "The wet earth smells the same. The wind and fire still dance in the night... And now..." He paused again—this time for effect.

"Open your eyes."

A collective intake of breath. Fingers pointed, and heads leaned together. Some campers swiveled in their seats. He waited for the rustling and the oohs and aahs to settle down before continuing. Almost all of them had come out from the cities, and he had made them sit with their eyes closed for so long to get them adjusted to the dark. When they finally opened them again with their backs to the fire, they could see the ancient heavens as clearly as if the world were brand new. So many stars filled the night sky that it glowed.

"Shhhh." He brought them softly under control again. "Sometimes out here ... under this sky, you get the feeling you can travel back in time."

The old cowboy paced himself, like he had all the time in the world. After giving them a little longer to take it all in, he told them they could turn around if they wanted to and he slid his folding chair closer to the fire. Once he had their full attention again, he began.

"Now, I have to be honest with you. My family didn't get this story from my father. He never was the kind to talk much about himself. It was the Queen who told it to us first. And that was some years later. So, it's mostly her version of things. But the Chief ... he backed her up on every bit of it. So, I believe this is what really happened."

Chapter 1. Cow Hunters

The first time Queenie saw Billy and the Chief, her world was about to change forever. Theirs was, too. But, none of them had any idea what was about to happen, what they'd have to do to survive, or who they would be when it was over.

It was 1914, and she was in Tantie, Florida. Her father had gone to the back of Raulerson's store to buy provisions, and she had nothing better to do than sit there in the afternoon shade, fanning herself and taking in her surroundings like she always did.

Crack!

The sound echoed through the trees. A rifle shot? Queenie sat up straight, instantly awake. Eyes wide, she tilted her ear toward the sound. On alert.

Crack. Crack!

The soft, deep thuds of horses' hooves striking sand.

A yodeled, "Yee ...yee ... haw!"

Other voices answering, "Whoo! Waaa-hoo!"

No. Not gunshots. She shook her head and grinned to herself. "Cow hunters," she said out loud, "and they're making a show of it." She glanced over at the docks along the creek. No fishing boats. Good. Still early for fish boys. There probably wouldn't be any trouble.

There wasn't much to Tantie. A few rough buildings scattered along sand trails up near where Taylor Creek feeds into Lake Okeechobee from the north, a sawmill, a school, a church, a store, and some small, mostly log, houses. Only a handful of folks collected their mail there, and most of those who did actually lived out in the Florida jungle some distance away, in hunting or fishing camps or small homesteads they had carved out of the wilderness.

And soon, Tantie would disappear all together. The Florida East Coast Railway Company had laid out a new modern town it called Okeechobee on the prairie a mile or so to the northwest. The new train station with "Okeechobee "written on it already loomed on the horizon, and they had renamed the post office in its honor.

The railroad people claimed "boom times" were coming, but they hadn't got there yet. In fact, it would be almost another half a year before the first locomotive even rolled into town. So, life in Tantie that day was just about the same as it had always been, ever since the first white settlers found their way to the lake's north shore some twenty years before.

Crack!

"Yeeeee-haw!"

Hoof beats pounded louder as four of the scrawny Florida ponies that cow hunters called marsh tackies rounded the last curve in the trail at an easy lope. Three of the riders slumped back in their saddles. The leader stood tall in his stirrups, swung his sixteen-foot bullwhip around his head in a big, lazy circle, and then snapped his hand down so fast the girl could hardly see it. The whip cracked like lightning.

Queenie couldn't help clapping her hands under her chin. Her mouth still hung open in a giddy grin. "Yes, cow hunters!" she exclaimed to nobody but herself and clapped again.

About a year earlier, before she ever heard of Tantie, Queenie's mother had brought home the popular novels about cowboys and Indians out in the Wild West. Those stories grabbed the girl's imagination in a special way and held it so tight she raced right through them, hardly taking time out to breathe. For a while, she dreamed almost every night about riding herd on the western prairie, her six-shooter at the ready.

Then to her great excitement, she discovered there were cowboys and Indians in Florida, too. But Florida cowboys were a different breed from the cowboys she had read about in her books. They even went by a different name. They called themselves cow hunters.

The four in Tantie that day fit the Florida mold. They wore floppy old hats and tie-up brogan shoes instead of stiff-brimmed Stetsons and tall boots. Three of the four still rode flat, old-style military saddles left over from the war. Cow hunters could make do without saddle horns because they didn't use their ponies for roping cattle the way western cowboys did. Instead, they sent catch dogs into the bushes and swamps to roust them out. Once the cows were out in the open, the cow hunters kept them under control by cracking their bullwhips and flicking their heels.

The girl squinted, trying to get a good look at the riders as they pulled up to Raulerson's. As if he expected someone to be watching, the leader of the cow hunters nonchalantly looped his bullwhip and tied it to his saddle with one hand as he slowed his pony to a stop at the side of the store with the other. As if on a signal, he and his three companions swung their legs high over the backs of their horses and dropped to the ground all at the same time. They landed with one big thud, even making a show of dismounting and tying up their tackies. Then, they wiped their brows with the sleeves on their forearms, slapped their hats against their pants to get the dust off, resettled their hats on their heads, and stepped into the shade of Raulerson's porch, laughing and pounding each other on the back.

"Waaa-hoo!"

Queenie was still grinning at all the commotion the cow hunters had made when two boys came half-running, half-trotting, around the same curve. One, a sandy-haired white boy, looked tall for his age, which seemed to be about a year or so younger than she was. Like most Okeechobee fish boys, he wore faded denim overalls, a broad-rimmed straw hat, and no shoes. The other was a Seminole Indian. About the same age, slightly shorter, a little wider and darker skinned than she was. Barefoot, too, he had on one of those long, light-colored cotton shirts some Seminole men still wore. It hung down below his knees. A sash held it tight at his waist.

She could tell right away the boys were trying to catch up with the cow hunters. They slid to a stop in the sand when they saw the ponies tied up at the store. Even though their chests heaved from the running, they bounced on their toes, gave each other a couple of quick looks, and sprinted toward the store faster than before.

When they got to the hitching post, though, they didn't touch anything. Instead, they nosed up as close as they could get to the cow hunters' horses and gear. They studied each piece seriously as if trying to memorize every detail, pointing and talking and nodding to each other all the while. Once they had seen all they could see, they pumped some water from the store's well, plopped down on the edge of the porch, and waited for the cowmen to come back out.

Queenie settled in to wait, too. With so much new front-door trade, it could take the Raulersons some time to get around to her father's business at the back door.

Before long, three of the cow hunters came back out. They took up prime spots in the shade of the overhang and started talking and laughing. Although she couldn't make out their words, the energy in their voices reached out to her on the wind.

She wished she was up there by the porch with the boys. Every now and then, they elbowed each other or did little jigs in response to what the cow hunters were saying. Queenie was sure the cow hunters were telling stories.

The tales Florida cow hunters had to tell were every bit as exciting as anything she had read in her books. Like cowboys out west, cow hunters lived wild and free in the wilderness. They rode horses, slept under the stars, and always kept their guns at hand because they never knew when they'd run into a bear or a panther or a rattlesnake or a rustler.

But on top of all that, Florida cows often snuck away to hide in the swamps. When that happened, cow hunters had to be on the lookout for alligators, too. *And* they had to deal with other things that guns and dogs and whips couldn't help with, like hurricanes and lightning storms, flash fires and swamps so thick with mosquitoes and black flies you could choke to death on them.

Oh, it was true. Cow hunters thought mighty highly of themselves. But the thing was, they had adventures to tell, and more than almost anything, Queenie *loved* adventures.

Chapter 2. Different Ways to Skin a Cat

Queenie saw the two boys again the next afternoon, out in the woods near a Seminole camp. Her father was discussing things with an Indian man who wore a dark vest over his long shirt and so many scarves wrapped around his head that they looked like a thick, wide hat.

She had climbed up a big oak tree, as she often did, to get the lay of the land. She hadn't been there long before she noticed the boys a little ways off in the woods. This time, they seemed to be stalking something. She scanned the trees and bushes around them to see what they were after.

There. A scrawny, tan-colored cow with uneven horns picked and chewed its way slowly between clumps of fan-shaped palmetto fronds. The boys had knotted boat ropes together to make lassos and were sneaking up on it from different directions, trying to get close enough to throw a loop around its neck.

Suddenly, the cow lifted its head, its ears straight up at alert and aimed directly at the sandy-haired boy. The boy stopped stone-still, but too late. The cow mooed and started away from him in a jerky cow trot, straight toward the Indian boy's hiding place. Queenie lost sight of it behind another clump of palmettos and pine trees.

But then she heard a "Whoop!"

The cow crashed back through the bushes with both boys in full pursuit. They hollered and flailed their ropes in the air. The cow ran right past her tree into the middle of a shallow pond and stopped in belly-deep water. From there, it gave first one boy and then the other a lazy eye before settling in to chew the tops off the water plants.

The boys danced around the edge for a while, but they couldn't outmaneuver the cow. Every time they made a move in its direction, it shook its horns, blew water out its nose, and shuffled over to a different part of the pond.

This all changed when the Seminole boy called out, "It heard you! *Everything* could hear you!"

The sandy-haired boy called back, "I was driving it to you! We'd of caught the thing if you'd just learn how to throw a rope!"

Then, another "Whoop!" And some pushing and shoving and rolling around on the ground that ended with the two boys lying in the grass laughing. The cow raised its head and peered across the pond at them. After a moment, it stuck out its long, pointy tongue and slowly curled it up to flick a drop of water off the tip of its nose.

It was all so cute and funny Queenie couldn't help laughing out loud, herself. She climbed down, walked over to the boys, and offered what she considered to be encouragement. "You'd have probably done better if you had a catch dog."

The boys sat up to face her, and the sandy-haired boy rolled his eyes, which were the most amazing blue, and as clear as the water in the springs up in the middle of the state.

"Of course we would've," he snorted in a Cracker drawl. "But, we don't *have* a dog. And what makes you think you're in any position to tell *us* anything about cow hunting, anyway?"

The girl knew a challenge when she heard one. She threw it right back at him. "I'm betting I know a lot more about it than *you*!"

"A *colored* girl? In a fancy *dress*?" He dismissed the idea by puffing up his cheeks and blowing air out between his lips. "Puh!"

Queenie could have let it go at that. Although her hazel eyes and black hair, which curled as much as it kinked, told a tale of mixed blood, the milky chocolate tone of her skin made it clear. She *was* Colored. *And* she was a girl. But that blue-eyed boy needed taking down a notch or two for thinking either one of those facts meant she couldn't know more about cow hunting than he did.

True, she'd never heard of Florida cow hunters until a few months back, when her father decided to move her family toward the big lake. As their small steamboat zigged and zagged its way down the Kissimmee River's vast open prairie, she hadn't been able to believe her eyes when she saw dark silhouettes of men on horseback circling huge herds of cattle in the distance.

And then, about halfway down the prairie, a colored cowman who owned his own ranch invited them to stay a while. For almost two months, her mother set up shop every morning on the ranch-house porch to teach reading and writing to colored children from the nearby ranches and settlements. The girl and her father earned their keep helping out with chores.

But Queenie spent every spare minute shadowing the ranch's cow hunters. Her wish had come true. Of course, the cow hunters didn't give her a gun or let her ride in a round-up like she did in her dreams. They did, however, answer her questions and let her follow along close enough for her to be sure she knew more than this blue-eyed boy.

Looking down at him with her fists on her hips, she said, "I spent a fair amount of time just now learning cow hunting. *First hand*! From *colored* cow hunters on a *colored* ranch." That ought to have put him in his place.

She could tell he was evaluating the truth of her claim by the way he narrowed his eyes and shot a questioning look at the Indian boy. When the Indian raised his eyebrows and gave an "I-don't-know" shrug, the blue-eyed boy threw back a test.

"Where?"

"A few days north of here. About halfway down the Kissimmee Prairie."

"How big a ranch?"

"Not exactly sure. But bigger than I could see all of. They run over a thousand head. Sold three hundred down in Punta Rassa last year alone." She threw in the last few details to make up for not knowing the actual answer to his question.

The blue-eyed boy turned to the Indian again, but his friend only shrugged again.

"How'd you find all that out?"

"I spend my time watching and listening when I get the chance. You'd be surprised what you can learn ... *if* you pay close enough attention." She had him now. "Like you two were doing with the cow hunters yesterday. Only I was out there on the prairie *with* the cow hunters and saw it *all* for myself!"

Queenie loved the way the upper hand felt when you got it. But the boys were so darned young and serious about everything that she backed down a little. She dusted off the front of her skirt. "Plus, this *isn't* my fancy dress."

"But, it *is* fancier than the one you were wearing yesterday." The blue-eyed boy recaptured some ground. He apparently paid more attention to his surroundings than Queenie had given him credit for. And he kept a keen eye out for the details.

"And yesterday?" He sniffed in disgust. "Those boys turned out to be just a bunch of new hands come to town looking for moonshine. More likely to find trouble. Not much good for anything."

With that, he screwed up his face until one of his blue eyes squinched shut and conceded, "But I reckon there *is* more than one way to skin a cat."

Now, Queenie had not been in Tantie long, but she had been there long enough to learn that catfish had skin instead of scales which made skinning catfish a big part of the Okeechobee catfishing business. Fishermen spent a lot of time arguing over who was the fastest, and they were always spying on each other's techniques and trying to come up with their own special tricks for doing it faster. It was one of those points of frontier pride.

So, she wasn't entirely sure, but she took that to mean the boy had called a truce.

Chapter 3. Each Other's Faces

The blue-eyed boy *had* called a truce. He gestured toward the shade of Queenie's tree with a toss of his head, and the three moved out of the sun. They sat and talked for a while, starting to find out a little about each other.

The blue-eyed boy kept his introduction short. "My pa and me, we stay in a palmetto-thatch shack. Down on the beach. Been there most my life." Eventually, he added, "We scrape up a living fishing out on the lake." As if that wasn't obvious from the look of him.

The Seminole had a lot more to tell. "There are many in my family," he offered. "Mother, father, sister, aunts, uncles, cousins, grandfather, and grandmother." The other boy nodded in agreement as the Seminole counted his relatives off on his fingers. When the Indian finished the list, he looked up and said seriously, "We are members of the Bird Clan."

He explained that the Seminole Tribe was divided into seven clans, and each clan was divided into families headed by elder women like his grandmother. His family stayed at several different camps in the woods, one of which Queenie and her father were visiting that day. They moved from one to another depending on the season and how good the hunting was.

But, his family had always built their camps near the big lake. So, except for the times every year or so when all of the Seminoles got together down in the Everglades, he had never traveled very far from where he sat right then.

"Home," he said holding his hands out, palms to the sky.

The funny thing was both boys went by the name "Billy." The blue-eyed boy offered, "My pa started calling me that the day I was born."

The Seminole explained that under the customs of his people, he had recently chosen his American name, Billy Jones.

Queenie thought that was a funny name for an Indian.

Then the boy explained, "In the history of my people, great warriors and..." He seemed to correct himself and spoke haltingly, "...Great leaders have taken those names. I honor them so that I may always remember." He tapped his chest over his heart twice with the knuckles of his right hand.

Later, after they all got to know one another better, they'd call each other Billy, the Chief, and the Queen. But that first day, the boys called the girl Queenie, like everybody else did, and she thought of them as *her* "two Billies," or when she needed to keep them straight in her mind, as her "blue-eyed Billy" and her "Indian."

Queenie had a lot more story to tell. First, she was slightly more than a year older than the boys. Second, until four years before, she had lived in the big eastern city of Baltimore, way up north in the State of Maryland. So, she started out feeling superior and bragging about Baltimore's tall buildings, cobblestone streets, and electric trolley cars.

"It's not like here." She gave the blue-eyed Billy a smug look. "There's lots of colored people. We have our own schools and stores. My grandfather owns one ... a store, that is. His house alone is bigger than Raulerson's, bigger than the sawmill even." She wrinkled her nose at the blue-eyed boy and made a face that said, "So there!"

But neither boy was impressed. First, they didn't believe half of what she told them. And then, Billy took her in an entirely different direction by asking the obvious question. "So, why'd you come here, then?"

Now, how Queenie came to be sitting under that tree in the middle of the Florida jungle on that particular day was a long story that had begun way back before she was born. Learning from recent experience, though, she started with the short version. "My daddy brought us here. Some folks say he just has the wanderlust ... but he's actually on a quest."

It didn't work. The boys sat there squinting at her with their mouths open like they had no idea what she was talking about. So, she gave them the details.

"You see, my daddy's mother and father were slaves in Alabama before the war. After they got freed, they wanted to go back to Africa more than almost anything in the world. About the time Daddy was born, they heard that somebody in Carolina was arranging for a boat to take freed slaves home. So, they moved to Charleston to catch that boat. But, something happened."

"What was that?" the blue-eyed Billy asked.

"Don't know." Her father had never told her what had stopped them. Even he didn't seem to know for sure. "All I know," she continued, "is they didn't get on the boat, and my daddy grew up thinking things would have been a whole lot better if they had. So, as soon as he finished his studies at the Friends School, he set out to find a place in America colored people can call their own. That's why he left Charleston and came to Baltimore."

"Sounds like he should've loved Ball-ti-more." The blue-eyed boy exaggerated his drawl. Then he widened his eyes and leaned toward her. "So, why'd you leave?" He paused to look over one shoulder and then the other as if checking to make sure no one was listening and whispered in a deep low voice, "Is he on the run?" He sat back again, elbowed the Seminole, and giggled at his own joke.

"Ugh!" Queenie narrowed her eyes at him and shook her head in exasperation. "No. My father is *not* on the run." She wasn't going to let that boy get her goat, though. "He says, 'Even in Baltimore, white folks still have all the power and most of the money.'"

The Indian grunted and nodded.

She continued, "So, when Daddy heard there was a Colored-owned town in Florida ... by the name of Eatonville, up there, near Orlando ... northeast of Kissimmee..." She indicated the direction with her head. "He had to come down and see what it was like. We loaded all our things on the train and here we are." She swung both hands up as if she had completed a magic trick.

The boys had fidgeted while she told her story, looking over to check on the cow every now and then and throwing acorns and twigs at each other. But, when Queenie told this part, the blue-eyed boy shook his head. "Don't see why he just don't pick a place and be done with it."

"It's not that easy..." She had a sudden realization and asked with more than a little indignation in her voice, "You don't know much about my people do you? Our history and all."

The boy looked at her warily. "Why would you expect me to know *anything* about your people? You're the first Colored I ever talked to, except for him..." He gestured with his chin toward the Seminole. "And his family. I can tell you *they're* right decent folks. That seems enough to know." He said this last with the conviction of someone who meant what he said.

The Seminole didn't act surprised to be called "colored," but Queenie had never compared herself to the Indians. They weren't anything at all like Coloreds. Yet, her eyes flitted from his arm to hers. His was darker. Even his eyes were darker.

And the white boy had made a good point. Two actually. The truth was, with him growing up in that part of the wilderness, how could he know anything about colored people? Only a couple of colored cypress loggers and the colored woman whose children her mother was teaching lived anywhere near Tantie. They had all come down within the past year to help build the railroad or cut cypress trees, and they almost never left the colored quarters the cypress company had started on the other side of the creek.

And, the more she thought about it, his other point was a good one, too. If folks were good people, what *did* it matter what color they were or what their history was? Finding herself less certain that she actually held the moral high ground, she decided not to push the issue.

She returned to the boy's first question. No sooner did she start to explain why her father hadn't picked a place to call home yet than she discovered there was a lot more the boys didn't know.

All they'd heard about the war to end slavery was that folks on the prairie couldn't wait for it to be over. With no plantations or slaves to protect, cow hunters didn't have much of a dog in that fight. Mostly, they tried to avoid getting caught by Rebel soldiers. The Rebs would pull their guns and order them to drive their cows north to feed the Confederate Army. Then, they'd keep the cow hunters up there and force them to fight the Yankees. A lot of cow hunters hid their herds and tried to lay low until the war was over and they could start shipping cattle to Cuba again.

The boys didn't know much geography either. They'd never heard of Eatonville and weren't sure where Charleston was. They had a vague idea how to find the Florida prairie town called Kissimmee. But that didn't mean they were stupid. Queenie wasn't sure she'd even know any of that stuff if her mother hadn't made her take her lessons and her father hadn't started his quest.

But the real revelation was that none of those things interested the boys. All they really wanted to know about was the train. Queenie had actually traveled for three days on the railroad, and they pestered her to hear all about it. So, she took a side track and answered their questions.

Chapter 4. The Negro Seminoles

To Queenie's surprise, however, as soon as she satisfied their train curiosity, the blue-eyed Billy pulled her back to where she had left off in her story. "So, how'd you get from Kissimmee to here, then?"

"We didn't come straight."

The boy rolled his eyes again. Then he wrinkled his brow and bobbed his head to keep her going. He'd made his point. Everybody knew it was impossible to come straight to Tantie from Kissimmee, what with the way the river twisted and turned and all.

She started over. "About two years ago, Daddy heard there was another colored town, a smaller, cypress-logging town on the Gulf side of the state called Rosewood. So, we packed up again."

"Train again?"

"Nope. Ox cart."

That took her down a peg. People in Tantie were all too familiar with ox carts. The boys looked at each other and chuckled at her comeuppance.

Then Billy asked a different version of his first question. "So what made your pa think things'd be better here?"

Another good question. Things were *far* from better in Tantie.

"You're right," the girl conceded. "There's nothing much for colored folks to brag about here." The only lodging her family had been able to find was a small rough shack with a dirt floor in the quarters. Didn't come near Rosewood standards, much less Eatonville, or, God knows,

Baltimore. "But, my daddy didn't come here looking for something *better*. He came here looking for the Negro Seminoles."

Billy squinted and repeated "Negro Seminoles" slowly to himself like the words didn't make sense. The Indian boy nodded again, as if he had heard the story before.

"Way back before Florida became part of the United States, slaves had started running away to Florida to live with the Indians," Queenie explained. "The Spanish liked having both of them here because they fought on the Spanish side every time the Americans started something. Life was good." She focused on the blue-eyed boy.

"But everything changed about a hundred years ago when the Spanish turned Florida over to the Americans. Almost the first thing the American government did was order the army to move all the Seminoles out of Florida, Indian *and* Colored."

When Queenie said those words, she suddenly realized maybe the blue-eyed Billy was right. She and the Seminole had more in common than she'd thought. She cleared her throat to cover the momentary confusion caused by that new idea.

"The plan was to send the Indian Seminoles west … to Arkansas or Oklahoma … and to turn the colored Seminoles over to slave owners in the South," she continued more thoughtfully. "But, neither one of them wanted to go. So, they stood together and fought. How they fought against the Army!"

Queenie's eyes watered up. "They were so brave! Many of them died fighting. And most of those who survived did get sent away to one place or the other. But a few bands led by great warriors … like Billy Bowlegs…" She caught the Seminole's eye and tipped her head to let him know she understood why he had chosen the name "Billy."

"They didn't give in!" she continued. "Just when all seemed lost, they escaped into the swamps around Lake Okeechobee and stayed there until the Army was forced to give up looking for them."

Billy squinted over at his Indian friend as if trying to verify this point.

The Seminole's eyes were fixed on the girl, as he said in a low voice, "Abiaka."

Queenie didn't know what the word meant.

"Abiaka, the one the Whites call Sam Jones," the Indian explained.

"Oh." Queenie thought she understood. "That's where your other name—"

"Billy Bowlegs went to Washington and saw the power of the Whites and their government." The Seminole tipped his head as he interrupted her. "He chose to stop fighting and left this place to save his people. It was Abiaka… He is the one who refused to go. He is why we are still here this day."

After a pause, he answered her unfinished question matter-of-factly, "I chose both names because I see through both their eyes." He said the words as if confessing something. Queenie didn't quite understand, but now the Indian's eyes were shining, too.

The blue-eyed Billy looked away without saying anything.

After a short silence, Queenie picked up *her* story again, almost in a whisper, "Anyway, after we'd been in Rosewood a while, my daddy heard a rumor that a band of Negro Seminoles was still hiding out … that they lived in the swamps south of here even now. So, he wanted to see if he could find them."

When the Seminole boy nodded, she felt better and continued with more energy. "We packed up again and headed down the middle of the state. We found colored families here and there to stay with along the way," she explained. "Like the rancher I told you about. But, we didn't come across one single Seminole of either kind until we got off the steamboat here." She concluded, "And now that Daddy's got Indian Seminoles to talk to, he's trying to find out everything he can. So's he can make up his mind whether we should keep moving south or not."

This time the Indian boy shook his head.

"Wh—"

"They have gone," he answered that question before she could finish it.

"Oh." The girl's shoulders sagged in resignation. "We were afraid of that." But, then she got hopeful again. "Do you know where they went?"

Another shake of the Seminole's head. "Just that they left the jungle long ago and did not come back."

She sighed and shrugged. That was all either of them knew to say on the topic.

But the blue-eyed Billy took this impasse as an opportunity to shift the conversation back to the part that interested him the most. "So, if you couldn't find any Seminoles, what kept you on that ranch long enough to give you the idea you know so much about cow huntin'?"

"My momma's a school teacher."

The boys shied away from her and made faces at each other.

Queenie continued anyway. "There's no colored schools out here on the frontier. So, when a teacher stops by ... especially a college-trained one like Momma." She emphasized that fact by puffing up and making a face at the boys. "Folks try to keep them around as long as they can. They bring little ones in from all the surrounding ranches and camps to get their lessons. Gives us a place to stay." It also gave her family a little extra spending money and a chance to barter for books and things.

But Billy's question had challenged her on the subject of cow hunting again. "Anyway, I was there *long enough*!" She got ready to start sparring again.

To her surprise, he didn't push back. Instead, he wrinkled his nose, chewed on a piece of grass, and shifted direction one more time. "So then, what exactly *is* a quest?"

He had done it again. Caught her by surprise by paying attention. But this time, his question opened the door for her to show him that cow hunting wasn't the only thing she knew a little something about. After all, she *had* finished almost all of her high school courses already. She could teach these boys a thing or two.

Queenie smoothed her skirt and settled herself down into her most mature and scholarly voice. "A quest is something heroes do."

She paused for effect, making sure she had their attention. "They make a promise to find something. Like a missing treasure. Or to do something that's important, but that seems like it's impossible to do. *And then...*" She looked from boy to boy to build suspense. "They keep at it until they get it done. No matter how hard it is, how far they have to go, or how long it takes!"

"And when it's over..." She held her hands together up against her chin as if she was praying and took a deep breath. "People tell the tales of their deeds. Some are even written down in books and told over and over again ... forever!"

"I have heard such stories at night by the fire," the Indian boy responded thoughtfully.

Then, Billy caught her off guard again. "So, your pa's a hero, then?"

Before the girl could clap her hands and say, "Yes, he is," her father strode out of the palmetto scrub looking every inch a hero. Tall, broad-shouldered, and handsome. A coffee-and-cream-colored man with purpose in his step and the sun at his back.

"Come along, Your Majesty," he said tipping his head to acknowledge the two boys and gesturing at Queenie to stand up. "It's time to go help your mother."

Chapter 5. The Queen's Schooling

Up at dawn the next morning, Queenie finished her schoolwork and chores by the time her mother started collecting the little ones from the colored quarters for their lessons. That freed her up to go off with her father.

They headed down to Taylor Creek again. He had set up a meeting with some Seminole men from a different clan who had come from farther south to trade otter skins and venison at Raulerson's. The girl sat on the ground off to the side. Supposed to be listening, but nothing new was going on in the conversation. She had a difficult time keeping her mind from wandering. When the men moved a little farther away, she didn't get up and follow them. Instead, she leaned back against the tree to wait in the shade.

Thinking back, Queenie never was sure exactly how much time passed before she heard the whispered, "Shhhhh. Whatever you do, don't move."

She opened her eyes and started to turn her head toward the voice.

"I said don't move!" This time louder. A command.

She froze and found the blue-eyed Billy's face with her eyes. He stood perfectly still several paces away, but he indicated she should look downward by quickly glancing from her eyes to her feet and back. Then she felt something heavy slide across her left leg. Breath sucked into her chest. Her eyes widened. She shifted her gaze down and sideways without moving another muscle.

The biggest, blackest snake she had ever seen. Over five feet long. At least two inches thick. Shiny black, darker than coal and weaving its way toward her lap.

"You can talk," the boy offered. "Just don't move."

"Get it off of me!" she hissed through clenched teeth.

He paused. "Best not to try. No telling what it'll do. Just stay still, and it'll likely go away."

She started breathing rapidly. Couldn't keep her chest from heaving.

"Shhhh," he whispered again. "You want to stay calm." He closed his eyes as if trying to figure out what to do next. Then, with his attention back on her wide eyes, he suggested. "Shift your mind to something else. Like…" He paused again, taking his time. "Like what you been up to this mornin'?"

Was he trying to carry on a casual conversation? Was he crazy?

"Talk," he ordered in a calm tone. "Use your normal voice. It'll irritate him. Make him choose another resting place." He raised his eyebrows and moved his head slightly, indicating she should answer. The snake folded itself over both of her lower legs and looked straight at her face.

"More watching and listening?" the boy coaxed.

She tried. "Yes." Her voice did *not* sound normal at all.

"Figure anything out, yet?" He leaned slightly back, waiting.

"No." It came out as a squeak.

The snake coiled itself in layers on her thighs like a fat boat rope on a dock. It seemed to be settling in instead of planning an escape.

The boy widened his eyes and raised his eyebrows again, prompting her to keep talking. He *had* to be crazy.

"You?" She took in a quick shallow breath and looked up at the boy, not panicking, but close to it.

"More questions than answers."

He was too calm.

"So, what exactly is it you're always watching and listening *for*?" he asked.

"Anything..." She fought for control. "Almost everything." Still the pitch of her voice kept rising.

He nodded for her to continue.

"It's part of ... my ... schooling..." She almost didn't get the words out. She couldn't do it. Couldn't catch her breath.

"Do something!" Through her teeth again, but this time as a plea.

He cocked his head. "Okay."

Okay?

The boy took two giant steps, picked the snake up matter-of-factly, and started petting it. Then, he draped it over his shoulders as if it actually was a boat rope. But a boat rope with round, black eyes that peeked out from behind his ear and a forked tongue that flicked in and out between bony snake lips. Its long black tail coiled itself lazily around his arm.

Queenie jumped up. Fit-to-be-tied. Eyes blazing.

"Seems to me, you *could* use some more schoolin'." The boy sounded nonchalant, but grinned wildly. "At least when it comes to the jungle and its critters."

Without looking, Queenie reached down and grabbed the first things her fingers touched, a handful of dirt, acorns, and twigs.

"Use my normal *voice*? It'll *irritate* him?"

She hauled back and threw the whole handful at the boy as hard as she could. Dirt and acorns and twigs exploded from her hand like birdshot from a shotgun. He sidestepped them all with a nifty light-footed jig, still grinning like a fool. She picked up another handful and charged him.

He backed up, thrust the snake out between them like a shield, and shifted to a serious tone. "Best be careful."

She pulled up short. No… The way he handled the thing, it had to be harmless. She hunched her shoulders and took a menacing step forward.

He bobbed and weaved, having fun again, but still semi-serious. "This here's a good one. You wouldn't want to hurt *this* kind."

She seethed.

"It's an Indigo. Good to have around. They clear out the rattlers and rats."

She made another move. Trying to get past the reptile.

He dodged and kept talking. "You can tell them by the color. Indigos're right blue in the light." He sidestepped her again, all the while holding the Indigo out between them where she could get a good look at it. "And by the head. See? It's round."

She glanced down involuntarily.

"Not a triangle like a rattler or a cottonmouth." He danced sideways.

Queenie hesitated. The boy was right. She did have a lot to learn about snakes. And the jungle. And how many *other* things? Frustrated, she threw down the handful of dirt and twigs, pivoted on her heel, and strode away.

"And he's just a baby." He raced around to get in front of her and skipped backwards as she kept walking. "They get three, four times bigger."

She stopped.

"You can hold it if you want to." The boy extended the Indigo toward her with two hands as if offering her a gift.

She just looked at him through narrowed eyes. Who did he think—

"They're known to be gentle."

Queenie sighed so deeply her shoulders rose and fell. Then, she slowly stretched both arms out toward the boy. He carefully laid the snake over them.

Later, after she had carried the Indigo deep into the palmettos and let it go, she and Billy sat back down in the shade. When he said, "I'm sorry… Probably shouldn't of done it like that," the apology came out of the blue.

Queenie rejected it with a sniff and turned aside.

"But you did learn something."

He obviously hadn't taken her slight to heart. Even his voice could twinkle.

"Didn't you?" He grinned again.

The boy was insufferable. Conceding he was right didn't come easy. "Yeah," she threw at him. "Not to trust the likes of *you*."

That he seemed to take to heart. "I said I was sorry."

She didn't respond. Not even when he hung his head so low his chin almost touched his chest.

"And you got to admit…" He picked up a handful of dirt and let it dribble through his fingers. "Your kinda schoolin's a mite different than most girls."

That did it. The dam burst. Without thinking at all, Queenie blurted out, "But that's the thing! I'm not *like* most girls. I *hate* women's work, keeping house, cooking, and sewing and things like that. I want to *go* places and *do* things."

She stopped for breath and to see what the boy was making of all this. He snapped the twig he had been fiddling with, raised his eyebrows, and tilted his head back a little. She took that to mean she should continue.

"And the other thing is … I'm the only child in my family. That means my daddy doesn't have anyone else to pass on everything he knows to. And he knows so much! Learns something new practically every day. So, about the time we left Eatonville, I made a deal with them … my mother and father, I mean."

She spoke excitedly. She never got a chance to share her secrets, and the boy sat there chewing on a stem of grass and looking at her with those blue eyes.

"If I get my school work and chores done in time, I can spend the rest of the day with my father. At first, he just let me work with him around whatever house we happened to be staying in at the time—"

The acorn landing in her lap stopped her.

"That don't sound like much of a step up from cooking and cleaning to me." The boy drawled, smiling broadly by the time his second acorn hit her on the arm.

"Well…" He *did* have a point. At first the only thing she could think of to throw back at him was a defense. "It's that … things are *different* when you're a girl."

Then she went on the attack. "But it didn't stay like that. After a while, Daddy started taking me with him to bargain for work or to gather information. Or, sometimes, to swap stories. I was helping. My job was to be a second set of eyes and ears."

And she knew she was good at it. Sometimes, she saw things he didn't see or heard things he didn't hear. Plus, it gave her a chance to learn new things firsthand, like with the cow hunters.

"In the beginning," she continued, "Daddy only let me sit close enough to the men folk to listen in on what they had to say. And, then, only if I kept my mouth shut and didn't draw attention to myself."

"Haw!"

Acorns and leaves erupted into the air as the boy almost choked trying to stifle a giggle that shook his shoulders. He looked at her sideways and almost couldn't get the words out through the fingers that covered his mouth. "*That* last long?"

He was infuriating. Queenie glared at him, stuck out her chin, and decided to ignore his attempt at humor. "And, no! That job *didn't* last long!" She *was* a help to her father. "Soon, Daddy started telling me his thinking on things as we walked from place to place. And after a while, he started listening to some of what I have to say—"

Another acorn hit her arm.

Chapter 6. Moving On

This time Queenie ignored the acorn. Let the boy sit there grinning like a fool. So what? It didn't matter how afraid she'd been of the Indigo or how smug he acted about it. She knew better now, and she was sure of one thing. She was learning more about a lot more things than the ordinary fourteen-year-old girl living in the year 1914, no matter where she was growing up.

That's what she would miss about the frontier. The girl sighed. She hadn't put that thought into words before and was surprised how sad it made her feel.

Of course, her father hadn't made the announcement yet, but she could tell they were getting ready to move on again. The night before, she had told him, "I talked with a Seminole boy today, Dad. He seemed to know a lot of history and things. He said the Negro Seminoles didn't stay in the Everglades. He thinks they've been gone a long time."

Her father answered, "I know, Sweetie. That's what I've been hearing, too." He reached over and ruffled the hair on top of her head. "Good work, though."

Queenie and her father sat at the table in their cabin in the Cypress Quarters. Including Queenie's mother, there were only two grown women in the Quarters. The other's name was Ruby and she had two small children. All she had to pay Queenie's mother for giving her children their lessons that day was one squirrel. Its well-seasoned meat simmered in the cast-iron Dutch oven on the pot-bellied woodstove, giving off a tempting aroma that filled the small room.

"Critter and sweet potatoes for dinner tonight." Her mother tossed the words over her shoulder as she lifted the lid. "With some field greens I gathered this afternoon."

Queenie's mouth watered. Her mother could work wonders with squirrel, but she had used the word "critter." Having studied all her parents' secret codes for years, Queenie could tell by the way she'd said it she wasn't happy about how things were going here in Tantie. Plus, the way her mother settled her shoulders as she served up the plates meant she was thinking seriously about how to say whatever she wanted to say next.

"Pickings are getting slim around here," she started, still facing the stove. "Not much work for me. Most of the cypress and railroad workers aren't here yet. Won't get here for months. And Ruby told me that only a few of those who'll come at first'll be women, if any. Almost none with children for me to teach."

Queenie had to agree. They'd come to the lake looking for a long-lost tribe of colored people, and that Indian boy and the Seminoles her father'd talked to were the only dark faces she'd seen all day, other than her mother and father, of course.

Still, she liked something about the place. It was young, like those boys, full of energy and possibilities, not set in its ways yet. Like places she'd read about in stories, it felt exciting. As if anything could happen. She wasn't ready to leave.

"And Ruby's barely scraping by, herself." Queenie's mother continued, pointing at the pot with her wooden spoon. "Don't know how we'll—"

"Tantie's got a school," Queenie offered out of the blue. She'd noticed the small one-room building near the creek. "Maybe you—"

"She can't," her father cut her off.

Before the girl could react, her mother gave him the eye. "They already have a teacher, Honey."

"It's a school for Whites." Her father ignored his wife's unspoken warning. "They'd never let a colored—"

"Anyway, our children need me more." Queenie's mother stopped the discussion by setting a heaping plate of squirrel, sweet potatoes, and greens in front of her husband with a thud just hard enough to make little drops of gravy fly half an inch in the air. That was an obvious signal to shift the conversation to something else.

After holding his wife's gaze for an instant, Queenie's father fulfilled the request she hadn't put into words. With a look of appreciation on his face, he leaned over the plate and breathed in the sumptuous steam through his nose. "A meal fit for a king." He patted his belly and beamed. Queenie's mother smiled back and turned to fill another plate. Their unspoken discussion was over.

Queenie wanted to roll her eyes. What did they think they were protecting her from? She understood that Whites every place else weren't likely to let Coloreds into their schools. Not even to teach. But, this place could be different.

Yet, she also knew better than to jump into the middle of this conversation between her mother and father. This was their one recurring argument, and they were set in their positions. She'd heard it so many times she knew it by heart.

It went like this. Her mother had been raised on the teachings of Booker T. Washington. She believed in the American ideal. Even though everything was "separate but equal" between Whites and Coloreds now, she trusted that education and hard work would change all that over time. All the Coloreds had to do was stay out of trouble and show what they could do. Eventually, the Whites would come around.

After all, hadn't her father been able to establish a successful store in Baltimore? Didn't he send his children to Morgan College? Didn't they have a good life? That's why she was willing to spend her time down here in Florida teaching one colored child at a time to read and write.

"Every little bit I can do will help," she'd say to get herself going again when she felt frustrated by the slow pace of progress.

Queenie's father actually agreed with her on the education part and the role she played in it. Still, he'd pace the room and argue, "But Dubois is right, honey." He'd turn to Queenie and explain that he was talking about W.E.B. Dubois, a colored leader who had been to Harvard. Then he'd continue, "Dubois says accommodating white people like Washington preaches is only half-a-step up from slavery. Maybe back before I was born…" Then, he'd remind Queenie he'd been born on the day free colored people in America lost their rights, the day President Rutherford B. Hayes handed control of South Carolina back to the southern Democrats by withdrawing the federal troops.

Then, he'd pick up his argument again. "Dubois says we should put pressure on the Whites to give us our rights back. But Douglass, now…"

He *always* went back to Frederick Douglass for inspiration. He'd looked up to Douglass all his life. He'd even moved to Baltimore to meet him, but the man had died before he got the chance.

"In my mind, he's the one that hit the nail on the head," her father'd continue. "Like Douglass said…" He'd emphasize this point by jabbing his index finger into the air. "We can't count on the white man to do it for us. We'll never be free till we don't depend on anybody but ourselves."

Nobody ever won this argument. Queenie's mother'd eventually rub her father's shoulders and neck, saying, "I know. You're right, honey. It's just…" Usually, she didn't need to finish the sentence. All she needed was for him to reach up and pat her hand where it rested on his shoulder, and they'd start talking about whatever else had happened that day.

The night before, however, their conversation had continued on when her mother said, "It looks like we've gone about as far down the state of Florida as we can go."

Her father nodded. There was no need to announce the conclusion to *that* conversation. Everything indicated that there were no Negro Seminoles or other colored communities left to hunt for. *That* turn of events had to signal they'd be heading off to someplace new sometime soon.

But to where? Queenie didn't know. All she knew was this time she wasn't sure her parents were right. The Whites and Seminoles seemed to get along just fine, and the boys didn't seem to care what color she was other than at the very beginning.

"Dadgummit," she said to herself. This time she didn't want to go.

An acorn hit her left shoulder.

"Talking in your sleep?"

The words brought Queenie's attention back to the real world. Finding herself staring at that sandy hair, that white face, those blue eyes, it took a moment to reorient herself.

"Lost you there for a while." The boy tossed an acorn in the air and caught it.

She nodded and was surprised a second time by the realization that he was acting like a friend. Living her whole life in one colored community after another, she'd never had a white friend before. Not many friends of any kind, actually. Not since they left Baltimore, anyway. They were always moving. Plus, she'd spent most of her spare time lately with her father.

"Yes," she answered after shaking the cobwebs out of her head. "But I'm back now."

Chapter 7. Billy's Dream

Back in the present, Queenie wasn't completely ready to forgive the boy for scaring her out of her wits with the Indigo, friend or not. Still, he did know more about the jungle than she did, and even if she would be there only a little while longer, it would be good to have someone who could teach her things about it. Plus, she was curious about him. So, she started by asking about the one thing she thought he'd know something about, fishing on the lake.

Billy took the bait. "My pa staked out a fishing ground some years back. It's small but good. Right near the mouth of the creek." He squinted over toward the girl. "The two of us row out to the ground and lay the net to surround the fish..." He made a circle with his arms to demonstrate. "After a while, we row our boats together and haul the net wings back into the boats." He showed the circle getting smaller and smaller with his hands.

"Then you pull the fish to shore?"

"Naw." He blew out a short breath that made it clear the girl didn't know anything about fishing. "Do that and all you'd end up with is a lot of dead fish. Got to keep them alive till the run boat comes by with some ice."

He was right. She didn't know anything about fishing, but she wasn't inclined to give him an inch. She widened her eyes, shook her head, and lifted her hands palm up as if to say, "So, get on with it."

"That's the thing about a pound net." He actually seemed eager to share his fishing secrets. "It's got two wings ... not long like a long seine. Short enough for two boats to handle. And it's got a pocket in the middle. When you pull in the wings, that forces all the fish into the pocket. And that's where they stay, milling around till it's time for me and my pa to scoop them out with our hand nets."

"Sounds harder than sitting and listening," she jabbed.

But, he slipped the punch. "Not as hard as some. We're independents." His pa refused to join one of the new five or six-man long-seine crews some of the big boat captains had started running once the state had finished dredging the new canal down at the south end of the lake. There was big money to be made now that they could ship catfish out of Fort Lauderdale.

"But, it's not worth it to my pa. He says, 'Too many people. Too many places to be at ... and too many times you don't get to set for yourself.'"

Billy and his pa worked alone, still using their smaller two-man pound net. Or, sometimes, when his pa felt like it, a trot line like in the old days. And they sold their catch directly to the run boats that picked it up out on the water.

"We take less per haul, that way." He shrugged. "But we don't have to worry about skinning and gutting the cats ourselves. Never gonna make much money. Not compared to the hauls the long-seiners are making."

Then his blue eyes lit up. "But that don't matter in the long run." He paused to take a deep breath, as if considering whether to tell her this next thing or not, before facing her eye to eye. "Because you see. I am gonna be a cow hunter."

"What's your pa say about that?" Queenie had wondered about that question. From what she knew, it would likely be a problem. "My daddy tells me Okeechobee fishermen hate cow hunters," she continued. "He says that's the main reason we have to stay clear of town on Saturdays. It's too dangerous what with the two always getting into brawls over one thing or another."

"Pa won't say nothin'!"

The force with which he said it caught the girl by surprise. He had blurted it out before she had even finished asking the question, and he clearly intended it to be the only thing he'd say on the subject. But her father had taught her a trick or two about how to handle a conversation. She held her tongue with great difficulty, and eventually, the boy stepped in to fill the silence.

"Okay. Sure, there's trouble between the two sometimes. But, we're not part of it. You see, I've got cow hunting in my blood." He added the last proudly. "And my pa? He don't care too much about anything, anyway."

It seemed a struggle for the boy to keep going. She looked at him like she wanted to know and bit her lip. Her daddy's trick worked again.

"Fact is, I was born on a ranch up near the Kissimmee, north of Basinger. But, my ma … she died soon after, and that broke my pa. He couldn't stand being in that place any more. So, he gave up what he was doing before and took to drinking. And then fishing. As soon as I was old enough, he found us a place down on the beach. Now he spends all his time doing either one or the other."

He paused to take another deep breath. "It's okay for him down on the lake. So long as he stays far enough away from folks and has enough moonshine to drink. But, that's not for me. The prairie's right over there." He pointed beyond the new Okeechobee train station that marked the horizon. "And my place is somewhere out on it. One day, I'm gonna get back. On the lake, I'll never be nothing but one more poor fish boy. But, a man can still make his fortune hunting cows!"

Then, he explained how cow hunting down there by the lake was different. Up on the Kissimmee, people had started staking out ranches years before. Down by the lake, the land was still wide open. No fences and no landowners to bother with. Wild cattle still roamed the scrub. Like in the old days, all a man had to do to get his start was round up a few and brand them. He could set the best ones loose again to build his own herd or drive the whole bunch to one of the ports on the Gulf Coast and sell them at the docks to get his stake.

"And not only that!" He continued, working himself up. "Out on the prairie, cow hunters live like kings. Money or not! Run their own lives. Hunt deer and hogs and turkeys in the swamps and woods. Whenever they like. Sit by the campfire and do nothing at all. If that's what they want. Just listen to the owls and look at the moon—"

"Or search for the path of stars that leads people who are good in this life to the Shining City in the sky." The Indian boy seemingly appeared out of nowhere. "You'd think he was part Seminole." The boy continued as he nodded to Queenie, smiled, and sat down.

"I didn't notice you coming." Queenie said it, but the Seminole boy's sudden appearance seemed to have caught Billy off guard, too.

"That is because we are taught when we are very young how to be silent. I have been trying to teach him…" The Indian tipped his head toward his friend. "How to move unheard and unseen through the jungle, but…" He stopped and shrugged in a way that indicated the cause was hopeless.

"And you speak such good English!" Queenie blurted that out, too. She was embarrassed by how forward it sounded the minute she said it, but it *was* true. The Indian seemed to know a lot of words. Yet he was overly careful, took his time using them. That made him sound a bit stilted and formal. Not at all like you'd expect an Indian to sound. Or even a Cracker.

Fortunately, the boy didn't take offense. Instead, he explained good-naturedly, "Yesterday was not my day for talking." Then, "Thank you. I was first taught by a missionary from Oklahoma, but he has gone. Now, I learn from the railroad people." He tilted his head toward his friend. "And I get a lot of practice trying to teach *him* Seminole ways. In case he is ever lost in the jungle and must survive on his own."

Chapter 8. The Hound Dog

The blue-eyed Billy gouged deep scratches in the dirt with a twig while his Indian friend said all this. He looked uncomfortable, as if he couldn't figure out whether to be embarrassed that he got caught carrying on about the moon or upset that his friend was exposing his weaknesses to a girl.

Queenie almost felt sorry for him, though not quite. She still owed him for the Indigo. *And* it gave her an idea. A way to get even and to make the most out of the little time she had left on the frontier in the bargain. She'd get him to take her out on Lake Okeechobee. It might not be an adventure, but at least she'd see something new, something she may never get another chance to see.

"That the kind of schooling *you're* getting?" she asked, referring to the Indian boy's comments and raising her eyebrows when the white boy looked up.

He glowered out from under the frown that pinched his forehead.

Turning to the Indian, Queenie rubbed it in some more. "Oh, and he led *me* to believe he already knew *everything* there is to know about the jungle." She wrinkled her nose at the blue-eyed boy.

He continued to glare.

The Seminole glanced quizzically from one to the other and said nothing.

Still talking to the Indian, Queenie asked, "How about the lake, though? He *does* know something about the lake, *doesn't* he?"

The Seminole held his tongue, but nodded slightly in response.

"Well, *I've* only seen it once. On the steamboat between the Kissimmee and here. And it was getting dark." She gave an exaggerated sigh. Then she turned to the blue-eyed Billy again. "And you *do* have a boat, don't you?"

He scrutinized her through slitted eyes. "Yeah," he mumbled and pointed warily at a wooden rowboat tied up on the creek.

"Well, you know what I'd *love* to do?" She stretched out the word "love." Lingered over it.

Neither boy replied.

"I'd love to learn *all* about the lake. And since you know *so* much about it…" As she said the word "so," she tilted her head and tossed the most coy sideways glance she could muster in the blue-eyed boy's direction. "You'd be the perfect one to *teach* me. Wouldn't you?" She blinked at him several times as if sending a secret code. "After all, I'm just *dying* for some more *schooling*."

Billy's cheeks glowed pink. He looked from the Indian to the girl and back again before grunting out a small breath.

The Seminole's face remained expressionless, except for the edges of his mouth. They twitched up and down as if fighting off a laugh.

Eventually, Billy shrugged, shook his head, and tossed aside the acorns he'd been crushing in his hand.

The girl could read him. He was getting ready to agree.

"I reckon I could do it."

From what she'd seen of him before, however, she expected him to try to reclaim some control over the situation. She waited.

He took his time, spit out the stem of grass he'd been chewing on. "But, it'll have to wait till morning." He explained, "We already finished one haul, and Pa plans to go back out again this afternoon. If we do, he'll be taking tomorrow off. Stay by the hut to dry the nets and smoke the scale fish we'll be keeping for ourselves."

"Tomorrow then!" Queenie clasped her hands together and gave him a wide smile. Then, to knock him off balance again, she switched to the most proper and sincere tone she could muster. "I am *so* looking forward to it, Billy. Thank you ever so kindly." She could hardly keep from laughing out loud because the boy sat there with his mouth open and a puzzled look like he couldn't figure out what had happened.

The Indian broke the spell. He shook his head again and sighed. "Good." As the other two turned to him, he slapped both palms lightly against his knees. Then he raised his eyebrows, rubbed his stomach, and let out a deep breath.

"Tomorrow, we go to the lake. Today, I am hungry." He unwrapped a big piece of pumpkin bread and held it up.

Billy chuckled and patted his belly, too. "Eating sounds like a right good idea. Got to keep up my strength." He caught the girl's eye with a wry glance. "Seems I'm gonna be *lecturing* in the morning." Without waiting for a response, he jumped up, and trotted down to his boat.

Queenie watched him go. Let him keep the little piece of ground he'd taken back. She'd gotten what she wanted. She'd been the one who got to offer the truce that time. And who knew? Maybe they'd find something exciting out on the lake.

Billy came back with a lunch that was almost identical to the one she'd packed earlier that morning, bacon and heavy biscuits left over from breakfast. The Indian's was mostly pumpkin bread. When she asked, he told her about some of the other foods the land provided his people and tore an inch-thick piece off for her to taste.

As she chewed the pan-fried dough, testing it for flavor, he said somewhat wistfully, "This is not our true bread. In the past, we made our own flour from coontie that grew wild in the jungle. But, settlers dug up all the coontie to sell, and it did not come back. Now we must buy flour from Raulerson. It is not the same."

"But, it's very good!" She bit off another chunk to prove the point.

"It is not the same."

She had no answer.

Billy jumped in and filled the gap by turning the conversation back to how much the two boys wanted to be cow hunters and how hard it was for them to get started. The Seminole boy joined in.

After listening for a while, Queenie sat straight up and clapped her hands together. She had an idea. "I know what you need to do!"

Billy sighed exaggeratedly and picked up an acorn to throw at her.

Before he could say or do anything, she continued, "Make a list."

"A list?" Both boys tilted their heads.

"My father says life's like a picture puzzle. The hard part's that each man has to decide what he wants his own picture to look like. Until you figure that out, you can't tell what pieces you ought to hold on to and what pieces it's safe to throw away."

The boys groaned and gave her "what-does-that-have-to-do-with-anything" looks.

She stuck out her tongue at them and went on, "And then my momma always finishes it by saying, 'And once you know what pieces you need, it helps to make a list and check each piece off when you find it.'"

"And," Billy broke in, "the first thing to check off my list ... is a dog."

Now, Queenie knew she'd told the boy the day before he'd be better off if he had a dog. But she hadn't meant he had to put a dog at the top of his list. She started to straighten him out, "That's as good a place as any to start but..." She stopped when she realized he had not been asking a question.

The boy's blue eyes stared right past her, over her shoulder toward the wire grass at the edge of the palmetto-sedge prairie. When she turned and followed his gaze, she could tell by the way the grass moved that something was working its way in their direction. Then, she made out the top of a brown and black head with long ears flopped over on both sides.

And then, eyes rimmed in black, followed by an almost black nose over a pink tongue.

Before long, a small, bedraggled black-and-tan hound dog revealed its whole self at the edge of the clearing. Still too cautious to approach, it focused its eyes on the blue-eyed Billy and barked a nervous, high-pitched young dog bark.

Billy talked to it matter-of-factly, "Hi, little buddy. It's okay. You look lost. Your pack leave you behind? Come get some water. Some biscuit?"

He sat there coaxing and cooing the pup closer and closer until it was nibbling the last of his lunch from his hand and drinking his water. He stroked the little hound's head as it sat close to him, panting. Soon, its eyelids drooped as it realized it was safe to relax.

"Wonder who lost him," he said to his Indian friend. "Looks like the runt of the litter. Probably nobody cares, anyway."

The boys explained that dogs had to be big and strong enough to run with the pack to be worth the food they ate. So, hunters tested young dogs by letting them loose in a hunt. Normally, a hunter would come looking for a lost dog he cared about. And the right thing to do was to give those dogs back. But, if a runt couldn't keep up, that was a sign it wasn't good enough. Most often, no one went out looking for it.

You could count the ribs on this scrawny dog. It had probably been out on the prairie for days. It was lucky it made it to them in one piece. They asked around the store, and everyone pretty much agreed the hound was likely theirs for the keeping, if they actually wanted it.

After looking the hound over carefully, Billy said, "He looks like he comes from good stock. Probably just needs some time to grow into himself."

Then he turned to Queenie and said with an unfathomable grin and a glint in his eye, "So, what's next on my list?"

Chapter 9. The Lake

That night, as Queenie tried to fall asleep in the quarters, her mind drifted off to a book called *Peter and Wendy* that her mother had brought home for her to read right before they left Eatonville. In it, a magical boy named Peter Pan sprinkled fairy dust on a proper young English girl about Queenie's age named Wendy. Then, they flew off to an amazing world called the Neverland where they had adventures with a band of lost boys.

There were times when the Florida jungle felt a lot like the Neverland to Queenie. It was so wild and full of danger. And the strangest things did tend to happen. Sometimes, when she walked through it, Queenie even imagined she was in that story. She didn't see herself as Wendy, though. No. She was Tiger Lily, the Indian Princess who lived in the Neverland and who stalked pirates and crocodiles with her knife clenched firmly between her teeth.

Of course, sad to say, fairy dust existed only in storybooks. But the blue-eyed Billy was certainly cocky, like Peter, and ... and this *was* Florida.

The next morning, she woke up so excited about whatever real-life adventures might lay ahead that she rushed through her chores and schoolwork and ran toward the creek. She and the Indian boy got there about the same time. Billy was already waiting for them. The hound danced around her as she walked up. It had clearly benefitted from food and companionship overnight and was bouncing around like the puppy it was.

"Pa don't think it's a bad idea to keep a dog around." Billy was all blue eyes and smiles.

Queenie had begged extra food from her mother and had wrapped it tightly in oilcloth to keep it from getting wet because she had seen the boat. Only twelve feet long and five feet wide, with a flat bottom, its sides didn't come up very high above the water line. Before getting in, she added the boys' food to her lot and retied the oilcloth.

This time she *was* wearing her oldest dress, a faded calico, with a full long skirt and a petticoat made of sturdy cotton. Arranging all that cloth in a way that left room for everyone else was a challenge. Eventually, she simply took a seat near the front of the boat and settled the hound dog on her lap. The boys jumped in and rowed toward the mouth of Taylor Creek.

The early morning lake took her breath away. Nothing but sky and water as far as the eye could see. The horizon was a sharp, straight line that cut the world in half, with bright blue sky at the top and gunmetal gray water at the bottom. Their boat seemed even smaller than it did before.

"It's so big," slipped out of Queenie's mouth without her even thinking about it.

"Yes. Big water."

When she narrowed her eyes and tilted her head to look at the Seminole, he added, "Okee chobee. That is how we say 'big water.'"

She hugged the dog and beamed at her Indian.

"Water's gray, today," Billy broke in, bringing the girl back to a more practical way of looking at things.

Queenie frowned at him. He was taking the magic out of it. Ruining the fun.

He raised his eyebrows. "Are you here for some schoolin' or not?"

For an instant, her jaw dropped into a surprised open-mouthed smile, but she quickly recovered. She assumed proper school posture, sitting up straight with her hands folded over the dog in her lap, and said, "I am."

She gave him her full attention.

"There's a fair to middling wind from the east kicking up a chop." He began the lesson, pointing and squinting toward the middle of the lake. "That's why you don't see more boats out there. We might oughtn't to stray too far from the creek."

"Ohhhh," Queenie moaned, disappointed. "Are you sure? I want to see as much as I can, and this may be my only chance to see it."

The boy pushed his cheek out with his tongue as he surveyed the sky in all directions and mulled it over. Then, he took a strong pull on his oar that turned them to the left. "We'll head south along the east shore. Stay in the lee. Shouldn't cause us any trouble."

At first, he was right. The water near shore was as smooth as glass and so clear they could see the lake's patchwork bottom of white sand and water grass as they floated over it. They hadn't left the mouth of the creek far behind before Billy pointed to a palmetto-frond shack set back a ways from the water's edge and commented as if to himself, "No smoke. Pa's prob'ly not up yet."

Queenie nodded respectfully. She intended to wait him out. She figured she could play student as long as he wanted to play teacher. But, caught up in the beauty, she got interested and slipped up. Reverting to her natural self, she started asking questions about this and that, about practically everything she saw. The boys looked at each other and shook their heads in wonder every time she came up with another one, but they did their best to provide her with whatever information they could.

A little down the shore from Billy's shack, the boys rowed right up to the edge of a low, green island that blocked the mouth of a small creek. When they got close enough, though, Queenie could see that it wasn't an island at all, but a tangled mat of plants with wide green leaves, grass, and weeds bobbing on the water's surface. Within it were smaller islands of darker green plants with amazing white flowers the size of saucers sticking up out of the water on long stems. Ducks and other water birds paddled in the gaps.

"Water lettuce." The blue-eyed boy explained that the plants were anchored in place by long roots. "And hyacinth. Makes fishing hard. Lines and nets both get tangled."

"Oh, look!" Queenie pointed at a small night heron walking on gawky long legs across the top of the plants rather than in the water. Her eyes filled with genuine excitement.

"Call them floatin' islands, because sometimes they get thick enough even a man can walk across them like that. But then they break loose in the wind and block the creeks, like this one."

The Indian boy nodded.

"Got to cut your way through when that happens. More trouble than you'd think." Billy shook his head.

Then, he pointed at three boats out in the lake that were maneuvering around two men standing in chest deep water. "Long seiners," he explained. "Likely the morning pull's hung up. Bottom starts getting rocky the further down you go."

After giving the men and boats a little more thought, he chuckled. "Out in the water hauling nets six days a week. Could be my pa's got a point."

The sun rose higher as they floated south. One continuous forest of tall dark trees ran all along the lake's eastern shore. In some places, the trees marched all the way into the water. In others, they stood as a green backdrop for narrow white sand beaches. The tarpaper shacks of long-seiner fish camps or the isolated huts of other more independent souls dotted the first few beaches. After a while, though, the beaches were empty, like lonely pale strips no man had discovered yet.

Billy did his best to show Queenie everything he knew about fishing and the waters of the lake, but he couldn't tell her much about the land that surrounded it. Only that many of the trees on this part of the lake were cypress, and she already knew cypress was the best wood for milling and building things.

"Hardly anybody comes down this far," he said. "Bottom's too rocky to haul seine. No roads. Just swamp. No reason to be here." He had never set foot on shore that far down.

Neither had the Indian, although he did know a little bit more about the land. Indicating the cypress swamp, he explained, "I hunt in such a forest when we camp near the place the white men call Indian Town." Indian Town was a long one-day's journey down this side of the lake.

"Will we pass it?"

"No. It is not on the lake." Nor was it a real town run by Indians, the way colored people ran Eatonville. But, the Seminole boy's clan had built chickees there long before the white men came.

Then, the Seminole diverted Queenie's questioning about the things he did not know by offering her a bigger idea. "The earth, the water, the trees, and the animals were created to fit a pattern. If you learn to read that pattern, your eyes can tell you much of what you seek to know."

That captured the girl's attention.

The Seminole pointed at the forest. "Those tall straight trees with light-colored trunks? Cypress grow to be very old, but only where the land is low and the water is high. Look closely. The forest changes when the land changes." He pointed out the wide, lighter green leaves of maple trees, which grew near the water rather than in it, to prove his point. "They turn red when the weather is cold and dry."

As they floated past a darker-green tree in the shape of a rounded dome, Queenie exclaimed, "I know that one! That's an oak! They get to be very old, too."

"Yes. That is the tree white men call oak." The Indian boy spoke somewhat solemnly. "In this place, such trees often reveal a secret. Oaks grow only where the ground is high. When my people first came to this land, we found great mounds in the swamp. Ancient people who lived here long ago built them. Because it is standing alone, that tree is likely growing on one of the mounds built by the ancients."

They floated and rowed. Soon, Queenie was able to pick out the different trees and a few mounds on her own, and she took mental notes when the boys told her about the alligators and turtles and different kinds of birds.

It had started out as a lovely day.

Chapter 10. The Wind

Some time after the sun passed its highest point in the sky, Queenie started thinking about lunch. Just as she opened her mouth to suggest they stop to eat, however, Billy said, "We'd best get back."

He pointed toward the west. Although the water near the boat was still smooth, choppy waves had moved much closer to shore than before. Now capped with white foam, they ran more to the south. Without the kids realizing it, the wind had been changing direction and getting stronger.

Then, Billy pointed at the sky above the cypress trees to the east. Hidden behind those trees, storm clouds had secretly been building. Their tops loomed above the trees, and they rolled ominously in the boat's direction. The boys started rowing toward Tantie. But, the wind, now from the northeast, picked up without warning. "Come on! I should have..." Billy ended with a mutter under his breath as he pulled hard on his oar. The boat started to respond.

They didn't get far. Within moments, one of the storms that had stealthily gathered its forces behind the trees burst out of the swamp and rushed onto the lake. The boys pulled for the safety of shore with all their might. The storm moved fast. The wind blew even harder than before. And, then, without warning, it shifted again. A gust caught the boat broadside and spun it. With the boat itself acting as a sail, they slid sideways out toward the roughest water.

The sky was still sunny and clear in that direction. But, now farther from shore, they could see a solid wall of dark storm clouds advancing from the northeast. The boys strained for control of the boat to no avail. The wind pushed it into the dancing whitecaps of the open lake. It rocked wildly from side to side. Queenie held on to the dog and the food for dear life.

The wind suddenly shifted again and blew even harder. One especially strong gust struck the boat like an invisible hand, slapping it down the back of a wave. As one side dropped sideways into the trough, the other side lifted up, and the boat almost rolled over. When Queenie reached for something to hold on to, the dog flew off her lap into the water.

She leaned over the side to grab for him at exactly the wrong time. Another wave hit the boat so hard it jolted the bow up into the air. Queenie's momentum took her over the side into the water, too. When she came up for breath, the distance between her and the boat was getting wider. Another gust! Another wave! The wind took the boat away!

The boys lost sight of the girl and the dog in the chaos of whitecaps as they struggled for control. To no avail. They went where the wind pushed them, bouncing with the waves past a spit of sand and trees that jutted out from the shore. Right before they careened past it, they caught a glimpse of the dog running out of the water onto the beach. They saw nothing of the girl.

Then, for the first time, they got lucky. The gusts slacked off. Only for a moment, but that was all the boys needed to force the boat into the more protected water behind the point. They hauled on their oars for shore. The instant the bottom scraped sand, they leaped out and dragged the boat up the beach to a safe place.

Chapter 11. The Alligator

The Indian boy stopped long enough to tie the boat to a stump. Billy took off running up the beach. He slowed only to bend down and grab a long, straight piece of wood. He carried it like a spear as he reached the trees and disappeared. All they had with them for weapons were their pocket knives. And they were far away from home in an area full of alligators, panthers, bears, and who knew what other dangers.

When Billy rounded the point, the full force of the wind hit him in the face. It grew stronger even as he ran through it. Where had the waves taken the girl? He squinted into the gale and searched both water and shore for any sign of her. Then, a gust carried the sound of barking to him, and he started running even harder.

Soon, the barking got faster and louder, and he could hear the girl shouting, "Get away! Go on. Go *away*!"

He ran through shallows and leaped over stumps. As he rounded another clump of trees at the water's edge, his worst fears were confirmed. The girl was backing up toward the cypress swamp. The dog ran back and forth between her and a huge alligator that couldn't seem to make up its mind which one of them to go after. Gators are fast on land, faster than people. Maybe even faster than dogs in a straight run. If it hadn't been for the hound, the girl would have been easy pickings. But the hound kept darting between them, harassing the gator and distracting it.

The pup kept changing directions and seemed quick enough to outmaneuver the beast on dry land. But the girl didn't run to safety when she got the chance. Instead, she picked up sticks and pieces of driftwood and threw them at the gator to take its attention away from the dog. As she did so, she unknowingly edged closer and closer to the cypress swamp where the gator would clearly have the upper hand.

Billy dropped his spear, picked up the heaviest piece of driftwood he could lift, and charged the gator from behind. When he got close enough, he swung the driftwood over his head and crashed it down right between the gator's eyes.

That only made the thing mad. More startled than hurt, it swung both its head and its tail in his direction, trying to sweep him into its teeth. That was a typical gator move. Billy expected it and jumped away. The giant reptile switched its focus to him. Billy prepared to jump to the side at the last minute once it started after him. That was the best way to escape a gator because it took a while for them to change directions.

Right as the gator started its charge, another piece of driftwood hit it from the other side, and the Indian boy took his turn jumping out of the way of the thrashing head and tail. When it started to launch itself toward the Seminole, Billy grabbed the log he had used before and rammed it into the beast's open jaws. They slammed shut with so much force they crushed the wood. The creature stopped for a moment to figure out what was in its mouth before shaking its head to get the splinters out.

That was all they needed to get away. Billy raced past the gator to the girl and grabbed her by the arm. He pulled her away from the swamp toward an ancient oak tree on an Indian mound they had seen as they floated down the shore. The tree's trunk was almost eight feet in diameter, and some of its branches drooped all the way down to the ground. Queenie was good at climbing trees. She easily scrambled up to where the branches hit the trunk, about seven feet above the mound. The Indian followed her up, as Billy turned back for his dog.

By then, the gator had shaken the driftwood out of its mouth. Its beady eyes focused on the nearest target, the hound, which still ran circles around it, barking loudly. Billy called for the pup. It stopped for an instant and tilted its head to listen. The minute it stopped moving, the gator lunged. But the dog sprang aside with inches to spare as the giant teeth crashed together. Then before the gator could turn to follow it, the pup ran as fast as it could to Billy under the big oak tree. He handed the hound to Queenie and clambered up the branch to join them.

"Couldn't leave him down there. Wouldn't be nice to tease the gators like that," he said as he found a place to sit on a nearby branch that separated from the trunk.

At that moment, the wind stepped up to a howl, pushing a heavy rain before it. Big, icy-cold drops thudded like stones against the oak leaves and branches above their heads. The three shuffled over to the more sheltered side of the tree and huddled together. Water filtered its way through the leaf canopy and dripped on their heads. Before long, the rain stopped almost as quickly as it began, and the wind slowed down to the steady push it had been before.

The big gator did not track them up the mound to the tree. After a while, it crawled down the beach and slid silently into the lake, disappearing beneath its surface. Queenie widened her eyes and shuddered. "Don't ever want to go swimming with that thing again."

Then she bent down toward the hound that was snuggled in the hammock she had created by stretching her skirt over her knees. She scratched its head and cooed to it. "Good thing I had a big brave gator dog when I needed one."

The two boys looked at each other, shook their heads, and rolled their eyes. In all likelihood, the dog had attracted the gator in the first place. *Plus*, they were the ones who had actually fought the thing.

Then, the wind and rain hit again. And stopped again. And hit again. It went on like that for hours. Storming and stopping. All the while, the wind kept shifting, and they kept changing their position in the tree. When it blew its hardest, it came at them from the center of the lake. By the time the storms started petering out, the sun was settling down toward the lake's sharp horizon.

Chapter 12. The Tree

As soon as they felt safe, the two boys made Queenie promise to keep the dog up in the tree so's not to attract any new gators. Then, they jogged down the beach to get the boat. They returned on foot. Billy carried four good-sized pieces of wood, and the Indian carried two slightly larger pieces of wood and the oilcloth package of food Queenie had wrapped that morning.

That's when they told her the bad news. During the worst of the storm, waves had crashed so high up on shore that they had washed the boat away.

"The rope broke." The Indian offered it as an apology.

"So, we'll be staying up there for the night." The blue-eyed boy pointed up at the tree. They had come to that decision walking back.

Before Queenie could ask why, the other boy explained, "It is always dangerous on the beach in the dark." He directed her attention toward the water to make his point. The pink and orange reflection of the early evening sun silhouetted the heads and backs of several alligators that looked even bigger than the one they had fended off. The gators swam lazily closer and closer to shore.

Because of the waves and rain, everything was wet. "We do not have time to gather enough dry wood to keep a strong fire burning all night," the Seminole continued. "Without such a fire, the alligators are not the only danger. Many other creatures walk the jungle in the dark."

"So, it looks like all your experience sitting in trees'll come in handy." Billy grinned and dropped his load of wood. "There's just enough light left to build a sleeping platform." He pointed at the place where two large branches grew out of the tree.

With safety in numbers, Queenie lowered the dog to Billy and scrambled down the branch. She gathered grapevines to tie together the platform while the boys scrounged around for more wood. No sooner had the boys and hound disappeared down the beach than she noticed something in the fallen leaves and dirt between the ancient oak tree's roots.

A black stone. Bigger than the palm of her hand. Smooth and cool to the touch. And very heavy for its size. Not at all like the other stones she'd seen near the lake. What made the stone even more unusual was that someone had chipped the surface of one side, creating a number of shiny flat faces with sharply defined edges. It looked like a giant black diamond.

The girl had never seen anything like it. So beautiful, and the solid weight of it felt good in her hand. She decided to keep it.

As she searched for a place to store the stone, she snagged her skirt on a thorn. That triggered an idea. Taking the pocketknife her father had given her from its hiding place in the dress's waistband and keeping an eye out for the boys, she cut the petticoat away from her dress. That gave her one big piece of cotton cloth to work with. She started tearing it into long, sturdy strips about two inches wide. She hated the sound of cloth tearing. Still, even though it made her jaw clench and sent a chill up her neck, she kept ripping off strips.

By the time the boys got back, she had almost enough cotton strips to hold the platform together. They needed to add only a few wild grapevines for extra strength. Before she climbed up into the tree to help with the construction, she tied the remainder of the petticoat across her chest like a sling. That gave her an easy way to carry things such as the black stone, which she slipped inside. She hardly felt the weight of it nestled there against her side.

While they worked on the platform, small furious storms blew in and out as if something big and dangerous was chasing them. They grew weaker as the time between them grew longer and longer. The boys had been right. Even using the matches Queenie's father made her always carry in a small oilcloth packet, everything was so wet a fire wouldn't start. With no fire, the tree definitely provided the safest place to spend the night.

By the time they climbed up onto their platform to stay, a shadowy dusk was sneaking stealthily out of the cypress swamp onto the lake. From their perch in the tree, they heard the night sounds starting up around them. Queenie was sure she saw dark shapes working their way onto the beach from the water.

She had fashioned another hammock out of her skirt for the dog. It curled up and nestled there. The three kids made themselves as comfortable as possible on the small, uneven platform and watched the reflections of the sun's last rays fade into darkness.

Earlier, they had opened the oilskin-wrapped lunch the Indian had saved from the alligators on the beach. The cured meat, biscuits, and crusty bread inside had fared remarkably well. They ate most of the food, giving the dog only enough to keep him calm, then wrapped the rest back up for safekeeping till the morning.

Now, there was nothing to do but sit up in the tree in the dark. The boys seemed to have settled in. Against the backdrop of night sounds, Queenie heard the scrape, scrape, scrape of their pocket knives as they carved long, sturdy sticks into pointed spears.

Chapter 13. The Bag of Wind

Queenie, on the other hand, chomped at the bit, simultaneously excited by everything that had happened and bored by having nothing to do. After the wind and rain stopped long enough for the novelty of their situation to wear thin, she had to say something.

"Well, at least now I can say I know firsthand how Odysseus felt when his men opened up the bag of wind." It simply popped out of her mouth the instant it popped into her head.

The scraping stopped. "Odd who?" Billy asked.

That's how the storytelling began.

When Queenie was little, her mother had held her in her arms at night and told her bedtime stories till she fell asleep. How she loved those stories, especially the adventures about heroes and beautiful maidens. Then when she got older, she discovered some of the stories weren't for children at all. They were classical tales her mother had read in books of history and literature. Some of them were actually, or at least partially, true. That opened up a whole new world, a world in which something exciting could happen to her, too.

And now? Neither of the two Billies had so much as *heard* of one of her favorite stories. It was her turn to tell the tale.

"Odysseus was one of the greatest Greek heroes," she started.

"Greek?" The blue-eyed Billy screwed up his face like he was thinking. The tip of his tongue stuck out between his teeth. He asked the Seminole, "That's some kind of Indian, right?"

The Seminole raised his eyebrows and shrugged.

Queenie shook her head and started over. "No. No. Greek is what you call the people who live in Greece."

That only made matters worse. This time, both boys narrowed their eyes and looked at her like she had said something stupid.

"Oh!" She figured out what the problem was. "Not grease like you cook with. Greece is the name of a place. It's a country like the United States. But, it's very old and far, far away … on the other side of the world."

She paused to make sure they understood and then continued. "And the story of Odysseus is one of the first stories ever written. It's about great heroes and creatures with magical powers the Greeks called gods."

The Indian boy grunted his approval. "We tell such stories at night by the fire."

She went on, "The story about Odysseus and the bag of wind begins when the King of the Greeks ordered all the Greek heroes to sail across the sea and destroy a city called Troy." When they just looked at her, she explained, "The Greek gods could watch everything that happened in the world from their home high up on top of a mountain called Olympus. They especially loved watching battles, and usually when they did, each god would help his or her…" She looked from one boy to the other to emphasize that point. "Favorite hero. But this time all the heroes in the world were fighting against each other at the same time. The gods started bickering mightily among themselves over which side to support."

The boys chuckled together.

"Zeus," she explained, "was the most powerful of the gods. When things started getting out of hand on Olympus, he threw a few thunderbolts to get the other gods' attention."

Billy grunted and asked, "Thunderbolts?"

"Yes."

He grinned and grunted and raised the stick he was carving into a spear above his head.

The Indian boy returned the salute.

Queenie smiled to herself. They were getting into it. She started back up with more energy. "Well, once Zeus had the other gods' attention, he laid down the law. He ordered them to stay out of the war all together. That left the heroes to fight on their own. The problem was the two sides were evenly matched. Without the help of their gods, neither set of heroes could beat the other side fair-and-square. So, the fighting went on and on. For ten whole years."

The boys stopped whittling and listened close. They even whistled a couple of times and raised their spears when she described some of the heroes and their fights.

"But then one day, Odysseus … the hero I'm telling you about … he came up with the idea to fool the Trojans into believing the Greeks had given up and gone home. They pretended to sail away, leaving behind a huge wooden horse with Greek soldiers hiding inside. The Trojans thought it was a peace offering. They opened their gates and they let down their guard."

The wooden horse was the most famous part of this story. "And so the Greeks defeated the Trojans," Queenie intoned theatrically and stopped for effect.

But the only response she got was a question from the Indian. "This is an old story?"

"Very old. One of the oldest."

"And the Americans teach this story in school?"

"Yes."

"Hunh." He blew his breath out through his nose.

When the Seminole didn't say anything else, Queenie started up again. "After Troy finally fell, one of the gods, his name was Aeolus, and he had favored the Greeks all along. Anyway, he decided to give

Odysseus a reward for coming up with the trick. 'Odysseus,' he said."
Queenie used a deep voice to sound pompous. "'What is your greatest
desire?' Odysseus answered, 'To go home.' More than anything, he
missed his wife and his son and the land he loved."

The Seminole nodded.

"It turned out this was a wish that Aeolus was able to grant because
he was the god who controlled the winds of the world. He gathered up
all of the winds ... except the calm west wind that would take Odysseus
straight back to his home island ... put them in a magic bag, and tied it
shut. Then he handed the bag to Odysseus and told him there was only
one thing he had to do in return. He had to promise he'd restore balance
to the world by letting the other winds loose again once he got home.
But..."

She paused to look first one boy in the eye and then the other. "And
this was a very big, but. Aeolus also gave Odysseus this warning:
'Whatever happens, you must not open the bag until you are *standing on*
your home shore.'"

Another dramatic pause. Neither boy whittled. They hung on her
every word, waiting to hear what happened next. Queenie loved it. She
beckoned them to lean close. They did. She switched to a low
conspiratorial whisper.

"Now, Odysseus had told his men what the god had said, but the
more they thought about it, the more it didn't seem to make sense. After
all, Odysseus was a great hero! Surely, the gods would have rewarded
him with something bigger than a quick journey home. The bag *had* to
contain something valuable. Unimaginable treasure. They started
speculating over what was *really* in the bag and worked themselves up
into a lather about it. When their home island came into sight, their
curiosity got the best of them. They untied the bag to see what was
inside."

"Woosh!" She threw her arms up fast and howled into the night.

That startled both boys so badly they shied away from her and almost fell off the platform. The hound tried to jump up, but its legs got tangled in her skirt.

"All of the ill winds came rushing out of the bag at once!" Queenie held the dog tight in both arms and suppressed a giggle as the boys shot her dirty looks.

"The winds blew long and hard in all directions at the same time. The most horrible of storms! Their island vanished! They lost control of their ship! Had to fight just to stay afloat! And by the time the storm ended, they were lost at sea and it took Odysseus a whole ten years to get home."

While she told them the end of the story, the boys regained their composure by rearranging themselves. Eventually though, Billy tipped his head and grinned.

"Maybe there's something to those stories. It *did* seem like somebody let all the winds out of the bag at the same time on the lake today," he chortled.

They all agreed to that.

Chapter 14. Seminole Tales

The Seminole boy stepped in next. "I have a story. It is also old."

Telling stories about heroes and magic around the campfire at night was a Seminole tradition, but the elders usually did the telling. This was the young Seminole's first chance to tell the tales, and he turned out to be good at it.

"It is also about the wind. But in this story, the wind is the hero. I will tell it as it was told to me."

He took a deep, solemn breath before starting. "In the beginning, the Creator made all of the animals and placed them in a shell to wait until the world was ready for them. Because the Panther combined beauty, power, and patience, the Creator wished the Panther to be the first to walk the world when the shell cracked open. It took so long that roots of a giant tree, like the tree we are sitting in now." He lifted his arms above his head and slowly spread them apart to reveal the tree that was protecting them. "Only bigger and stronger ... grew around the shell."

"When the day came that one of its roots created a tiny crack in the shell's wall, it was the wind who first noticed the crack. The wind whirled around and around inside the shell trying to make the crack bigger." The Seminole swayed in small circles with his eyes closed as the wind swirled bigger and stronger in his mind's eye.

Then he leaned forward and spoke directly to Queenie. "When the crack was big enough, the wind could have burst out into the world the Creator had made on its own. It had the power! But, it did not. Instead, the wind honored the will of the Creator. It woke the Panther." He sat up straighter and nodded his approval of the wind's decision.

"Only after the Panther had set its paws firmly on the land did the wind soar out of the crack and begin to explore the heavens. It became the air that we breathe."

"What came out next?"

He answered the girl with pride in his voice, "The third out of the shell was the Bird. It flew out on the wind. And after all the other animals had taken their places in the world, the Creator named the Seminole Clans and gave them each special tasks to do in his new world."

"What tasks?" She had to know everything.

"He gave the Panther Clan the knowledge for making laws and for making healing medicine."

"Your clan?"

The Seminole answered proudly, "Because the Bird can fly high above the world and see everything all at once, the Creator gave the Bird Clan the task of making sure all things are put in their proper places on earth."

"Humph," Billy snorted. "So, that's why you're always trying to tell me what to do ... and how to do it."

Queenie could barely make out his shoulders shaking at his own joke in the dark.

Then, since Billy didn't have a story he wanted to tell, Queenie took another turn. She told them about other adventures Odysseus had while trying to find his way home. They especially liked the story about the one-eyed giant called the Cyclops. He had locked Odysseus and his men in a cave, intending to eat them. When she told the boys Odysseus had saved them by using a stick he had sharpened into a weapon, they grunted and tapped the spears they had been sharpening throughout the night against the side of the tree.

A period of silence followed, after which the Indian boy asked somberly, "The wooden horse of the Greeks. It is possible the American Army knows that story. Yes?"

Queenie nodded confirmation. Until a few minutes earlier, she'd assumed everybody learned that story as a child.

The Seminole rocked slightly back and forth, his head bobbing as if he had figured something out. "They used much the same trick to capture Osceola."

"Osceola?" Queenie had never heard the name before.

"Osceola was a great leader in the wars against the American Army. They captured him by flying a false flag of truce," he explained. "Osceola would never have stopped fighting." The Seminole boy was adamant. "The only way the Americans could put him in shackles and take him away from this land was to trick him by offering a false peace. He made the same mistake as the Trojans."

Billy nodded. "Sure seems like two sides of the same coin to me."

The girl had to agree.

"But," the Indian continued, "our story does not end as that story does. The Army's treachery did not destroy my people. Coacoochee was with Osceola when the white men took him. He escaped and told Abiaka. That was the day Abiaka vowed..."

Queenie waited spellbound.

"...That he would never surrender."

Heat infused the Indian's voice when he said those words. Queenie thought she felt him shudder in the dark.

"From that day forward, Abiaka answered no flag of truce and listened to no offer from the white invaders. We signed no treaty." As he said this, his voice lightened and picked up a more dramatic tone. "And the war continued ... almost to this day."

Queenie looked at Billy, checking to see if the Indian boy was pulling her leg, but he nodded in agreement.

The Indian explained that the most recent uprising had happened only a few years before. A lying white man had convinced a few Seminoles from Indian Town that the American Government wanted to honor the Seminole people.

"He told them he wanted the bones of one of our chiefs for the great American museum in Washington."

But the man did not represent the museum. He bought the Indians whiskey, and when they had enough to drink, they led him to the hammock south of Indian Town near Big Mound City, where a well-known Seminole named Tom Tiger had been buried. He stole Tom Tiger's bones to put in an amusement park. When other Seminoles found out about it, they were outraged.

"Some members of the tribe were so angry they threatened to go on the warpath once again!" The boy was enjoying himself now. "Billie Smith came to Raulerson's Store in Tantie to warn the Whites. He told them, 'If Tom Tiger's bones are not returned within one moon, many white people will die.' I was there. I heard it with my own ears!"

Threatening war had proved an effective tactic. Within days, many of Tantie's white women and children had been sent to Fort Pierce for safety, and the St. Lucie County Sheriff was trying to find a way to get Tom Tiger's bones back.

"What did they do?" Queenie asked, transfixed.

"They worked it out." The reply came from Billy. "But not before my pa got out his rifle ... just in case," he teased the other boy.

The Indian glared back. "Around our campfire, we did not *want* to fight, but..." He paused a moment and decided not to finish that thought.

Instead, he said, "We were glad when the Sheriff and Billie Smith reached an agreement. He turned to Billy. "And we *did* get the bones back!"

They had been reburied in a secret place, possibly near where the three sat at that very moment.

Chapter 15. The Panther

Throughout these exchanges, Queenie occasionally saw the boys' eyes and grins flashing when the moon came out from behind a cloud. Mostly, the blue-eyed Billy listened and whittled the night away on his spear, without saying much.

Every now and then, they heard bumps and snorts below. The boys made educated guesses some were gators and others were hogs. The call of a Chuck Will's Widow fluted out above the background chorus of cicadas and frogs. After the moon came up, a congregation of owls surrounded them with a debate of hooted questions and answers. Eventually, all this commotion seemed to fade. The dog snored softly in the folds of Queenie's skirt, and the youngsters started nodding. They fell asleep.

Later, none of them could say how long it lasted. The dog's growling woke them up. It fought to untangle itself from Queenie's lap. She felt the hair all along its back stand up stiff in a ridge. She struggled to keep it from leaping off the platform into the darkness below.

In a flurry of activity, both Billies leapt to their feet and crouched on either side of her with their backs against the trunk of the tree. They looked down in the same direction as the dog, with their spears at the ready.

The kids all heard it at the same time. The padding of soft feet on the forest floor as it circled the tree. A low rumbling growl as it grew nearer. Then, the moon suddenly came out from behind a cloud again. It outlined the edges of a huge, tawny shape moving sinuously below them, its long, crooked tail waving high at alert. The dog barked in a deep, threatening voice they had never heard it use before.

A panther. Looking up at them. Its yellow eyes glowed in the moon's reflected light. Its fangs flashed as it opened its mouth to let out a ferocious screeching cry and gathered its muscles to launch itself up the tree.

Without saying a word, the blue-eyed boy had positioned himself in front of the other two, where he would meet the panther's attack head on. But before it could leap, something flew past his shoulder and hit the beast square in the nose. The panther's roar ended in a squeak of surprise, and it bounded away into the swamp. The two Billies turned to look at Queenie, the whites of their eyes shining in the moonlight. She had thrown her black stone.

"Another thing my father says: 'If it looks like you can't avoid a fight, it's best not to let them get close enough to bite you,'" was all the girl could think of to say.

After that, they couldn't go back to sleep. Too excited from their close encounter with the most legendary creature in the jungle, they rehashed their adventures of the day, and the stories started again.

It was during those darkest hours of the night that the girl told the two boys the true beginning of her story.

"Almost a hundred years ago, the most feared warriors in Africa were a tribe of women called the Amazons. They were strong and fearless. Never beaten in battle. And they were ruled by a wise and beautiful queen. But one day, an evil sorcerer betrayed the Amazon queen and killed her. Then, he shipped her daughter to America and sold her as a slave."

The boys were silent.

"And, to keep the Amazons from rising again," she continued, "the sorcerer put the Amazon princess under a spell. Neither she, nor her children, nor her children's children would ever have a female child so long as they were slaves. And so it was for generations. Still the blood of the Amazon queen flowed strong, even in the veins of her male descendants." Queenie stopped this time because her voice caught in her throat.

"My father," she struggled to say the words she had never spoken out loud before. "He was the first of the queen's bloodline to be born free in America. And *then* I was born."

"The curse has been broken." The Seminole boy almost whispered the conclusion.

"Yes." He had given her the strength to continue. "The power of the Amazons has been set free. One day, we will be strong again, and there will be a new Amazon Queen."

After a time in which nobody said anything, Billy asked out of the darkness. "Is that another one of the stories from your mother's books?"

"No," she answered. "It's one of the secrets my father told me."

Chapter 16. The Plan

The three were able to relax enough to drift to sleep only when the blackness of the night faded to predawn gray. When they awoke, the bright sunlight of the new day revealed the full extent of their dilemma. To the north, the way to Tantie, waves had washed away the beaches. As far as the eye could see, the tall trees of the cypress swamp marched all the way into the lake. Getting home would be no simple walk back up the shore.

While the two Billies and the dog were out scouting the magnitude of their problem, Queenie retrieved the black stone from the edge of the mound. She also unknotted the strips of her petticoat from their platform. Using some of them, she converted her skirt into pantaloons by pulling its back hem between her legs and tying it to the front of her waistband.

When she looked down to evaluate her handiwork, her fingers flew to her lips to suppress a giggle. Her mother would be scandalized. She could hear her scolding, "A proper young lady *never* shows her ankle." Well, technically, she *wasn't* showing her ankles. Her sturdy tie-up shoes still covered them. The rest of her legs, however, from the tops of her shoes to the tops of her knees, stuck out bare for all the world to see.

"Yes, mother," she retorted as if the woman was standing there before her. "But then, proper young ladies usually aren't stranded in the jungle." Still giggling, she jumped up and down and kicked a few bushes to test the modifications she'd made. They held. Good. They'd be easy to undo when she got back to civilization. But for now, she'd be able to move as freely through the underbrush as the boys.

Satisfied with her handiwork, she tied another strip of petticoat cotton around her forehead to hold back her hair. Smiling to herself, she packed the remaining cotton pieces and the black stone in the sling and hung it across her chest like a bandoleer.

Billy had left her the spear he carved during the night, in case she needed it. When Queenie heard the boys returning, she picked it up and stood at the ready, the spear's dull end planted firmly on the ground, her feet spread apart. The time had come to reveal her transformation from a poor little colored girl marooned in the Florida wilderness into a full-fledged Amazon warrior.

The boys stopped in their tracks when they saw her. Eyes and mouths popped open. Then both of them looked away as fast as they could. The Seminole focused on something above Billy's head. Billy's blue eyes searched the ground for things he'd never find. Both shifted their weight from foot to foot.

"What?" Queenie giggled again. They'd never seen knees before?

"It's … ah … em," Billy hemmed and hawed, but didn't look up.

"My skirt. It keeps snagging on things. See?" She stretched a handful of cloth toward them, showing a small tear. "It'd slow us down. And rip all to shreds, anyway."

No response.

"*And...*" She used the sharp end of the spear to point at the boys' legs.

Both boys looked down, first at each other and then down at their own bare feet. The Seminole's knobby brown knees stuck out below his long shirt. Billy had rolled his overalls up over his calves.

"Well … um." Billy raised one eyebrow and switched his gaze quickly from his feet to Queenie's face, still not dropping his eyes lower than her shoulders. "I guess—"

"This is *not* Tantie," she cut him off. "This is the jungle." She pounded the blunt end of the spear on the ground and struck her ready pose again. "And this is how *I'm* traveling through it."

The Seminole nodded.

Billy looked from his Indian friend to Queenie, pursed his lips, and closed one eye. Then, his face cleared and he snapped to attention. Knees straight and heels together, he rolled one hand in front of his body with a flourish, and bent at the waist in what passed for the frontier version of a bow. As his head came slowly back up, he grinned and said, "At your service, your Highness."

That boy was no end of ambiguities.

The initial shock of seeing Queenie's new attire wore off quickly. The boys had returned from their scouting mission in fairly high spirits, partly because they felt invincible for having survived the night and partly because they had come up with a plan. They told her about it as they finished off the little bit of the lunch left in the oilcloth wrapper. They fed the hound a special share for warning them about the panther.

As they scraped the last crumbs off the oilcloth, the Seminole boy explained how they had reached their conclusion. As they had seen the day before, the cypress swamp ran all along this side of the lake. The storm had washed away the beaches as far as the eye could see. If they took the direct route home up the shore, they could end up slogging through the shallows and cypress swamp with the alligators and who knew what else all the way. It would be slow going, and they had a long way to go.

"It is best to go east. Although the swamp is long next to the lake, I believe it is not so wide this far down. My uncle once told me he heard waves on the lake from the other side of the cypress when the wind was right."

"Why not wait here for someone to find us?"

"Nobody'll come looking here," Billy answered Queenie's question. "Seiners don't work this far down because of the rocks. The run and supply boats stick to the deeper water in the middle. Even if someone does come lookin', it'll likely take days for them to find us. And we're already out of food."

The Seminole boy added, "On the other side of the swamp, a high ridge of sand runs from Tantie to Indian Town. It is along this ridge the American Army built its trail to Jupiter after it lost the big battle near Tantie. But that was long ago. Before we were forced to flee." His voice tailed off with a mix of pride, followed by something almost like sadness.

"I have taken this road to Indian Town many times," he picked up again. "Once we find it, we will walk home within one day. We may even find someone with food to share."

Minutes later, they turned their backs to the lake and headed into the dark heart of the cypress swamp. The puppy sniffed the air and wagged its tail when Billy draped him over his shoulders to keep him from floundering around and attracting alligators. The boy nodded his thanks when Queenie offered to carry his spear.

They waded through water that was soon knee-deep and got deeper in places. Not easy going. The swamp lay completely in shadow. Tall cypress trees grew high overhead, their ghostly-gray branches coming together to shut out every ray of light. Vines, some with inch-long thorns, hung down from above. With no trail to follow, the Indian led them along the highest ground he could find, using his spear to test the depth of the muck and to brush aside the giant webs of orange and black spiders that blocked the way.

The kids climbed over and around smooth brown cypress knees that stuck out of the water, some higher than their own knees. They sank ankle-deep into soft, black mud that sucked at Queenie's shoes as they waded through stagnant shallow pools covered with green slime in an effort to avoid deeper channels of dark, almost black water. Occasionally, birds flushed from the trees above with a clatter. And more than a few dark shapes slithered or swam away from the disturbance they made.

But the Indian boy was right. In hardly a matter of hours they saw the first narrow shafts of sunlight between the trunks of the trees ahead. Then, the water gradually got shallower.

As soon as they set foot on dry ground, Billy put the dog down. The instant the hound's paws hit the sand, it took off at top speed into the palmetto bushes and disappeared. Billy laughed. "Looking for something to eat. His stomach's been growling in my ears for the last mile."

The Seminole continued leading them east. They crossed through palmetto scrub and grassy highlands shaded by pine trees. After a while, they came across two sandy ruts that wandered between trees and bushes from right to left.

"The army's trail," he announced. "But now people have forgotten our wars. Today most call it the Old Wire Road," he added, pointing at remnants of a telegraph wire that ran alongside from tree to tree, connecting glass insulators.

To Queenie, it really wasn't much of a road at all. Especially not by the standards of a girl who had grown up in a big modern city. With so little space between the trees and bushes on both sides, an ox cart could hardly push through. She didn't say anything, though. It was the road home, and they were going to take it.

Chapter 17. Outlaws

They started up the Old Wire Road toward Tantie and almost immediately smelled bacon.

During the past few days, the Seminole boy had been teaching Queenie some of his language. The two boys had also shown her some of the secret signals they had developed for sneaking up on cows and for other reasons.

Seeing his friends' eyes go wide when they smelled the bacon, the Indian gave three signals. His raised palm stopped them on a dime. Then, he ran the length of the first finger of his right hand across his upper lip from left to right. That was their "silence" signal. Letting them know he'd go see who was up ahead was a little more complicated, but once they got the message, he slipped soundlessly into the palmettos.

After the Indian disappeared into the understory, Billy relaxed a little. He whispered to Queenie, "It's not safe to just go barging up to everyone you run into out here."

That was particularly true if you weren't armed with anything more than a pointy wooden stick. Queenie didn't remind him that she had often walked similar woods with her father. She had already been *schooled* in the need for caution.

A few moments later, the Indian boy was back. He signaled them to be quiet again. They huddled, and he delivered the bad news in a low voice. "It is John Ashley and some of his gang." As if he knew what

Queenie was going to ask, he explained, "John Ashley is an outlaw and a murderer."

Ashley had started out delivering moonshine as part of his family business. One thing led to another, and he ended up killing a Seminole down in the Everglades west of Fort Lauderdale. "Desoto Tiger." The Seminole spoke the victim's name gently, paying it the respect due the dead. "We learned of his death when a dredge found his body in the river. We know it is Ashley who killed him because Desoto Tiger marked his hides with a secret mark. The trader who bought his hides from Ashley found Tiger's mark."

Ashley's family lived north of Jupiter near a coastal settlement called Hobe Sound. After the Palm Beach Sheriff tried to arrest him for killing Desoto Tiger, Ashley and his boys hid out in a hammock between Indian Town and Jupiter. Every now and then, though, they ventured south to taunt the Palm Beach Sheriff. For a while, they raised havoc as far south as Miami, selling moonshine, stealing things, and, some said, killing anyone who got in their way. Then, they disappeared. Nobody had seen them for a couple of years.

"I heard John Ashley went west over a year ago." Billy's statement questioned whether the Seminole had identified the right man.

"That is what I heard, too. But he is here now." The Seminole explained that he had gotten close enough to eavesdrop on the outlaws' conversation. Ashley had told his henchmen he was in a hurry to get to Upthegrove Beach, one of the fish camps they had passed on their way down the lake. He wanted to see a girl he knew there.

This side of Jupiter, Ashley and his boys had come across a man with a car. The four outlaws had robbed him. Last night in the storm, the car's wood spoke wheels got stuck in a mud hole. Now one of the outlaws was passed-out drunk, and the other three were trying to figure out what to do.

Queenie and the two Billies decided the wise thing for *them* to do would be to go back toward the cypress swamp and steer a wide berth around the outlaws. Before they could even take one step, however, they heard loud cries from the direction of the bacon smell. Then they heard gunshots and more hollering.

As soon as they realized the noise was headed in their direction and coming fast, the hound dog tore around the curve in the road with a slab of bacon in his mouth. The sound of two shouting men followed close behind. One, large and slow-moving, lumbered along. The other, a short, thin, bow-legged man, looked tightly-wound and mean.

Billy dived off the road to the east. Queenie and the Indian fled into the bushes to the west. They weren't quite fast enough. The men caught a glimpse of something. They stopped.

The smaller man said, "Someone's out there." He aimed his gun in the direction the girl and the Indian had gone and signaled his mate, "Come on." They started directly toward the place where the two kids had stopped fawn-still to avoid making a sound.

But before the men could leave the road and enter the palmetto scrub, a voice behind them said, "Good mornin', gentlemen."

The men whirled, guns aimed at the voice. There stood Billy, leaning on his spear with its point in the ground disguising it as a walking stick. He continued, "Please don't shoot my dog for stealing your vittles. He's a cur and a scoundrel, but he's still a pup, and he's the only hound I have." He took a few steps toward them, faking an exaggerated limp, and stuck out his hand, "Perhaps I can do something to make it up to you."

The bigger and obviously drunker of the two men put his gun away and reached his hand out to greet the boy. If the other man had done the same, Billy could have jumped away and fled back into the scrub. But the little man was either not as gullible or not as drunk. He kept his gun aimed at the boy. When his friend got close enough, the short man barked, "Grab him!"

The big man almost fell down in surprise at the order, but instead of shaking hands, he lunged and took hold of Billy's arm. The little outlaw followed with a gap-toothed grin that did not indicate good humor as the big man dragged the boy up the road toward the bacon smell. Billy didn't resist. He leaned heavily on his spear and limped all the way.

Chapter 18. The Rescue

When the outlaws were out of sight, Queenie and the Seminole moved a little farther off the road. After telling her he'd be right back, the boy disappeared. Some time later, he came back and reported things were not good. He had reached Ashley's campsite soon after Billy and the two men. The outlaws were still drinking, but they had started mixing coffee with their whiskey. Ashley, however, was the least drunk of the lot.

The Indian shared what he had seen and heard with the girl. "Billy was doing a good job trying to talk his way out of it. Ashley asked him, 'What are you doing out here?' Billy answered the question straight. He pointed out his overalls and said, 'I haul nets for catfish. Lost my boat in the storm yesterday and I'm trying to make my way home.' Then, he asked if Ashley could use his help getting the car out of the mud in exchange for breakfast and what his dog had stolen."

"What did Ashley say?"

"Nothing. Before he had a chance, Billy saw something that looks like blood on the car seat. His face gave him away. After looking in the same direction, Ashley told the big outlaw holding Billy's arm, 'Tie him up.'

"The man tied Billy's hands and looped the rope around the car's bumper. Then he asked Ashley, 'What you gonna do with him?'"

"What did he say?"

"He said nothing. Just took a sip from his mug and frowned."

After the Seminole described these events to Queenie, they agreed that Billy was in trouble and started planning a rescue. She smeared mud all over her face and pulled at her hair till it stood out in every direction from her headband. Then she shifted the petticoat sling to hang from her right shoulder. The Indian picked up his spear, and they set off toward the bacon smell.

The girl had gotten pretty good at moving silently through the bushes, at least good enough to sneak up on a bunch of drunk outlaws. With the Indian in the lead, they worked their way close enough that she could see he had told it right. The passed-out outlaw still lay face down in the shade. Billy sat on the ground next to the car, his hands tied in front with the end of the rope looped over the bumper. The girl and the Indian split up and waited for the other three outlaws to put their guns away and sit down to eat.

As soon as they did, Queenie burst out of the bushes nearest Billy without warning. She looked wide-eyed at the handsome dark-haired outlaw, John Ashley, and announced in a voice that kept getting louder until she shouted, "Thank goodness you *caught* him! HE *STOLE* TOM TIGER'S BONES! THE SEMINOLES *ARE RAMPAGING!*"

As she did so, she lurched a few crazy steps toward Ashley and stopped when she stood directly between him and Billy. Then she whirled to face the boy, turning her back to the outlaw. Before Ashley and the others could stand or protest, she slapped Billy in the face with her left hand and crouched down. She made a show of searching his overall pockets with that hand, while she used her right hand to cut the rope that bound him with her pocket knife. She kept yelling, "Where are *they*? WHERE ARE *THE BONES?*"

But Ashley was no dummy. He stood up and yelled, "Grab 'er!"

Then he lunged toward the girl, with the least drunk of the other outlaws, the small mean-looking one, not far behind. Queenie was ready. As soon as he made the move, she sprang up from her crouch and whirled toward him all in one motion. She had let her sling slide down her arm to her right hand. As she rose and turned, she swung the sling up and around as fast and hard as she could. Hidden in the petticoat cotton, the heavy weight of the black stone gathered speed as it flew in an arc toward Ashley. It hit him square on his left jaw. He went down.

The instant she began to spin around, Billy jumped up and grabbed his walking-stick spear. He swung it over hand and conked the second outlaw on the head before he could draw his gun. Right at that moment, the hound dog came running and barking into the camp, and the Indian burst out of the bushes behind the last outlaw standing. He swung his spear with both hands the way he'd seen white boys in Tantie swing baseball bats and caught that outlaw behind both knees, then once on the top of his head. Now all four outlaws lay crumpled on the ground.

Queenie and Billy fled into the bushes. The Seminole took one look at the unconscious outlaws spread out across the road and stopped long enough to grab the remaining biscuits and fatback from the frying pan before disappearing after his friends.

Chapter 19. The Chief

Not much later, Queenie and the boys stopped running in the cool, damp shade of an oak hammock. The Indian signaled them to be quiet. He'd come right back. Queenie and Billy sat down with the dog and caught their breath while they waited.

When the Seminole returned, he had good news. All four of the desperados had revived. Instead of chasing the kids, however, the outlaws were trying to push the car out of the mud.

"They are very angry." The Seminole grinned. "But they have decided it is smarter to keep moving away from Jupiter than to stay here looking for us. Plus, they are not sure how many attacked them."

At this news, the three relaxed, and soon began eating the Ashley Gang's breakfast. As they did, they started retelling the story of their heroics, laughing and congratulating each other on how quick and clever they had been.

Queenie found a pool of rainwater and was washing the mud off her face when she said to Billy, "Well, we can only hope if you ever run into John Ashley again he doesn't recognize you as the crippled fish boy who appeared out of the bushes on the Old Wire Road."

Billy stuck out his jaw on the right side of his face where she had slapped him and rubbed it with his left hand. "Nothing to worry about. The way you hit me, my face'll likely never look the same again."

She narrowed her eyes at him. After all, she *had* saved his life.

Then, as if acknowledging that fact, he reached over and brushed a smear of mud off her cheek with his thumb, saying, "One thing's for sure. He's not likely to recognize *you* as the crazy woman going on and on about Tom Tiger's bones. All got up like an Amazon and all."

The Indian boy looked up to the sky and shook his head. Then he crowed, "I have nothing to fear! They never saw me at all! Like the chiefs of old, I came and went as the mist. But I struck a mighty blow!" He beat his chest with one fist and did a hopping little dance around the other two.

"You are the Chief!" They clapped in time with his steps and chanted their approval. "You are the Chief!" And that's how the Chief got his name. From that moment on, they never called him anything else.

When the Chief finished dancing, Billy turned his attention back to Queenie, "And you should've seen the looks on their faces when you howled, 'The Seminoles are rampaging!' Ooooooo-eeeee!"

The Chief joined in, pulling at his hair and mimicking her wild gestures. They all doubled over with laughter as they continued to replay the story, enhancing their roles in it, and finishing off the last of the gang's biscuits. This time they shared only the crumbs with the dog. He had already feasted on the Ashley Gang's bacon. It was turning out to be quite an adventure.

Chapter 20. John Tiger

After the kids finished eating, they stretched out in the deep shade on the hammock floor and dozed on the soft bed of leaves, catching up on the sleep they had missed the night before. When the hound woke them up by licking Billy's face, they all realized their stomachs were growling again.

Billy asked, "Okay, Chief, now what do we do?"

Once the Chief laid out their options, it became obvious that Billy's question was actually serious. No matter how they figured it, home was a long march away. The Ashley Gang was ahead of them on the only road that took them straight there. The cypress swamp and lake lay to the west. *And,* the Chief informed them, another swamp called the Alpatiokee bordered the high ridge they were on to the east.

"Alligator water?"

"Yes," the Chief replied with a small smile. He looked pleased that Queenie was such an apt student of his language. The Alpatiokee was wide and deep in places, full of sloughs and ridges *and* alligators. It flowed all the way to the Everglades south of the lake.

"It is a bad place to be lost," he explained. "Part of it is called The Hungry Land because once, long ago, my people fled there to avoid the army and almost starved to death." The Alpatiokee could be that inhospitable.

Only one choice made any sense. They would follow the Old Wire Road south. That would take them farther from home. "But," the Chief explained, "we cannot be too far from Indian Town and Joe Bowers' Trading Post. There we will find food. And, it is likely, we will find others who will be taking the road to Tantie soon." That would also give John Ashley time to get off the road at Upthegrove Beach.

They had to get moving, however. They had spent most of a whole day trudging through the cypress swamp, escaping the Ashley Gang, celebrating Billy's rescue, and catching up on their rest. By the time they made up their minds and headed south, the afternoon was wearing on. They might not even make it to Indian Town before nightfall.

They didn't get far. Once again, the smell of food cooking over a campfire stopped them. This time, however, the smell came from somewhere in the scrub, east of the road toward the Alpatiokee.

Having learned their lesson, this time Billy grabbed hold of the dog before it could go looking for trouble. As the Chief disappeared into the palmettos to spy on whoever was doing the cooking, Billy and Queenie stepped out of sight of the road. They sat with the hound as quietly as they could, trying not to swat at the mosquitoes that swarmed in the still air after the night before's rain.

The Chief soon returned. He squatted down next to his friends. "It is the camp of one Seminole who is traveling," he reported in a low voice, "but I did not find the one who made it."

"That is because you have much work to do on your tracking skills, little nephew," a deep voice spoke out of the palmetto bush nearest his back.

All three kids jumped to their feet.

"And tell our uncles you also need to work on listening," the voice continued in English that was a little better than the Chief's as its owner stepped into view. The young Seminole man who spoke those words was apparently very good at those and many other skills, too. Even the hound hadn't realized he was there.

A taller and bigger version of the Chief, the Seminole's long shirt and sash were similar to the boy's. Except his shirt was fashioned out of small pieces of bright colored cloth sewn together in complex patterns.

"John Tiger!" The Chief whooped and started toward the older Indian in greeting, but he caught himself and stopped before he got too close. After exchanging the properly calm Seminole greetings, the Chief introduced John Tiger to his two friends. He explained that Tiger was the son of one of his mother's aunt's daughters. He had also been raised a member of the Bird Clan until he got married and became a member of his wife's clan. The Chief had known Tiger all his life, although he had not seen much of him lately.

"I am on my way home. My new clan has a camp for trading near the City of Stuart. It is the first time I have gone there," Tiger explained. "Trading is good," he added. "The train brings many new people every day. The price for pelts and meat is high. I sold enough to buy my wife a new sewing machine." He held the front of his colorful shirt out to show off his wife's handiwork.

But, the kids weren't that interested in his shirt.

"Stuart?"

"The train?"

Queenie and Billy asked their questions simultaneously. Queenie followed hers up by turning to the Chief and adding, "There's a city called Stuart *nearby*?"

"I have never been to Stuart." The Chief looked down. His response sounded like an apology.

John Tiger came to his rescue. "Stuart is not near. It is on the other side of the Alpatiokee where the river meets the ocean."

That at least explained why Queenie had never even heard of the place. Her family had traveled down the middle of the state to Tantie. She tried to visualize the Florida map, but she couldn't conjure up anything on Florida's east coast between St. Augustine and Palm Beach.

"I have never crossed the Alpatiokee," the Chief continued his defense.

"Me, neither." Billy tagged along. "Hearda Stuart, but never had reason to leave the lake before." He grinned.

Queenie pinched her eyebrows together as if getting ready to aim her next question at him.

"Plus, you can't get there from Tantie. There's no road," he added hastily and looked from the Chief to John Tiger for support.

Tiger confirmed Billy's claim. "You are right. No road crosses the Alpatiokee. But that is not important at this moment." He pointed to the western sky. "The sun is low. You cannot reach Tantie or even Indian Town before the light has gone. You are welcome this night to stay by my fire."

The kids looked from one to the other.

Tiger completed his invitation. "I have food." He sniffed the air.

The question was never in doubt. John Tiger's camp was only a short distance away through the palmetto scrub and pine trees. The smell of gopher tortoise stew bubbling in the pot on his fire drew them to it like a magnet.

Chapter 21. The Queen's Stone

Later, as they sopped up the last drops of stew, the kids explained why John Tiger had found them wandering the edge of the Alpatiokee like castaways. With help from his friends who kept adding details, the Chief described their adventures of the last two days. By the time he got to their escape from the outlaws, night had fallen.

The Chief practically danced around the campfire in excitement as he told the story. He demonstrated how Queenie had whirled about to hit John Ashley with her sling and how the two boys had whacked the other outlaws with their spears. Instead of cheering their heroics, however, Tiger looked pensive.

He spoke seriously. "John Ashley is here. That is not good news. He is a danger to our people. To all people. You did well to escape as you did."

But the girl was caught up in the Chief's bravado. "Don't worry," she blurted out. "If he tries to cause us any more trouble, I'll just hit him on the other side of his head with my stone!"

"Your stone?" Billy and John Tiger asked.

"Oh." Queenie had told the Chief she carried a stone in her sling when they planned the rescue. Now she realized she hadn't told Billy. She hefted the stone through the cotton of its sling, savoring the perfect weight of it. "It's just a stone I found."

Then to John Tiger, "It's a strange stone, actually. Maybe you can tell me what it is." She took it out of the sling and held it toward him in both hands.

Black as the night itself, the stone was almost invisible. The three young men drew closer in silence, trying to get a better look at it.

Then there was a spit from the fire. The resin in a pine knot burst into flames. Firelight danced and shimmered on the stone's shiny surfaces and sharp edges as if it came from within the stone itself.

A communal intake of breath. John Tiger's entire body flinched backward. His hand flew up, palm facing the thing in Queenie's hands as if to ward it off. Unconsciously, the two boys did the same, putting distance between themselves and it.

After steadying himself, Tiger asked in a low voice, "Did you take this from a grave?"

"No... No! I would never...!" Queenie was horrified at the suggestion. Her parents had taught her to be respectful. "I found it. Between the roots of the big tree. The tree we stayed in to escape the alligators."

Tiger turned to the Chief. The Indian boy nodded. "I saw no grave." He also affirmed that they had spent the night in a giant ancient tree that grew on one of the mounds built by the first Indians. They all held their breaths until Tiger spoke again. It seemed like forever.

"So, this stone was lost ... or left ... under the tree..." Billy and the Chief relaxed. Tiger studied Queenie long and hard. "For *you* to find."

She nodded eagerly, anticipating a pronouncement. Instead, she got another question.

"And it is with this that you chased away the panther and freed him from John Ashley?" He pointed at Billy.

Another nod. Queenie saw the two boys watching her with wide eyes. "Do you know what it is?" she asked more softly than she intended.

Tiger reached out and touched the stone for the first time. He took it in both hands. Then shifted it from hand to hand to test the feel and heft of it. After a moment, he shook his head.

"*It* does not yet know what it is. This is a stone of the ancient people who left here before we came to this land. It could have become many things ... and may yet still ... because its maker has not yet finished his work." Then, he returned it to Queenie. "In your hands, however, it has proved to be a stone of great power." Tiger locked eyes with the girl in the firelight. "That is all I know to tell you of such things."

After that, the boys couldn't wait to get their hands on it.

"When you told me you had found a stone, I did not realize it was *such* a stone," the Chief said as he lifted and touched it, giving it the respect due all things of ancient power and lore.

Billy handled it thoughtfully. When he returned it to the girl, his gaze held her eyes. He grinned, bowed his head. "Your stone, your Majesty."

Once again, she couldn't tell how he meant it.

Chapter 22. Revelations

Queenie didn't have long to think about Billy's intentions. As she tucked the stone back into her sling, the blue-eyed boy chewed his lower lip and turned to John Tiger. "So, you saw a train at Stuart?"

The Chief nodded his approval of the question and leaned closer to hear Tiger's reply.

The older Seminole answered. "Yes, many trains. One comes from the south and one from the north each day."

The two boys gave each other quick little looks. Billy went on, "You know, the railroad men say the train'll make it to Tantie within the year."

The Chief's head bobbed again in agreement.

Billy continued, "They're saying it'll bring a boom."

"A boom?" Tiger wrinkled his forehead and looked from one boy to the other.

Billy pursed his lips and furrowed his brow, too. Seeing that he was struggling to put together a definition, Queenie suggested, "Good times?"

Billy's face brightened. "And a lot of new things happening all at once."

John Tiger raised his eyebrows and grunted. "The railroad men may be right, then. I made much money in Stuart. That is good." He tapped the small sewing machine box on which he sat to emphasize his satisfaction. "And I saw many things I had not seen before."

"What kinda things?" Billy's eyes flitted to the Chief's.

"There are many people in Stuart. Many more than Indian Town and Tantie together. And all of them are rich. They live in big houses." He raised both hands to demonstrate. "Made of fine wood. Painted many colors. With glass in the windows." He shook his head. "Some even have electricity machines."

"Elec ... tricity?" Now, the Chief's brow wrinkled.

Billy nudged him with an elbow. "Remember? The railroad men say they'll be putting electricity in the station at Tantie?"

The Chief nodded, but didn't look convinced.

"Electricity's the stuff that fills those glass balls with light, right?" Billy turned back to John Tiger for verification.

"Yes. They do not burn. Yet, they glow in the night like little lanterns." Tiger held his fingers about three inches apart to demonstrate their size. "There is electricity in the Stuart train station."

The boys glanced at each other and leaned forward again.

"You wish to know of the train?" Tiger anticipated their next question.

The boys nodded so enthusiastically Queenie had to smile with them.

John Tiger granted their wish. "When the train comes, it makes a great noise. People swarm to it like bees, talking and trading. Then it leaves and everyone vanishes as fast as they came. Even those who get off the train." He shrugged and arched his eyebrows simultaneously. "Two times a day this happens. First a train comes from the south and then another comes from the north."

"Sounds like a boom to me." Billy rocked ever so slightly back and forth.

"And!" Tiger raised a finger to his lips as if he had remembered something. "Do you wish to hear of another new thing I saw?"

All three kids said, "Yes."

"I saw new fish."

"Fish?" Billy sounded skeptical and disappointed. "What could be new about fish?"

"The fish themselves. They are new … at least to me." Tiger's eyes widened. He sat straighter, as if preparing to tell a great myth. "One I saw was shining and silver. As long as a man is tall. With a mouth this wide." He held his hands a foot apart to demonstrate. "And scales so big." He pointed at the palm of his hand and drew a circle around it.

"Ain't no fish like that in any river I've ever seen." Billy leaned forward, making it clear he knew something about fishing.

"Perhaps you have not seen this river."

Put in his place, Billy slouched back into the shadows. The Chief chuckled quietly and shot his friend a sideways glance.

"A wide and deep river they call the St. Lucie surrounds the City of Stuart on three sides. I was told that when the white men first came, it did not open to the ocean. It ran as fresh as the rivers on this side of the Alpatiokee. But that was before the railroad when the people who lived there had to sail all the way to Fort Pierce to get supplies or to ship their goods to the north."

Both boys nodded. Although they'd never been there, they knew Ft. Pierce was about thirty miles north and east of Tantie. There had always been a road between those two.

Tiger continued, "The white men soon grew tired of sailing so far for everything. The river was too shallow. They could use only small boats and the trip took much time. So they dug a ditch from the St. Lucie to the ocean."

Tiger rocked on the sewing machine box as he spoke. "They call this ditch an inlet because it let the ocean in. And the ocean has changed the river."

"Changed the river?" Queenie had seen firsthand how the Kissimmee River had been dredged so steamboats could use it. And Billy had told her that dredging the new canal from the lake to Fort

Lauderdale had made fishing more profitable. Yet, this was the first time she'd thought about how doing that kind of thing might change the rivers themselves.

"Yes," Tiger continued. "Now the river flows fresh only when the ocean is falling. It tastes of salt when the ocean is rising. The great silver fish lives where the water tastes of salt."

When none of the kids said anything, he continued with a second fish story. "And I saw another new fish. It was green. Or blue?" His hands turned back and forth, indicating he couldn't find the right word. "The size of a large boy." He pointed at Billy. "It had a spear on its nose and a sail on its back. This fish was taken from the ocean itself."

Billy shook his head. "Fish like those'd wreak havoc in a net," he ventured.

"Yes. You are right. Both of these fish are strong," Tiger agreed. "But they do not use nets. I am told they are caught on a very long line attached to a strong reed they call a rod."

Tiger's eyes flashed as he continued. "And I am also told that both of these new fish want very much to live. They fight the line. Fly out of the water and shake their heads to throw off the hook!"

Queenie hadn't been all that impressed by Tiger's description of Stuart. After all, she'd seen glass windows, painted houses, motor cars, electricity, and the such before. But, she'd never heard of anything like John Tiger's giant flying fish. They sounded like something not of this world, creatures of pure imagination that belonged in her storybooks.

"They must be beautiful," slipped out of her mouth.

"They are," Tiger responded immediately, a tone of respect in his voice.

"I wish I'd seen them." She sighed.

The boys leaned back, slightly rocking as if sharing her sense of longing.

Chapter 23. The Quest

"Well." John Tiger shrugged, breaking their wistful silence. "It is not far."

All eyes swung back to him.

"Stuart," he explained. "It is not near. But it is also not far. I traveled less than one day to get to *this* place from Stuart." He pointed at the ground.

The kids' mouths flew open. The two boys leaned their heads together, bounced in their seats, and talked in hushed tones. It reminded Queenie of the first time she saw them in Tantie, back when they rounded the bend and caught sight of the cow hunters at Raulerson's store. She held her breath.

In a matter of seconds, Billy turned to face her, his eyes twinkling in the firelight. "Odysseus was all in a rush to take the straight way home. Right?"

"Yes." Queenie breathed again, but didn't say more. By then, she knew him well enough. He'd drop the other shoe when he was ready.

"And what did it get him?"

She bit her lower lip and raised one eyebrow. He didn't really want her to answer that question either.

"Does anybody ever go on a quest just to see something new?"

"Like the train?" the Chief added.

"And everything that comes with it," Billy finished the thought.

Queenie almost clapped. "And great flying…"

The boys bounced in their seats.

"Oh no!" She stopped herself. Fingertips flew to her mouth. "We can't! Our parents." She shook her head like someone who had said something terrible by accident. "They don't know. We have to go hom—"

"John Tiger can tell them," the Chief broke in. His eyes pleaded with the older Seminole.

After a moment's hesitation, Tiger grunted and replied, "I can."

"As soon as you get to the Trading Post at Indian Town, you will send word to our families?" The Chief coaxed his new co-conspirator.

After scrutinizing the three kids for a moment, Tiger answered, "I will."

Queenie was torn. The boys clearly wanted to go to Stuart, and she was sure that they wouldn't if that meant leaving her behind. John Tiger's message *would* put her parents' minds at ease as fast as if she went straight home and told them herself. Still, they probably would *not* be happy to hear she'd gone gallivanting off to the coast with these two boys on some crazy quest to see what their future would bring.

On the other hand, she'd spent her whole life reading about other people's adventures, pretending to be Tiger Lily as she walked beside her father through the woods. Now she was having an adventure of her own, a *real* adventure. Why should it have to end so quickly?

After all, she'd be leaving the jungle one day. This could be her only chance. And she *was* almost grown. And ... what with the alligator, the panther, and the outlaws, she and the boys *had* proved they could take care of themselves. And she *was* a descendant of the Amazon Queen. And she *did* have the stone, now. And Stuart *wasn't* all that far. *And...* The more "*ands*" she added...

She'd be safe. Her parents were smart and supportive. They always wanted her to learn new things. Of course, they'd understand. They'd be excited for her.

"You'll make sure they don't worry?" she asked John Tiger.

Billy and the Chief hooted and elbowed each other.

Tiger nodded, maintaining a serious demeanor even as he grinned with the boys. "I will send word tomorrow that you have taken my canoe to Stuart and that the elder of my clan will welcome you to our camp."

Later they worked out the details. "The Alpatiokee is narrow here," Tiger explained. "I will show you a game trail that follows mostly high ground to a creek that begins deep in the swamp. My canoe is tied there. That creek is small, but it will take you to Stuart's river."

To come home, all they had to do was pole the canoe back up to John Tiger's hiding place and take the military trail up to Tantie, exactly as they had planned all along.

It sounded so easy that Queenie joined the boys in a more subdued version of the whole hooting and elbowing thing. They really were going to see the train. *And* the great flying fish. *And* whatever else they could find in the new City of Stuart.

After a while, the breeze died down and the mosquitoes came out from their hiding places under the palmetto fronds. John Tiger unrolled his mosquito bar and hung it above them, creating a small tent made of cheesecloth mesh that let the air in while keeping the flying insects out.

All four crawled inside and their talk wound down. At first, it meandered from the events of the day to their plans for the morning and speculation about the new things they would find in Stuart. Eventually, the safe presence of the older Indian, the fire, the dog, and the mosquito bar won out. The kids relaxed into a pile, like a litter of exhausted puppies, and fell into a deep sleep.

Chapter 24. The Alpatiokee and Beyond

Their quest. That's what Queenie was dreaming about when they awoke at dawn. A breakfast of hard bread, a thankful goodbye to John Tiger, and they set out to the east. In an instant, they entered a magical world. The Alpatiokee was mysterious in the morning. A narrow band of fog hovered about knee high over the wetlands and reached into the spaces between the palmetto bushes that marked the edge of the path they followed along the high ground.

The shape of a deer with its head held high at alert appeared out of the mist ahead of them. For a moment, low-slanting rays of the morning sun outlined its silhouette in gold. And then it was gone. At one point, the Chief gave them the "be still" signal. He pointed off to the side of the path and sniffed the air.

"Musk," he announced in a low voice. "Rattlesnake."

"What do we do?" Rattlesnakes were one of the things Queenie's father had taught her to be wary of in the woods. She sniffed. She smelled something. Was *that* the snake?

"We wait. He will go where he is going." The Chief explained that Seminoles seldom had trouble with rattlesnakes because the two had come to a mutual agreement years before. They respected each other and left each other alone.

By the time he finished, the smell had moved away, and morning in the Alpatiokee started back up again as if there had been no interruption. The kids heard, rather than saw, a family of hogs grunt and squeal its way across the path in front of them. And birds surrounded them. Seen and unseen. Buntings, jays, and mockingbirds in the air. Quail underneath the palmettos. Calling and chirping, flitting and flying as they greeted the new day.

They made good time and reached the creek in a couple of hours. John Tiger's canoe had been carved out of the trunk of an ancient cypress tree using fire and small axes many years before. Fourteen feet long and almost four feet wide, it provided plenty of room for the three kids and the dog if they sat single file. Moments later, they slipped soundlessly into the tiny creek John Tiger said would take them to the wide St. Lucie River.

John Tiger had poled his way as far into the Alpatiokee as he could. They spent the first part of the trip pushing aside bushes and ducking under branches, making sure snakes and other critters didn't drop into the canoe with them. The slow current from the rains the day before helped them follow the channel which grew wider as it left the swamp.

Once they found that channel, they could have let that current take them lazily all the way to the ocean, but they were in a hurry to get there. As soon as the space between the bushes and trees grew tall enough, the Chief stood up in the dugout and poled them along at top speed.

Orchids and ferns that looked like green hands grew on the trunks of cabbage palms that crowded the water's edge. The dark, curved branches of oak trees arched overhead. Fuzzy air plants with spiky leaves and bright red flowers that sat at the top of long, thin stems lined their edges. In some places, they looked like thin, hairy arms reaching across the river to shake hands. Sleek otters, with long, pointed tails and fur so deep a brown they looked black, washed their breakfasts in the river and chirped at them from the shore before turning quickly and waddling into the bushes.

When it got the chance, the sun peeked through the branches. Individual rays highlighted the curved shells of turtle families lined up from smallest to largest on half-sunken logs.

A little farther down the river, Billy pointed at an alligator dozing in a patch of sun. "Funny," he said, "that's the first gator I've seen this side the Alpatiokee."

As the Seminole grunted his agreement, the gator realized the dugout was approaching, slid down muddy banks, and disappeared into the water. The Indian shook his head. "He seems afraid."

"Of a dugout canoe?" his friend questioned. "That ain't normal."

"But that's better than me having to be afraid of them," Queenie chimed in, stretching the folds of her pantaloons over her knees. In the past few days she'd come face-to-face with enough alligators to last her a lifetime.

"Look." The Indian pointed at a muddy spit of land that sloped down to the water's edge. "That is why they are afraid." The bodies of dead alligators lay at sixes and sevens on the muddy bank between palms and oaks.

"They didn't take the skins or the tails." Billy whistled between his teeth.

"They weren't trappers or hunters," Queenie broke in. "I saw the same thing coming down the Kissimmee. Two men from up north stood on the deck of the steamboat and shot at everything that moved."

"But the skins and the tails. That's money. And food." Billy shook his head again.

"They already have money and food," the Seminole concluded flatly, and gestured at another carcass with his chin.

"Yeah," Queenie concurred. "The men on the Kissimmee were on holiday. They made money and liquor bets about who could kill the most. Like a game to keep them from getting bored. There's really not much to see coming down the Kissimmee, you know."

Both boys looked at the girl as if she was crazy.

She tried to explain, "The prairie's all the same ... swamps and bushes, swamps and trees."

The Chief stopped poling.

Flustered, Queenie added, "And what's wrong with it anyway? Alligators are horrible! They want to eat us! Why not kill them all and get it over with?"

"The Creator put them here," the Chief answered in a low voice. "This is their proper place."

After that, the kids rode the river in silence for quite some time. Queenie pondered the dilemma of people moving into the alligator's place, but with no success. Eventually, she simply wanted to put the fact that she'd upset boys out of her mind.

Leaning back against Tiger's sand-filled firebox at the front of the canoe, she tried to imagine if this was how the great Egyptian Queen, Cleopatra, had felt when she floated down the Nile. Then she remembered her dream. She'd tell the boys about it. That would win them back.

"Last night I dreamed that we were Knights of the Round Table. We'd already set out on our quest! And we'd already passed three tests: the alligator, the panther, and the outlaws! Tests and charms always come in threes! We..."

Once again, her rambling excitement drew only blank stares from the boys. Billy, who was braiding the long thin strips of her petticoat into a stronger line he could use to control the dog once they reached the City of Stuart, screwed up his face. "The what's of the what?"

Queenie sat up straight and clasped her hands under her chin in delight. This was one of her favorite stories. She started again, without realizing she was starting in the middle. "The Knights of the Round Table were the greatest heroes of all time."

Billy furrowed his brow as if he still didn't understand. "Thought you said all the heroes at Troy—"

"Oh, no!" She realized her mistake. "That was a Greek story. This one's from England. England's another country."

Billy rolled his eyes as if disgusted. "We've *heard* of England." He looked to the Indian boy, who nodded in confirmation. "These knight fellas'll have to go some to outdo your Greek heroes, though." Billy shook his head and spit into the river, but he sat up to listen.

"Oh, they do!" Queenie accepted his unspoken invitation to continue and started over enthusiastically. "The greatest fighters in all of England were called knights. But, you see, not all of the knights were good knights."

Billy sniggered.

She ignored him. "In the olden days, evil dark knights roamed the countryside. They used their power to plunder the land and enslave the people. Then, a boy named Arthur became king, and he came up with the idea to send out a call for all knights who were pure of heart to join him. Together, they'd fight for what was good and right. The best and most handsome knights from all over the world answered his call."

The boys rolled their eyes. Probably at the word handsome. She rolled her eyes back. "They came to England to sit at his Round Table!" Seeing the looks on the boy's faces, she explained, "He had a round table made because a round table has no head. Everyone who sat at it was equal."

Billy nodded.

"But the knights had to earn their place at the table, to prove they were good enough. King Arthur put them to tests, and if they passed, he tapped them on the shoulders with his sword Excalibur." She demonstrated the gesture with the first two fingers of her right hand. "And said, 'Arise Knight of the Round Table.'"

Billy wagged his head from side to side and worked his tongue in his cheek. He seemed to be thinking about what she had said.

The boys gave her their full attention when she described the fighting contests King Arthur set up to determine who were the greatest knights of all. Gallant warriors strapped on heavy suits of armor. Bright flags snapped in the wind. Trumpets blared! Giant iron-clad horses thundered toward each other. Their hooves shook the ground. The crowd roared in anticipation, and the fairest maidens in the land tied colorful scarves on the knights' armor as a token of their honor and respect.

Before long, the boys were reliving their own adventures once again. This time with a new vision of their heroics in mind. Their spears became lances and broadswords. They swung them mightily. They smote the alligator-dragon and triumphed over the dark knights of the Ashley Gang.

The sounds of children's laughter interrupted Queenie before she could get back to the beginning and tell them the story of how Arthur became the king by finding a magic sword that was stuck in a stone. They had been so engrossed in her storytelling none of them had noticed they were floating past a small house that fronted the river.

A few minutes later, the river rounded a bend and opened up to spread half a mile across. Boats and rooftops dotted the right hand shore, right where John Tiger said they would. Because the river was so wide here, the current slowed. Still, with the Chief poling hard, they fairly flew over the shallows. All the way down from the swamp, the water had been the color of tea. Here, it lightened up and was so clear they could count crabs and small fish hiding in the water grass that covered much of the white sand bottom as they passed.

John Tiger had drawn good directions to the Seminole camp in the sand. They were traveling up the wide St. Lucie River from the south. They'd find Stuart ahead on the right at the point where the St. Lucie joined an even wider river from the north and a creek from the west to become one great river that flowed to the east.

A sharp spit of land stuck out into the St. Lucie right before it met the other rivers. On this side of that point, they'd find a creek. The Seminole camp would be about half a mile up that creek. Identifying its mouth was easy because John Tiger had also described the homes that marked it. They turned in, and within minutes, left the houses behind. At first, fields lined the banks. Then woods once again, and finally, the Seminole camp nestled in the trees.

Chapter 25. Stuart on the St. Lucie

The Seminole camp was small, only a few chickees arranged in a loose circle. The chickees were not like houses or even the huts fishermen built on the beach. They had no walls. Thick palm-thatch roofs supported by cypress poles and held in place by logs provided shelter from sun and rain. Bags and shelves attached high in the rafters protected the Indians' clothes, food, and other goods from the weather as well as from the dogs, hogs, and chickens that moved freely through the camp. Open platforms about two feet above the sand served as elevated floors on which the Seminoles worked and slept, rolling down the cheesecloth canopies of the mosquito bars as needed.

In the center of the circle stood one chickee under which a fire burned. The Chief explained that Seminoles cooked and ate there as a family. He pointed out how the long logs radiated from the center of the fire like the spokes of a wheel. "We shove them to the middle as they burn. Until they are too short, they are a good place to sit."

Pots of stew and sofkee bubbled over the cook fire. Their smells wafting on the breeze reminded the kids they were hungry again.

As soon as they entered the camp, the largest of the camp dogs rose from its shady spot under one of the platforms and moved toward them warily. Before any of them could react, Billy's hound stepped forward to face him. The Seminole dog stood with its feet apart, dropped its head, and growled. Its hackles rose at its shoulders.

That didn't deter Billy's hound. He dropped his whole front half, chest, two front legs, and chin to the ground, leaving his hind quarters up in the air as if bowing to a king. The large dog kept coming. When it was only a step away, the pup rolled over on his back, feet in the air and his tongue hanging out. He wagged his tail so vigorously his whole body wiggled from side to side.

That changed everything. The camp dog's tail slowly moved from side to side. It accepted the hound's tribute by sniffing its black nose. A voice issued a short command in Seminole, and the camp dog retreated to the shade of the chickees from whence it had come. Without moving, the Chief called out his thanks and asked to see the elder woman in charge.

The woman who had commanded the dog emerged from the chickee and introduced herself as the one the Chief was seeking. The weathered skin of her round face was even darker than the Seminole boy's. She was not quite as tall as Queenie, but heavier, with deep wrinkles converging on high, wide cheekbones and deep-set dark eyes. Her long straight hair was mostly gray, with only a few streaks of black remaining. A fringe of bangs cut across the middle of her forehead. The rest of her hair lay piled neatly on top of her head.

The woman's long skirt fell almost to the ground, so that the toes of her bare feet showed only when she walked. It and a shawl, which ended a bit above her elbows, were made of horizontal bands of different kinds of cotton cloth. But her beads drew all attention to her face. There were so many multi-colored strands stacked between her shoulders and her earlobes Queenie couldn't begin to count them.

The Chief introduced himself. Seminoles usually treated visitors well. Plus, only a few hundred Seminoles still lived in Florida, and almost all of them knew each other, at least somewhat, because the clans regularly got together in the Everglades for the Green Corn and Hunting Dances. In this case, the Chief's grandmother's brother had also married into John Tiger's new clan. For any one of those reasons, it would have been natural for the elder to welcome them graciously.

All those reasons put together, the woman smiled openly and spoke animatedly with the Chief in Seminole. When she stopped, the boy turned to his friends, "She does not speak much English. We are invited to stay … and eat."

Three sets of young eyes flew to the cook fire. Billy, who had been a dinner guest in the Chief's camp several times before, nodded his thanks and took a step toward the food. Queenie stopped him with her arm.

"Excuse me," she said to get the old woman's attention.

Before she met the Chief, Queenie and her father had already picked up a few random Seminole phrases. Over the past few days, the Chief had given her actual lessons in his language, which he explained was called Muscogee. She joined her hands at her waist and bowed her upper body slightly toward the old woman in a gesture intended to show respect. Then, she said the Muscogee words she thought meant, "Hello. It is an honor to meet you. Thank you."

Fingers flew to mouths all around them. A twitter of conversation swept through the handful of Seminoles who had gathered loosely around the three to see what was going on. They spoke to each other so softly and quickly behind their fingertips that the girl didn't understand a word of what they said. Nor did she know how to read their expressions. What if she hadn't gotten the words right? Had she said something outlandish? Or even offensive? Her fingers flew to her lips, too.

The Seminole elder leaned closer to the Chief and said something softly but with a serious expression on her face. The boy nodded and responded with the same serious demeanor. Queenie held her breath.

When the elder turned back, however, the woman's eyes smiled at her. Once they crinkled the edges, the rest of her face followed. She spoke in Seminole, but she never stopped looking at Queenie.

The Chief translated, choosing his words even more formally than usual. "The elder says, 'You are welcome to our fire and our food. It is an honor to meet *you*, too.'"

The woman returned Queenie's slight bow as he translated her words. The girl acknowledged the greeting with a small smile and a tilt of her forehead while making eye contact with the elder. The Chief beamed from one to the other.

Then, Billy stepped forward and rubbed his stomach. "Thank you, kindly. I'm starvin'." The elder laughed and took his arm, leading him past the others toward the pots that bubbled on the fire. He raised his eyebrows at Queenie as he sauntered by.

When Billy reached the closest steaming cauldron, he grabbed the huge wooden spoon that hung next to it, dipped it into the stew, and sipped the broth directly from it. Queenie's startled hand flew to her mouth. She looked at the Chief to see how he responded to this horrible breach of manners, only to find that he held the bowl-sized spoon from the other pot out for her to take.

"Here. It is sofkee ... made from corn."

Queenie hesitated. Was it some kind of trick the Seminoles played on newcomers? No. She didn't believe the Chief was the kind to play jokes at other people's expense. Still, to be sure she asked, "We all use the same spoon?"

"Yes." The boy extended it again. "And you are a guest. You may eat now."

Still doubtful, Queenie accepted the wooden utensil and took a small sip. The sofkee turned out to be a wet Seminole version of grits. Familiar and filling. When Billy finished his bowl-sized spoonful of stew, he handed the spoon to the Chief who stirred around in the pot until he found whatever morsel he wanted, and Queenie handed the blue-eyed boy the one she'd been using. After they passed the spoons around three times, Billy was the only one still eating.

Queenie took it all in. Seminoles apparently helped themselves from the pots whenever they wanted, rather than sitting down to a meal. Most of those who had gathered to greet the kids had gone back to whatever they had been doing before they arrived. The Chief spoke with the elder woman in Muscogee while they ate, bringing her up to date on the news from west of the Alpatiokee.

After two more spoonfuls of stew and sofkee, even Billy patted his full belly in gratitude. Telling the elder they'd be back, they set out to do what they had come there to do, explore the booming new world of Stuart.

With the dog secured on its new petticoat leash, the kids started up the sandy trail that led north from the camp. Within minutes, the scrubby woods gave way to small fields. Soon, they passed houses with yards and gardens. By the time they found the railroad tracks half an hour later, the boys were wide-eyed in anticipation.

Stuart turned out to be even more than John Tiger had been able to describe. A shiny brand new train station that looked just like the one the railroad had built in Okeechobee stood next to the tracks. The one main road between the tracks and the wide east-flowing river was smooth. It had been hardened with crushed stone brought in from somewhere else. Businesses lined that road and the tracks. A bank. A hotel. A drugstore right across from the station in a sturdy-looking building made of square man-made stones. Most of the stores were two stories tall and had their names painted on their walls in bold letters for all the world to see. Some of the houses and a huge building that was rising up along the riverfront were even three stories tall.

And so many people. The kids would later learn that the State had made Stuart a real city earlier that year, and over seven hundred people lived there. Seven hundred. And that number did not include the other people, the people who had come to town from surrounding areas with names like Palm City, Jensen, and Salerno. Or the new people who arrived on the train.

And all those people were constantly coming from and going to somewhere. People on foot. People on horseback. Buckboards, ox carts, bicycles, and motor cars. More motor cars than the boys had imagined even existed. And, then, all the activity doubled as the residents of the town started gathering to greet the afternoon train, just as John Tiger said they would.

The train came from the north, rumbling, and vibrating its tracks, as tall as three men standing on each other's shoulders. Its whistle let out steam when it hooted, and its stack belched black smoke as it crossed the river. Steel wheels screeched on steel tracks as it braked to a stop next to the station.

A flurry of activity. Men's voices called out, "Stuart ... Stuart on the St. Lucie!"

Passengers stepped down from the train on little step stools. Some were met by what seemed to be friends or family. Others strode purposefully to businesses in town. Still others carried their suitcases to a nearby hotel with a sign that read, "The Stuart House." A handful of the debarking passengers stood there waiting in the shade looking lost. Queenie concluded they were tourists because of the way they searched the faces of the people around them until local men called out their names and started loading up their travel trunks and other belongings to cart them off to wherever they had made arrangements to stay. A few wearing funny hats carried fishing poles. John Tiger was right again.

Stuart had turned out to be more exciting than the kids could ever have imagined.

Chapter 26. The Tourist

Queenie and the boys stood off to the side of the road and marveled at all this hubbub. Suddenly, they heard something that sounded like a gunshot followed by a shout. Then the sounds of crunching, crashing, and galloping hooves. A car had backfired. That had startled one of the horses lined up to collect its load of tourists. The horse had bolted away from the station with its empty wagon careening wildly behind it.

No. The wagon wasn't empty. A small fair-haired girl in a white smock bounced around in its back cargo section.

Billy reacted before anyone else had a chance. He took off running toward the place the horse was headed. He got there right before it did and ran alongside as the wagon's front wheels flashed past him. Then he grabbed its sideboard, put one foot on the running board, and swung himself up and over. Within seconds, Billy had positioned himself in the driver's seat and gathered the reins. He pulled the horse in.

The Chief, Queenie, and the hound dog had joined the chase a step behind Billy. As he slowed the horse to a walk, the Chief grabbed its bridle and started soothing it. Queenie threw the dog into the wagon to keep it out of trouble. Then she stepped up onto the running board to check on the girl. The child wasn't hurt. She wasn't even upset. She laughed and hugged the hound as it licked what looked like candy off her face.

Queenie kept an eye on the girl and the dog from the running board while the boys guided the horse back to the station. One of the Yankee tourists had stepped out into the road to meet them. Behind him stood a woman in a well-tailored Yankee dress with her hair pulled back in a bun. Behind her stood a girl a bit younger than the two Billies, and behind her a slightly younger boy.

The Chief turned the horse's lead over to the local who came forward to claim it. Billy then handed the girl down to Queenie, who handed her to the tourist. After checking for bumps and bruises, he turned and handed the smiling child to her mother. The mother also checked for bumps and bruises while obviously trying not to cry.

Queenie and the boys turned to walk away, but the Yankee stopped them in their tracks by clearing his throat, "Ahem."

They turned back to face him.

He wore a dark suit with a starched white collar. His shoes were shiny and black. A gold watch chain hung in a lazy loop out of his vest pocket, and his round wire-rimmed eyeglasses magnified his eyes to twice their real size. The kids had never seen the like.

The tourist took one step forward as if he intended to say something. Then he stopped and peered at the three of them one at a time through those glasses. First at Billy. Then at the Chief. And then at Queenie. Finally, he harrumphed, and spoke in a manner that matched his suit.

Apologetically at first, "I should have known better than to leave the child in the wagon unattended." He seemed to be talking to the crowd that had gathered to watch all the excitement as much as to the kids. "But this is our first trip to Florida. And, truthfully, I was not fully prepared ... ahem ... for quite how wild and wooly it all is."

Then, he focused on Billy, "Young man, will you tell me your name? So that we may properly ascribe to you our debt of gratitude."

Chapter 27. The Cow Hunter, the Indian, and the Amazon

Queenie knew Billy had never seen so many people standing still in one place before. Nor had he ever been the focus of so much attention. He seemed both embarrassed and amused at being the center of this production. She read his face as he fumbled around in his mind, trying to figure out how to play his role. Then he made his choice.

Adopting a casual pose with his weight on one foot, he answered with a grin, "Billy'll get the job done, sir."

The tourist was quick. He flipped the jest of Billy's pose back on him. "Billy it is, then." He nodded. "So, tell me, Billy. Exactly what *job* it is that you usually *get done* around here?" The man actually fluttered his hand to indicate the general direction of the town when he said "around here."

Billy took his time to chew on the question for a moment. Then he looked at Queenie, gave her the slightest wink, and answered, "Folks call it cow huntin'."

"Cow hunting … hmmm." The tourist was enjoying this introduction to Florida. Queenie could almost see the wheels turning in his brain as he tried to make sense of Billy's answer. Then, he abandoned any attempt at clever comeback. "You have me there. I know little— No! I know *nothing* of cow hunting. But from the way you halted the runaway, I can surmise only that you must be good at it. We are in your debt, Billy the Cow Hunter." He emphasized that statement with a tip of his head toward the boy.

Then, he faced the Chief and said, "No, don't tell me." This time he lifted his index finger in front of his nose before pointing it at the boy. "You are ... you are ... a Seminole Indian. Right?"

The Chief took his cue from his friend and made the most of his moment at the center of this spectacle, too. In a quick sequence of individual gestures, he stood taller, spread his feet apart, puffed out his chest, and crossed his arms over it. Then, he lifted his chin toward the man and answered calmly in a strong but low voice, "I am."

The tourist gave a self-satisfied nod as if he was proud to have gotten it right. Queenie thought it looked as if the Yankee was trying to remember things he had read in a tourist guidebook while preparing for this trip. Suddenly, though, he switched his focus to her.

This time, he paused and studied her from head to toe. Then he did it again before speaking, "And you are... You are... Let me see..." He pursed his lips and patted them with his forefinger as he tried to puzzle it out.

Just then, the girl caught a glimpse of her reflection in the train station window behind the man and understood his dilemma. She stood there, covered in mud and dirt, wearing sturdy leather shoes and pantaloons fashioned out of a skirt tied up with petticoat strips. The sling that stretched across her chest bulged with the shape of the black stone, and her hair stuck out in all directions from her headband. Her mother would have been horrified. Heat and color flooded into her cheeks.

But, she'd be danged if she was going to curtsey politely and explain, "Why, sir, I really am a proper young colored girl from Baltimore. It's just that, you see, I've been lost in the swamp for a while."

Her decision made, too, Queenie stuck out her chin and struck a pose that mirrored the stance the Chief had taken on Billy's other side. Now, the casually confident cow hunter was flanked by two powerful warriors. She answered in the same deep tone the Chief had used, "I am an Amazon."

"An Amazon?"

"An Amazon." She was pretty sure that wasn't in the tourist's guidebook.

But, the man recovered quickly. "Well, then." He half-turned toward his wife and spoke over his shoulder. "Josephine, please remember when you make our journal entry for this day to include that, upon arrival in Stuart, our Sally's life was saved by a Florida cow hunter, a Seminole Indian, and an ... an Amazon."

When he faced the kids again, he smiled and his hand came out of his pocket. "Thank you, Billy. Thank you all." He nodded to each of the kids separately. Then he placed something into Billy's hand and said he hoped they would accept it as a token of his family's "deepest gratitude." But they really *did* have to get on with loading their belongings if they intended to get settled at the inn before nightfall.

While all this was going on, freight and mail had been unloaded and loaded. A few new passengers had boarded the train. As the tourist and his family attended to their things, the train's steam boilers rumbled back to life. Once again, the stack belched smoke, and the engine roared as the cars clunked into motion one at a time and started rolling, slowly at first, to the south. The hound joined the town dogs barking, and everybody waved as the train picked up speed and disappeared down the track.

Only then did the kids look at what the tourist had placed in the palm of Billy's hand. Three silver dollars. Grinning, Billy put two of them into the button-down pocket at the front of his overalls. After consulting with Queenie, who knew more about the ways of city life than he and the Chief did after all, he took the third dollar into the drugstore soda fountain. When he came out, he carried the first bottled sodas the boys had ever tasted. They had been on their quest for less than one day and they had already found treasure!

The boys knew that the same Florida East Coast Railway Company was laying tracks to the new town of Okeechobee it was building out on the prairie. They knew that sometime the next year, those tracks would start bringing trains like the one they had just seen. But, so far, all they had brought to town was a few motor cars full of surveyors and land developers. Nothing much about life on the lake's north shore was different that before. At least not yet.

Until they got to Stuart, they had no idea what changes the train and the new city would bring. Or what those changes would mean to their lives. They still didn't comprehend the full extent. Now at least, they had an inkling. Big-eyed, overwhelmed, and wound up by the prospects, they could hardly stand still.

Chapter 28. Hunted

The kids laughed about their latest adventure. Walked and watched, talked and listened, and searched the glass-fronted store windows of downtown Stuart for new things to talk about. The evening of a wonderful day was about to begin.

Then without warning, the Chief stopped short and gasped, "Hide!"

Jerking his friends by their arms, he led them roughly around the corner of the nearest building, into the late afternoon shadow. He smashed his shoulders and the back of his head flat against the wall and motioned for them to do the same. Then, he gave the "be-silent" and "stay-where-you-are" signals and inched his way slowly back to the corner, his shoulders pressed firmly against the siding.

Queenie gave Billy a questioning look. He shrugged and raised his eyebrows. They waited without saying a word.

The Chief leaned slightly forward and turned his head slowly till he could see around the corner of the building. He pulled his head back as soon as he did. "Ashley!" he hissed, directing the other two even farther away from the street into the alcove of a doorway.

The three scurried farther out of sight. As they peeked one eye each out of the alcove, a car came into view. It drove past slowly, the two men inside it scanning both sides of the street. The Chief was right. It *was* John Ashley. He was driving the same car they'd seen on the Old Wire Road. Now, though, he had only one passenger, the short scruffy man who had ordered Billy's capture on the trail.

The blue-eyed boy's breath came out in a hiss.

"But how can they—" Queenie started.

The Chief shushed her again by raising his index finger up to his lips before she got the words out. After a minute had passed, the Indian whispered, "They did not see me." Then, he dusted his shirt off and pulled himself tall and straight with his shoulders back. Giving them the "stay" sign again, he strolled nonchalantly out of the alcove back toward the street.

Queenie had lost all of the bravado she had displayed the night before when bragging to John Tiger about defeating the outlaws. This was Ashley's turf. He and his thug looked a lot more dangerous driving down the streets of Stuart than they had when they had been drunk and stuck in the mud out in the jungle. The dog growled, but Billy held its petticoat leash short and didn't say anything.

More than a few minutes later, the Seminole's low voice beckoned them to the street corner. "Come with me." He gestured with his whole arm, leading them with quick choppy steps across the street in the opposite direction from where Ashley had been headed and looking back every few steps or so. When they reached the far side of the train station, the Chief turned. "You must meet someone."

Before them stood a Seminole woman dressed in unusually bright, but traditional, Seminole clothes. Not only her clothes, however, set her apart. Very large and very dark-skinned, she carried a very big purse and led two small black hogs on leashes like dogs.

Billy shook his head as the hound and hogs greeted each other nose-to-nose, grunting and tail wagging like long-lost friends. "Some kind of hunting dog..." He didn't bother to finish the thought.

"This is Anna Blue," the Chief said. "Anna, these are my friends. Billy and the Queen." After a pause in which the three nodded politely to each other, he continued, "Anna is a member of John Tiger's clan. She trades at the station," the Chief explained, "and stays at the camp."

The woman smiled.

"Where'd Ashley go?" Billy demanded of the Chief, acknowledging the woman with a tip of his head, but not waiting for the formalities to get over with.

"I did not get to the street in time to see." The Chief apologized by tilting his head and raising both shoulders as he turned to face Anna.

The large Seminole woman's smile shifted to a thoughtful look. "He came off the ferry. From the direction of Fort Pierce. And he turned toward the new hotel." Her English was slightly better than the Chief's. She pointed toward a road a bit farther down the tracks from the station.

"How could he be here?" Queenie asked nobody in particular. She still couldn't believe he actually was. "We saw him just yesterday on the Military Trail ... way on the other side of the Alpatiokee."

Anna scrutinized Queenie for a moment, pursed her lips, and frowned before answering, "That road meets another at Tantie. It is also a Military Trail. It goes to Fort Pierce."

"But in one day?"

"It took us only half a day," the Chief reminded the girl, who looked embarrassed at asking such a dumb question.

"And they have a car," Anna offered. "Cars are very good to have. I would like to own a car." After a slight pause, she brought herself back on point. "And the road to Fort Pierce is what white men call a corduroy road." Seeing Queenie's confused look, the Seminole woman shrugged as if it didn't make any sense to her either and explained, "They have laid logs across the wet places. They call it that because it has ridges like a cloth they wear." She shrugged. "It is very bumpy, but still a good road."

After another pause, during which internal calculations were visible on her face, she continued, "Yes. It is the long way to go, but a car could travel from Jupiter to Tantie to Fort Pierce and here in one day." Another pause, followed by a nod. "Yes, it would be good to have a car."

"But he *said* he was stopping to see a girl." Still focused on Ashley, Queenie looked to the Chief for confirmation.

He nodded.

"Ah. That I know something about," Anna said calmly. All eyes turned to her again. "I was near the street as he talked with a man. He said, 'No account girl wasn't home.'" The big Seminole woman mimicked the outlaw's drawl, then continued in her own voice, "So now he's looking for someone else."

"Did he say who?" Queenie didn't want to hear the answer. This really couldn't be happening.

"Just someone he had 'some unfinished business with.'" She mimicked the outlaw's threatening, serious tone this time.

The kids traded wild glances and fidgeted. What to do now?

Anna observed them. "You met Ashley yesterday?"

Three sets of eyes flew back to her. Three heads nodded.

"Is it you he is looking for?" She looked concerned at the prospect.

All three nodded, and Queenie's, "Most likely," sounded like an apology.

"Come." Anna nodded and led her hogs across the tracks toward the other side of the city. "There is a hidden way to the camp. You will be safe there. Ashley will not dare come to the camp, and he will not stay long in town. We will send word to Sheriff Baker in West Palm Beach that he is here."

They followed the hogs into the head of a narrow trail that immediately disappeared into oak scrub. The kids told Anna the details of their meeting with Ashley as they walked. She frowned and then smiled, but hurried them along nonetheless.

That night, her stomach once again full of the elder's sofkee and stew, Queenie cleaned herself up in the fresh water of the creek. She scrubbed her skin shiny in the moonlight with fine white sand from its bank and borrowed a skirt and shawl from Anna to wear while waiting for the fire to dry her dress. She even combed the tangles out of her hair. She had been truly embarrassed by the reflection she had seen in the train station window. Now, she also had another, bigger motive. If she didn't look like an Amazon, John Ashley probably wouldn't be able to pick her out in a crowd.

The Chief explained their plight to the elder, and after consulting some of the other Seminoles, she came back to them. "Not safe now. Ashley still at hotel. But…" She tapped her chest lightly with two fingers. "We tell sheriff. Not stay long." Her words echoed Anna's.

The kids thought it over and found a source of relief in what she had said. Everyone who knew anything about John Ashley at all agreed on one thing. He would be leaving soon because the sheriff from Palm Beach wanted to arrest him so badly he'd come all the way to Stuart to get him. He'd be gone the next morning, if not that night. And they hadn't intended to spend the next day in town anyway. They'd already decided to go look for the ocean and the great silver fish.

The river was an especially good place to hide because Ashley was in a motor car. For all the cars and carts and bicycles in Stuart, there still weren't many roads. Only a few near the business section were hardened with crushed rocks. The rest were almost as bad as the old Military Trail, rough parallel ruts cut and grubbed through scrubby oaks and pines. The river was still the best way to travel around Stuart, and it would take them places Ashley and his car could never go. They'd couldn't even run into him by accident.

Dry and in her own clothes again, her petticoat strips packed away in her sling, Queenie convinced herself that everything would be fine. Ashley'd give up and move on. He'd be out of their lives by the time they got back. Even if he wasn't, the Seminoles would hide them till he did leave town. Oddly, enough, or maybe not, given all the excitement of that day, she slept well on the elder's platform under the mosquito bar.

Chapter 29. Zack

They set off in the dugout early the next morning. No sooner had they rounded the point into the wide river than they saw their first obstacle. The railroad bridge crossed the St. Lucie right where all the rivers came together. Made of concrete and steel, it sat low on the water. The drawbridge was down even though no train was coming. Several men picked their way gingerly across it on foot.

At first, the bridge appeared to block their way completely as if the people of Stuart had fenced off the river the way cattlemen had started fencing off the land up on the Kissimmee prairie. When they poled closer, however, they discovered there was enough space between it and the water that they could float under it, if they lay flat in the dugout.

They faced another obstacle almost as soon as they came out from under the bridge. The ferry was pulling into its dock, loaded to the brim and struggling under its burden of one touring automobile, its four occupants, and their luggage. As it slowly bumped to a halt, the kids overheard the tourists worrying among themselves.

"The guide book was right," one of them said. After they left Fort Pierce, the Miami Highway *had* become almost impassable. They had been lucky to find a place to stay in Jensen.

"And now this! We had to wait *over an hour* just to cross this one river."

"And the road's supposed to get *even worse* south of here."

"If we can't make it the forty miles to Palm Beach before dark, what will we *do*?"

The three kids rolled their eyes at the fretting travelers and returned the ferryman's wave as they slipped behind his tiny barge to face the main east-flowing river for the first time. They poled swiftly across the shallows and paddled through deeper water to get around long wooden docks with buildings on them. Within minutes, they left the hubbub of downtown Stuart behind. It could have been a clear shot straight to the ocean.

But, as soon as they rounded the second dock, the Chief said, "Look!" And they knew they'd be stopping again.

The Chief squinted in the bright sunlight and pointed to the east. Straight ahead about a mile away, the river seemed to end. What looked like a sheer dun-colored wall rose so high it almost blocked the early sun. The water at its base lay gray in shadow. When they got closer, they discovered it was a giant sand hill, the first hill the boys had ever seen in their lives. They had to climb to the top.

Queenie surveyed the fifty-foot cliff of sand and sighed. So much for being a proper young lady. She went off into the bushes and tied her skirt up into pantaloons again. When she emerged minutes later, bare knees exposed once more for all the world to see, the boys knew better than to say a word. She tied the last strip around her head as she followed them up the crumbly embankment.

When they reached the top, the boys also wanted to climb the tallest trees they could find, just to see what they could see. Both climbs were worth the effort.

The Chief shook his head in wonder. "The gods of the Greeks." He turned to Queenie, grunting softly and nodding to himself. "Is this what they saw from their mountain?"

At first, she didn't know how to answer him. Then she realized. "And the first bird, too, when he flew out of the shell."

The Seminole studied her for a moment and then turned his attention back to the vista that lay before them. "Yes," he said in a voice filled with wonder.

The three surveyed the world from side to side. To the east, the land sloped down to another very wide river. The far shore of that river was merely a narrow strip of land. Beyond that was more water. That's all. Just water, the flat horizon, and the sky as far as the eye could see.

"The ocean." Queenie verified Billy's whispered guess.

Billy shook his head in wonder. "John Tiger is right. It *is* as big as the lake."

It turned out the hill didn't actually block the St. Lucie. Instead, the river took a sharp turn to the south. From their vantage point, they could see that the two wide rivers ran side by side, kept apart only by another narrow strip of land that dropped away from the hill they were on. Clearly, the St. Lucie would have to take another turn to get to the ocean. They couldn't see where it did, but they knew all they had to do was follow the river. Back to the canoe. They ran and tumbled down the sandy slope as fast as they could.

But once again, they stopped almost before they started. This time they found a boy sitting near the middle of the river at the end of a long, skinny dock. He worked a hand line around the shaded pilings. Taller and more filled out than Billy, he wore town-boy clothes, a plaid shirt and belted khaki pants. But his cuffs were rolled up almost to the knee like the blue-eyed boy's and his feet were bare. His light brown hair stood up on end and blew every which way in the breeze.

The boy watched the three approach through gray-green eyes slitted against the glare of morning sun on water. He looked to be a little older than Queenie.

"Name's Zachary," he introduced himself when his turn came around. "But everybody calls me Zack." He turned out to be friendly and talkative. As he worked his line, he told them about his family's business. They built boats.

"My uncle builds the prettiest sloops that ever sailed the river," he said, "but my father agrees with me that times are changing. We have to think more modern. His last big one was a steamer. But wood for fuel's getting hard to come by. And me? I think the future's in those internal combustion engines like the ones they're using in automobiles. Some of the new motor yachts the Yankees on the Point bring down for the winter have them. Fast! Gasoline engines and V-hulls. Speed! That's the thing! That's where it's headed!"

Billy agreed. One thing he had seen a lot of in his day, other than catfish, was boats. "There's a mix out on the lake, already. Still steam, sail, and oar, mostly. Me? I row," he said, flexing his arm to show off his rowing muscles.

"But ever since they started shipping the cats out of Lauderdale, the big fish houses've been sending out run boats with motors to collect the cats. Say they're more reliable, and they do cut the time in half. And now, most of the *new* freight boats're getting motors, too."

While this conversation was going on, the Chief unrolled one of John Tiger's hand lines. With a nod of approval from Zack, he put some of the town boy's bait on the hook.

Meanwhile, Zack picked up where Billy left off, "That's what I've been telling them. Nobody listens to me now. But, you wait and see. I'm gonna go to engineering college and come back and show them how to do it. There's big money to be made taking people out the inlet for sailfish. A sailboat's not fast enough. Plus, you don't have enough control. And steam? Steam is—"

He never finished the thought because he and the Seminole boy both pulled in pan-sized silver fish with black stripes at the same time. "Throw it back," Zack told the Chief as he tossed his back into the river. "Too small. Let's hold out for some big ones."

Chapter 30. The Great Silver Fish

"Speaking of big ones." Billy scratched his head and squinted his eyes. "You ever heard of a big silver fish? Wide mouth? Scales like this?" He repeated the hand gestures John Tiger had used to describe the fish he had seen.

"You talking about tarpon?"

"Dunno what it's called." Billy shrugged. "Been told this fish grows to the size of a man, though."

"Uh-huh," Zack agreed. "That'd be a tarpon!"

"And what about a blue and green fish with a spear on its nose and a sail on its back?" Queenie asked.

"That'n'd be a sailfish. The ones we have to go out the inlet for." Zack corroborated everything John Tiger had told them. "Those're the fish we're getting famous for."

"Famous?"

"Yep," Zack explained with more than a little pride in his voice. "Tarpon and sails're what's putting Stuart on the map. This is the best place to catch both of them in all of America. The world maybe. Used to be only a few rich sportsmen knew that fact, though, a couple a presidents, some tycoons with estates on the Point, and all." He gestured across the river toward the thin strip of land to the east that separated the two rivers. "But, then, some Yankee reporter got wind of it and spilled the beans. Since that's got out, there's no end of tourists coming down on the train to try their hand right alongside the big shots and pol-i-ticians."

"Tourists?" Billy repeated the word as if he had never heard it before. "What do you mean tourists?"

A glint in his eye, Zack leaned forward and pushed Billy's shoulder with his hand. "I tend to think of them as Yankees with money." He chuckled as if he had revealed a scandalous secret.

Billy and the Chief exchanged raised eyebrows and shrugs.

By then, Queenie was getting used to the boys not knowing the oddest things. "Like little Sally's father yesterday," she explained.

The boys' mouths formed round "Ohs" of recognition.

Before they could say anything, Zack continued his own thought. "Got more money than they need anyway. But that's what we *like* about them. They don't stay long, but while they're here, they buy all kinds of things. And they're willing to pay top dollar."

Billy and the Chief shook their heads slowly.

Then Zack slapped his leg. "Come to think of it, I might be able to show you one!"

"A tourist?" Queenie couldn't help teasing.

That brought the boy up short. He gave her a sharp look that quickly converted into a broad smile. "Yep. And maybe a tarpon, too … if we're lucky."

Within minutes, Zack and the Chief had rolled up their hand lines, and the four of them were poling down the river on their way to the Sunrise Inn. Zack said that was where most of the tourists stayed when they came for the fishing.

Zack kept the conversation lively. He knew all about the water in those parts. He also knew pretty much everything about everything else, too. He regaled them with stories about who was who and what was what as they floated past the few homes and businesses that dotted the riverfront.

Then, the biggest structure Billy and the Chief had ever seen came into view. A huge rectangular building. Three stories tall, with three lines of glass windows running the length of all four sides.

"The inn," Zack announced.

The Chief poled up to the inn's dock. No sooner had they tied up, however, than the dog took off like a streak. Queenie and the Chief gave Billy one of those "not-again" faces before they all started out after the hound.

But this time he didn't go far. When they rounded the first corner, they heard the sound of children's voices. They found the hound licking little Sally's face, while she giggled and hugged him. That child always seemed to be eating and making a mess of herself when she did.

Sally's brother greeted them while her sister ran into the building, calling, "Mother! They're here! The cow hunter, the Indian, and the Amazon! They're hee-er!"

That attracted more than Sally's mother. By the time Miss Josephine came out the door drying her hands on her apron, a mix of inn guests and employees surrounded the four.

Zack, being both the oldest and most experienced in dealing with such people, did the talking. He explained that his friends came from a town out in the Florida jungle, on the other side of the swamp west of Palm City. Some tourist eyes got wide. Other tourist heads nodded in recognition.

"I'm trying to teach them a little about sport fishing. Anyone catch anything worth talking about this morning?"

"One of the guests just brought in a good-sized Silver King," offered a young inn employee Queenie recognized as the driver of the runaway wagon the day before. "That what you're looking for?"

"Perfect!" Zack pumped him on the back, and the inn employee hurried ahead, showing them the way. The six older children, followed by various younger and older guests and Miss Josephine carrying little

Sally, took off after him with the dog dancing and jumping to nip at Sally's feet.

When they rounded the corner, the Chief stopped so fast Billy bumped into his back. The biggest and most beautiful fish either one of the boys had ever seen hung from a sturdy wooden stand. No. they corrected themselves. The biggest and most beautiful fish they had ever imagined. Longer from nose to tail than a man is tall. As big and fat as an old Okeechobee alligator. And John Tiger was right. It shined like polished silver in the sunlight, and its scales were as big as their hands.

The Chief gazed at it reverently. He told the employee in a humble voice, "This is a great fish. You will not have to hunt again for days."

That generated puzzled looks all around until Zack figured it out. "Oh, no," he said. "Nobody *eats* Silver Kings. Tarpon's what they call a *game* fish. The kind the tourists come here for. Call themselves *sportsmen* to let everybody know it's a game. They don't have to fish for food." He paused to laugh at his own joke.

"They hang the kings up on a rack like this so's they can take their picture standing next to them. Show the folks back home how good they are at it. Sometimes though, when a king's big like this one, they stuff it and take it back north to hang on the wall. Like a trophy."

The boy sounded proud of the system he described. "This is what I was telling you about. This is where the *money* is!"

The Chief looked at Zack as if he were a creature from another world. His brows lowered. His eyes narrowed. Sucking breaths in through his mouth, his head shook slightly from side to side and the dark skin of his face grew even darker. The unexpected and strange reaction surprised Queenie.

However, before anyone else could say anything, Miss Josephine took the Seminole's comment in a different direction. "But that *is* where Horace is now. Out with one of the other men, trying to catch something good enough to eat for dinner."

She paused to shift Sally to her other hip. "But, truthfully? I doubt they've got the hang of it yet. It's likely we'll go hungry tonight." She dismissed any dilemma that might present by flicking her wrist in the air and laughing.

"Wait a minute." Her words had given Zack an idea.

Queenie and the dog played with Sally and her siblings while the three boys engaged in deep conversation with first one, and then another, of the inn workers and guests. A short time later, they came back and informed the girl they had negotiated a business arrangement. They would spend the rest of the day out on the water. The inn guests would pay them for any good eating fish they brought back before sundown. She could come with them or stay here, but they were going fishing.

Of course, Queenie went fishing.

Chapter 31. Salerno

Zack knew what he was doing. He directed the Chief to Salerno, a rough fishing village not half a mile to the south. It sat tucked inside the mouth of a wide creek that entered the St. Lucie right where it took its turn toward the sea.

"Only a few folks live down here on the Pocket now," he explained as they poled toward the dock. "Mostly fishermen." He pointed out isolated rough shacks shaded by the pines that lined the shore. "But things're moving fast," he continued. "Business picked up a couple years back when Mr. Mulford ... he's the promoter of the town ... started giving away one town lot here to anybody who buys a farm out west. Like they're doing out in Palm City. Changed the name to Salerno last year to attract more folks."

Still, Salerno was a lot more like Tantie than like Stuart. The fishermen's shanties that lined the waterfront were only a couple of steps up from the fish camps the long seiners were building on the lake. There were a few new houses like those in Stuart here and there off the water on small town lots, but most of those were in various stages of construction.

"Even built a tram track to the docks. Come, take a look." Zack beckoned and led them to a railroad spur that ran from the back of the fish house to the station. He pointed at a flat railroad car with some kind of metal contraption in the middle. Six barrels labeled "Fish" weighed it down, three on each end. Three men leaned into the railroad car, struggling to push it up the tramway.

"Shoots!" Zack shook his head. "Wanted to show you how they're attached a gasoline engine to that cart to move the fish up to the main track. Problem is it gives out on them as often as not. End up pushing instead of riding. Need a better design." He muttered the last to himself and shrugged. "Come on then. We'll get lines and hooks at the store. It's right up there, the other side of the ice house."

"Ice house?" Billy stopped and turned a slow circle in his tracks. He shook his head and whistled out a slow breath. Looking at Queenie, he said, "They're getting' ready to build an ice plant in Tantie." Then, he turned back to Zack. "Did all this come with the train?"

"Could say so." The older boy thought a moment. "If you've got a way to ship them, there's big money in fish. And now, there's also grapefruit and lumber and all sorts of other things people're growing. Train can haul anything. Hard part's getting your goods to the track." He grinned as he gestured toward the men struggling with the barrels of fish.

Chapter 32. A Different Kind of Cow Hunting

A few minutes later, the kids returned to the dugout, stowed their extra lines and hooks, and slipped out of the pocket that protected Salerno from the open water. Zack guided them out onto the wide St. Lucie toward the tip of the high, sandy peninsula that separated the two rivers. He called it "Mr. Sewall's Point."

They had reached the place where the St. Lucie took its turn toward the ocean at last. From that vantage point, they had a clear view of waves breaking to the east.

"The ocean?" the Chief half-stated and half-asked.

"Uh huh," Zack nodded. "From here you can see all the way out the inlet."

The Chief turned the boat toward the ocean waves and started poling, but Zack stopped him. "Whoa, Chief." He pointed across the second, wide river to the long island on the north side of the inlet. "*That's* where we're headed."

The other three shot him questioning looks.

"Can't go to the ocean through the inlet. Too dangerous," he explained. "Even on a calm day, it takes a lot better boat than this one to pass."

"This is a strong boat." The Chief looked offended by Zack's assessment.

Then Zack gave his reasons. "See the breakers? Onshore wind. Outgoing tide. I'm guessing they'll hit three, maybe up to five feet. Or more. You can risk it if you want to. But I'll be asking you to take me back to my dock before you do."

After measuring the waves with their own eyes for a while, the other three concluded that dugouts might be better suited for river running. They decided to trust Zack's judgment. The Chief followed his directions and poled left into the second river. Even wider than the St. Lucie, its water was a clear blue-green, rather than tea-colored like the water that flowed out of the Alpatiokee.

According to Zack, this second river ran hundreds of miles up the coast, all the way past St. Augustine. They called this section, between Ft. Pierce and Stuart, the Indian River.

"Can't say why, though," Zack offered, indicating the Chief. "Other than some Seminoles like you who stay at the camp on the creek to do some trading and that lady with the two hogs who meets the train, there's hardly been any Indians around here since before my pa was born."

Queenie looked over at the Chief to see how he reacted to this statement.

The Seminole didn't offer an explanation. He leaned harder into his pole and aimed the dugout across the river toward the silky smooth water in the lee of the narrow island, as Zack had directed. Before they had gone very far, however, they saw two men standing in the waist-deep water.

"Tourists," Zack said, and then explained how he knew. "See." He pointed at the men to support his conclusion and laughed. "Rubber overalls... Nobody but a tourist wears rubber overalls."

Plus, the men swished long thin fishing lines over their heads in slow lazy S's. "Yankees call that *fly fishing*," Zack went on, "because they use little feather baits that look like flies." He held his thumb and forefinger about half-an-inch apart to demonstrate.

The other three agreed that the way the fishermen worked their lines reminded them of cow hunters working their bullwhips before cracking them. Only, the fishing lines moved back and forth so slow they couldn't possibly crack.

Zack was right. They *were* tourists. The man closest to them turned out to be little Sally's father, Horace. He smiled and waved. Seemed to be enjoying himself even though it didn't look like he'd caught anything.

Then the Chief, who was standing up to pole the canoe, shouted, "Look!" He pointed toward the water not far beyond the second tourist.

Did that trigger a flurry of activity. Zack jumped to his feet so fast he almost dumped the canoe over on its side. The dog barked. Everyone's gaze followed the Chief's point.

A short distance upstream from the second fisherman, a disturbance broke the river's smooth surface. Underneath the roiling waters, two dark shapes moved slowly toward the tourist. The kids' actions attracted the man's attention. He followed their eyes, let out a howl, and threw his fishing pole high into the air. Then he started running toward the shore as fast as a man wearing rubber overalls can run in waist-deep water.

"No! No!" Zack called out after him, "It's okay. It's just sea cows!"

But the man made it all the way to shore without stopping to listen. The Chief poled across the grass beds to retrieve the tourist's fishing pole and got there about the same time as the two manatees. One was huge, at least eight feet long and as big around as four fat men tied together back to back. The other was smaller, the size of one fat boy. The little one tucked itself in close to the big one's side.

Queenie had never seen anything like them. Neither, it appeared, had Billy or the Chief.

The manatees' skins were a smooth brownish gray. Their small, dark, perfectly round eyes peered out over blunt flexible snouts that seemed to split down the middle, with whiskers that stuck out like a cat's. They used their long front flippers like arms without hands and worked their wide flat tails up and down slowly as they swam, not side to side like a fish.

Zack explained that was because they weren't fish. Manatees were air breathers that had to surface every now and then to catch their breath. When they did, they blew air and wet bubbles out of the tops of their heads with a soft "woosh." Those flat tails, round heads, and little bursts of air breaking the surface combined to create the disturbance in the water when they swam.

"We call them sea cows because they're fat and slow and graze on sea grass, like cows in a pasture," Zack called out to reassure Horace, who had showed more than a little courage by standing his ground as the exotic creatures and the canoe followed the current toward him.

When the canoe came within speaking distance, little Sally's father nodded greetings to the group. But he aimed his comment at Billy. "Sea cows, Billy? Are these the cows you Florida cow hunters hunt, then? I must say I had developed an entirely different visual image involving the four-legged variety when you described your profession yesterday."

Pretty sure Horace the tourist had spoken tongue-in-cheek once again, Queenie waited to see what would happen.

Not showing any doubt at all, Billy replied, "Cow huntin's cow huntin', sir. You gotta hunt 'em where you kin find 'em. But these 'uns do present a *par*-ticular problem when it comes to branding time." His equally wry answer came out in a drawl that was exaggerated even for him. His eyes twinkled, and he couldn't keep himself from smiling a little.

Queenie wanted to see how the tourist would respond. Before he could, however, Zack stepped in like someone who thought the whole conversation was serious. "No sir. We *used* to hunt sea cows, but they're asking us not to do that anymore. Some smart folks say we could be running out of them soon. So, we mostly just use them for looking at or swimming with these days."

At that, as if to prove his point, Zack took his knife and a few other things out of his pockets. Leaving them on the sand in John Tiger's firebox, he slid silently out of the canoe into the water with the tie rope in his hand and walked the canoe over the grass flat to Horace.

The sea cows worked their way closer. "These here're a cow and a calf. Bet they're part of the group that was feeding in the Pocket over by Salerno for a while. But a few days back, some tourist boys from up north hunted down the biggest one … the bull. My uncle told me they made such a show of towing it back to the dock you'd of thought they'd harpooned a great whale out on the cold Atlantic up where they come from or something. It's more likely, though, they accidently run across the poor thing grazing in the shallows, where it couldn't get away."

Then, Zack pointed at the other tourist, who watched all this from the shore. "Not much chance you're gonna catch anything else any time soon here, sir. Not after all the ruckus he raised. But, if you stand real still, the cow and calf'll likely swim right up to you."

Horace stood still, and they all watched as the two creatures nuzzled their way past his rubber legs toward the inlet. Once they floated lazily by, Horace offered that he had not been catching anything worth keeping even before all the excitement anyway. He intended to call it a morning.

He declined their invitation to join them in gathering clams and oysters for his dinner with a profuse, "No, thank you." He explained that fishing in waders had turned out to be much harder work than it looked. "And, frankly, I've had enough playing the role of hunter-gatherer for one day. If you need me, you can find me at the inn. Reading in the shade." He wiped his brow with his shirtsleeve to emphasize his point and started trudging toward shore, taking the other angler's fishing pole with him.

Chapter 33. The Ocean

As Horace slogged away, Zack said anyone who wanted to help him collect bait clams should join him in the water. All three did. As John Tiger had warned, this close to the ocean, the water tasted salty and stung their eyes and the small scrapes and scratches they had picked up sliding and tumbling down the hill.

They had a good morning. Zack showed them how to find clams with their toes and how to drag their feet along the bottom to avoid stepping on stingrays. He pointed out a flat fish the size of a dinner plate that scooted across the grass to get out of his path. It had a long whip-like tail.

"Step on them and that tail'll get you for sure," he explained. "It's got a barb at the end. Like a hook." He demonstrated by curling up his index finger. "Hard to get out. And some kind of poison, too. Hurts like the dickens." ·

After that, they made a point of slide stepping through the sea grass. The barefoot boys soon mastered the art of using their toes to bring clams to the surface without ducking their heads underwater. Queenie removed her shoes and joined them until Zack said they'd had enough and she assumed the job of cracking the clams with her stone to use for bait. They fished until the sun was high. Then, Zack showed them where they could scrape up some oysters for lunch. Once they had enough, Zack told the Chief to pole them north up the island.

That route took them past the strange leggy roots of trees Zack called mangroves that lined the shore. The mangroves were medium-sized trees with full leafy crowns that hovered above the water like giant green spiders with smooth, tan roots that sprouted in every conceivable direction for legs. Roots shot out from the trunks, from the branches, and even from other roots. The roots of different trees tangled together, creating an impenetrable barrier between the river and the island that was broken only occasionally by narrow, winding, densely-shaded channels.

"Safe place for the fry to hide," Zack said as he identified a variety of small crabs and fish that hovered in the small spaces between the roots.

Zack pointed to the top edge of a roof that was barely visible above the mangroves a little farther up the island. "That's the House of Refuge," he explained. "The government built it about the time my pa was born because every now and then sailors'd wash up on shore shipwrecked and needing help."

That year, though, the government was in the process of starting up something called the Coast Guard that was going to take it over. Zack gestured for the Chief to keep poling with his head. "Pull in at the dock. The keeper's not likely there, what with the changes being made and all. But folks have always used its dock for picnics and such. It's only a short hike to the House and the beach."

They ran up the slope that rose twenty feet in front of them. Even though they had no idea what to expect as they crested the high point, they were still surprised and more than a little awed by ... by ... everything they saw next.

The island was so narrow, only a few hundred feet, it seemed like the ocean should easily wash it away. But, a wall of reddish-brown rock ran like a spine down its middle and stood firm against the sea's advance. The House of Refuge sat on the highest part of that rock formation where it rose to face the ocean. When the kids stood at the highest point and faced west, they could see the peninsula that separated the two rivers and the hill they had climbed that morning.

What took their breath away, though, was the view when they turned around to the east. As far as the eye could see, they saw nothing but water. Water the likes of which they'd never seen before. Near shore it was the most amazing bluish-green. Darker patches, that turned out to be the shadows of small clouds floating above them in the sky, dotted its surface. Far away, the horizon was etched in a rich dark blue.

Zack explained that dark blue water marked a current that ran north in the ocean like a river. "My pa warned me that if I ever get stuck in it, I'll end up all the way across the ocean. In England."

"England?" Billy and the Chief looked from each other to Queenie. So, added to everything else, England, the land of King Arthur and the Knights of the Round Table, was just over there on the other side.

And the ocean was noisy. Not thunderous noisy like the Okeechobee waves crashing into the trees during the storm. The ocean made a rich, steady, resonant sound. Medium-sized waves broke on a sandbar about a hundred feet off shore, creating a low background rumble. Tiny shells clinked and tinkled as much smaller waves rolled them up toward the base of the rocks. Foam bubbles, left behind when the water retreated, hissed and crackled as they disappeared into the sand.

Although the ocean seemed gentle, Billy and the Chief soon discovered it was stronger than it looked. North of the House, the rocks disappeared into the beach. The boys ran down to the water's edge straight into the waves. Within a few steps, however, they hit a steep drop-off and lost control in the deeper water. The waves knocked them about until they could regain enough footing in the loose ankle-deep mixture of sand and seashells to scramble and claw their way back to dry land. Then, they whooped and laughed and turned around to run in again.

The dog barked and snapped at foamy wave tops until they disappeared into the sand. After a while, he got frustrated when all he caught was a mouth full of saltwater. So, he lay down in the shade to pout.

Later, they followed Zack to the rockier south side of the House. There, a great tangled pile of broken and twisted timbers perched high on the rocks. Billy and the Chief looked at each other as if how that pile of wood got there, more than ten feet above the ocean's surface, was a mystery.

After considering it for a while, Billy suggested, "Might ought to be keeping an eye out for the Cyclops."

The Chief whooped, and Queenie laughed her agreement.

Zack, however, had an explanation that turned out to be both more mundane and more exciting at the same time. A sandbar ran along the beach only a little ways out. They could see where waves broke over it. Those timbers were all that was left of a ship that had recently foundered on the bar and come apart. And the storm the other day had hit at high tide. When that happened, the waves threw things high up on the dune.

"Ships have been wrecking on these shores for centuries," Zack continued. "First, storms or bad luck got them. But later, according to what some folks say, pirates'd light fires up on the high point of the rocks here to lure them onto the bar. Once the ships were hard aground, their cargo'd be easy pickings."

Old maps even called this place "Gilbert's Bar" after the most famous of those pirates. Legend had it he used these very rocks as his base of operations back before the Civil War. "Nowadays, pirates're few and far between," Zack laughed, "but storms and bad luck still catch a ship now and then." He waved his hand at the pile of timbers and aimed his chin at it to emphasize his point.

And if pirates weren't enough, Zack's story got even more exciting. He spoke in a low voice as if telling them a secret. "There's a huge amount of treasure that's been lost in these waters. Started back in the early days when Spanish ships full of gold and silver got sunk by storms. And, sometimes, winds like the one that hit the other day'll shift the sand all around. When that happens, you can find gold coins and other things on the beach."

The other three kids looked at him with wide eyes and open mouths.

"Never found any myself," he backed down a little. "But, I know folks who did." Then, he perked up again and started jogging back toward the beach. "Who knows? Maybe today's my lucky day!"

Pirates and sunken treasure. Billy, the Chief, and Queenie couldn't stand it. They raced down to the beach and joined Zack searching the sand for flashes of silver and gold. Of course, they didn't find any. Just some broken crockery, a few bits of brass from the new wreck, and some old nails crusted with seashells.

Billy did find one thing he thought was worth keeping, a piece of pale green glass that had been in the sand so long its sharp edges had worn so smooth it felt soft. He knew it wasn't valuable like a jewel or anything fancy like that. Still he liked the touch of it. And for some odd reason, he thought it was one of the prettiest things he'd ever held in his hand. He put it in his pocket.

Time seemed to stand still and fly by at the same time. After a while, they gave up treasure hunting and ate a lunch of oysters and heavy flat bread the Seminole elder had given them. Then, they took turns cracking clams with Queenie's stone, readying their bait for the afternoon.

Finally, Zack said, "Time to get back to the river and earn our fortune." They ran to the dugout.

Chapter 34. The Snook

Zack showed them more about how the ocean tides worked. The current in the river had changed direction. Now, water was flowing up the island toward the north and getting clearer, deeper, and cooler. High tide was coming in.

Zack said the smaller river fish would be hiding from the afternoon sun. The big ones that came in with the tide would likely be looking to make a meal of those small fish and crabs hiding along the shady edge of the tangled mangrove roots that protected the shore.

"Like that one!" Zack stood up excitedly and pointed at a long silver fish with an underslung jaw and a black stripe running down its muscular side. It cruised slowly, inches below the surface of the crystal-clear water, toward the shadow of the mangroves. Zack hurriedly tossed his line toward it. He held the bait taut against the current, so that it drifted right in front of the fish's long snout. Nothing. The fish paid no attention whatsoever and kept moving its tail slowly back and forth at its own leisurely pace.

"Do tourists eat *that* kind of silver fish?" the Chief asked.

Obviously missing the steely tone in the Chief's voice. Zack answered enthusiastically, "You bet they do! They might even pay extra. That's a snook!"

Zack tossed his line again. Same result. "Top of the line for eating. Tourist or local." By the time Zack retrieved his line the second time, the fish had disappeared into the maze of channels through the mangroves.

"Darn. Never can tell about snook, though. Sometimes they sit there so thick you could hit five of them with one swing of a stick, but you can't get a one of 'em to bite for trying. Wish we had a net." He sighed as he sat back down and pointed for the Chief to continue the direction they had been going before the diversion.

But the Chief had come up with a different plan. He bumped the canoe into the mangrove roots, handed Billy the push pole, and knelt down to untie John Tiger's fishing spear from the side of the canoe. A long thin reed, the spear looked a lot like the skinny fishing poles the tourists had been using that morning, but it was stiff and strong and pointed at one end.

Spear in hand, the Chief grabbed one of the mangrove branches and swung out of the canoe onto an arched, leggy mangrove root. He picked his way from root to branch until he settled on a perch that hung low over one of the main channels through the trees. He turned to the other three and waved.

When Zack looked from the Seminole to the blue-eyed boy with a question on his face, Billy explained, "I never picked up the knack for spearing fish, but the Chief's right good at it. Says it's more reliable than using hooks. Don't matter if the fish care to bite or not. If he can see them, we get to eat them."

As if on cue, the Chief cast the spear downward with amazing speed. When he pulled it up, he showed the other three a snook that was about a third of the size of the first one they had seen. "This one good enough for the tourists?"

Zack's mouth hung open. "Shoots. Good enough to keep for myself..." He stopped in mid-sentence, pursed his lips, and narrowed his eyes at the Indian boy. Then he reached down into the bottom of the canoe and put a fresh clam on his hook. "Except, I can *catch* a bigger one."

That was the challenge. Zack against the Chief. Line against spear.

"Boys." Queenie looked to the heavens and shook her head with an exaggerated sigh.

Billy adopted a similarly disinterested attitude and shrugged. Even so, all four of them got caught up in the competition within minutes. Soon, the back of the canoe was filling up with mangrove snapper, flounder, and miscellaneous other fish. But all of the snook in the river seemed to be hiding in the mangrove channels where only the Chief could reach them.

He gave Zack a triumphant look with each new snook he tossed over to the boat. That only made the other three work harder. They bent their backs to the sky and searched for advantage beneath the surface of water that was still so clear they could almost count the grains of sand and blades of river grass on the bottom.

All three looked up when the Chief let out a shrill whistle. Tensed in his crouch, the Seminole directed them to look toward the mouth of the narrow channel with a small gesture of his head and eyes. A dark shadow wove its way lazily into his trap. Zack, Billy, and Queenie froze so they wouldn't scare it off.

"You'll *never* beat this one," the Chief called out to Zack, all the while tracking the fish with his eyes. It wasn't like the Seminole to boast, but this fish that was moving slowly into the channel was something to boast about.

Big. Real big. Sleek and silver. Light filtering through the mangrove leaves highlighted the long dark stripe running down its side. This snook had to be twice the size of the first one Zack had tried to catch. Still not as big as the great silver fish they had seen at the inn, but getting there. The Chief took his eyes off the fish for an instant to toss Zack a smug look. Then he waited for the snook to come to him with a harsh smile on his lips.

The sleek silver fish meandered its way into the shadows. Taking its time. In a moment, it would be directly under the Chief's spear. The

Indian's skin tingled with excitement. Muscles tight and prepared to explode, he crouched perfectly still, his spear raised as high as possible at the ready. Held his breath. Glanced at Zack, a smile of victory on his face, and took aim.

Bam!

Lightning struck the Chief.

The sound and force hit the boy at the same time. Light and color exploded all around him. He flew head over heels. The back of his neck and shoulders hit the water in the small channel with a splash. His body knifed all the way to the bottom. It bounced and lay there for what seemed like an eternity, hovering face up a few inches above the sand. Then, it floated listlessly back toward the light, legs and arms bobbing loosely at its side in slow motion as the current carried it into the mangrove roots.

"Oh, my God!" Queenie leapt to her feet. When the lightning bolt struck the top of the Chief's spear, she had blinked, and now he was gone.

"Come on!" Billy commanded himself and the canoe. He leaned into the push pole. The dugout shot toward the place where the Chief had disappeared into the shadows. "Come on!" He drove the dugout's bow hard into the mangroves. "Come on!" He used that impact to swing its stern across the mouth of the Chief's narrow channel and hit the water in a shallow dive as the canoe bounced to a stop against the mangrove roots.

Zack was trapped in the front of the canoe, smothered in mangroves. Queenie had a good view. The Chief bobbed right below the surface, one leg ensnared in the twisted mass of roots like a trap. The current held him under, trying to drag him deeper into the maze. Billy had not quite reached him, and the Indian seemed to be making a feeble effort to free himself. Somehow, he seemed to be alive.

Queenie hit the water, too, and came up only a few strokes from the two boys. The channel was deeper than it looked, and the current pushing the Chief into the tangle of roots was stronger than she expected. Billy held onto a mangrove root with one arm and lifted the Chief's head out of the water with the other, but the roots were slippery and the current kept trying to drag them both back down.

The Indian sputtered and flailed uselessly about with unfocused eyes.

Billy kept coaxing him, "Calm down. Hold on. … It's okay."

But, the injured boy didn't seem to hear. Billy slipped. He couldn't hold the Chief up and untangle him at the same time. They both went under.

The Chief's face broke water again just as Queenie got there. Completely under water, Billy was holding him up from below. She gulped in a deep breath and took Billy's place. He went up for air, but returned in an instant, working to free the Chief's leg.

The Indian grabbed Queenie's hair and neck and struggled against the mangroves by kicking his free leg. That made all their jobs harder. The only way Queenie could catch her own breath was by going all the way to the bottom and pushing off with both legs. She didn't know how long she could—

Suddenly, the Chief floated free. Billy's head popped up, and for a few moments, the three friends hung on to mangrove roots and to each other for dear life.

Back in the canoe, the Chief coughed up water, and amazingly, started to regain his senses. He sat facing the stern with his head and arms draped over his knees. Focus slowly worked its way back to his eyes. He shook his head and ran his fingers through his hair. He breathed so hard his shoulders bobbed up and down. He coughed again, made a face at Billy, coughed, breathed again, and gave a feeble "Okay" sign.

Sitting behind him, Queenie also fought to catch her breath from both the exertion and the excitement. She marveled and shook her head. How could he possibly be alive? She'd seen the lightning strike. It had been a direct hit.

Zack knelt in the bow and shook his head, too. He and the girl looked up at Billy to see what to do next. The blue-eyed boy leaned into the pole and backed the canoe out of the trees.

Chapter 35. Thunderbolts

Bam!

They had forgotten about the lightning. None of them saw where the second bolt hit, but it hit close by. Too close.

"Down!" Billy barked the order. "Now!"

The second part wasn't necessary. They had all been schooled enough in lightning lore to follow the first command without debate. Lightning generally took aim at tall pointy things. Standing up on the water in a thunderstorm was not safe.

Zack and Queenie crouched low on all fours. The Chief covered his head with his arms and curled into a tight ball on the floor of the canoe. Billy stayed upright only long enough to give the push pole another mighty shove. Then, holding the pole horizontal along the edge of the dugout, he squatted and curled up into a low egg shape as they shot past the mangroves toward the House of Refuge. Thankfully, it was not far away.

The two lightning bolts had struck without warning out of a perfectly clear, sunny sky. Queenie made a "what's-going-on" face and motioned up toward the sky with her eyes. "Where'd they com—"

Bam!

The third lightning bolt struck the island right beside them. A thin wisp of smoke immediately curled up from the spot it hit. While the sky was reloading, Billy took the opportunity to stand and shove the pole again. Back in his egg position, he pointed over Queenie's right shoulder.

Several thunderheads had been brewing way off on the other side of the river to the northwest.

"But—" Queenie started to ask.

Billy jumped up, pushed so hard and fast his face turned red, then crouched back down. "Some bolts get way out in front of the cloud. Never see those ones coming." His words came in short bursts. "Sometimes, you don't even get the rain. That happens. You've got a fire to contend with."

They both looked back at the island. The smoke from the third strike grew thicker and blacker by the second. "Don't think that'll be a problem today, though," the boy continued as he stood one more time and forced the canoe toward the shore next to the dock.

Queenie looked from the fire back to the storm clouds. One very small and very dark thunderhead had broken away from the others. It seemed to have taken a bead on them and was coming fast.

Billy drove the canoe ashore. It hit the sand, and the miracles kept coming. The Chief had not only regained most of his senses, he was almost strong enough to make it on his own. Queenie half-supported, half-dragged him up the sloping back of the rock formation toward the House of Refuge. They moved low to the ground, hunched over almost on all fours, partly to present less of a target and partly because the Chief was still weak. Zack and Billy pulled the canoe with its load of fish and oysters as high as they could up on the shore in the short time they had and tied it to a tree. Then, they scrambled up the incline after the other two.

All four reached the top at the same time and came to a halt. Everything on the ocean side of the island had changed! The water no longer lapped gently at the base of the rocks. Now, it reached two-thirds to the top of them. And much larger waves broke against the stone barrier in an orderly fashion like a marching army.

Bam!

They didn't see this one strike either, but Billy's sandy hair stuck straight up from his head like a halo. It was no time to be standing on the highest point of the island, admiring the ocean.

Behind them, a solid gray wall of water raced across the Indian River in their direction, a line of white splashes broiling up the river's surface in front of it. Then the first blast of a cold wind hit. As if they had been waiting for that signal, the ocean waves broke ranks. Transformed from an organized army into a frenzied mob in an instant, they splashed and jumped in every direction.

The sound of the storm changed behind them as the curtain of water crossed onto land. Raindrops striking palmetto fronds and sea grape branches rattled and clattered. It got louder as the wall drew closer, sounding more like an oncoming train than like anything else the kids had ever heard. Not even the storms on the lake had been that fast and furious. They ran as fast as they could to the House of Refuge.

Bam!

That bolt hit a wave top right in front of them a few yards off shore as they threw themselves on the floor of the covered porch. They crawled to the most protected outer wall of the House of Refuge and pressed their backs against it. The curtain of water burst over the House.

Safe at last, Queenie caught her breath and looked at the Indian boy. It was her first chance to find out how badly he'd been hurt. "Chief?" She touched his arm and gasped when he looked up at her.

The Chief's black eyes peered out through wide, dark circles. His chest still heaved as he gulped in air, and he appeared to know what was going on. Still, he seemed calm, maybe too calm, as if moving at a slower speed. He took his time, closed his eyes, and shook his head slowly from side to side. Gone from her again.

She called him back. "Chief."

The Seminole looked down at the middle of his right hand for a moment before holding it palm-out for Queenie to see. She took the hand in both of hers, gently lowering and turning it so she could study the small, dark circle of burned skin at its center more closely.

That first bolt had shattered John Tiger's fishing spear at the moment the Chief raised it to claim victory over Zack. The lightning had entered his body through the palm of his right hand and passed through him until it exited out the ball of his left foot. To the girl's surprise, the only injuries the boy had to show for it were the minor looking burn on his palm and a similar burn on his sole. Other than that, a dull throb in his head, and a ringing in his ears, the Chief said he was unharmed.

"Small things." He shrugged.

"No!" Queenie shook her head. "It's a miracle you're alive." She continued to hold his hand, staring at his palm.

But, the Chief shook his head again and said, "Every day, we die or we live." He shrugged. Then anguish distorted his face, and he pulled his hand away, saying, "Today, I became lost. I am thankful to have a second chance."

Letting out a deep breath, he fought for control of his face and turned away from her so that he sat facing the storm and the ocean with his back pressed flat against the wall. After watching his profile for a moment, Queenie leaned back against the wall next to him. She slid over so close that their shoulders touched and didn't pull away when he flinched. Instead, she reached out and took his uninjured hand in hers.

The Chief stiffened. She held on. In a moment, his fingers relaxed enough for her to slip hers between them. They sat there, under the protection of the House of Refuge porch roof, and watched a display put on by the heavens, the Chief's left hand grasped tightly in Queenie's right. She didn't want to let him go.

Zack and Billy watched and listened as Queenie tended to their friend. When the first tear slid down the Chief's cheek, though, they, too, turned their attention to the storm.

"Chief." Queenie leaned harder into his shoulder, the side of her head touching his so she could whisper privately, "I'm thankful, too."

They stayed that way, temple-to-temple, for some time before Queenie let out a long, slow sigh and pulled away to lean against the wall again. Lightning flashes illuminated the trails of tears that tattooed their faces. Their eyes closed. They had stopped watching the storm.

Thud!

Everybody, including the dog, jumped, eyes wide open now. Something had struck the shake roof of the porch, hard.

Thud.

Really hard. The kids looked at each other with even wider eyes. That was not rain.

Thud! Thud! Thud!

Within moments, the thuds came so hard and fast and loud that the kids couldn't hear to talk about what was causing them. Plus, they didn't have to. All around, white stones the size of quail eggs flew out of the sky, bouncing and rolling to a stop when they hit the earth.

Right after the next flash of lightning, Billy rushed out into the storm. "Ouch!" One of the white stones had hit his arm. "Ouch! Ouch!" They were falling fast and with force. He scrambled back under cover with a handful of the nearest pieces. Ice. He rubbed the back of his neck as he handed the first few chunks to the Chief to soothe his burns and cool his brow.

They had all heard stories about hail, but none of them had ever seen it before. So many hailstones fell so fast they piled up on one edge of the porch. Soon all five were licking and chewing them, verifying for themselves that hail really was regular water that had been frozen by the heavens.

The storm blew on. From their safe seats at the very edge of their world, they witnessed quite a show. Once the first wall of water passed by, the underbelly of the small but intense thunderhead shut out the sun.

It hovered above them like a low purple ceiling. Every minute or so, a bolt of lightning burst through its gloom with a brilliant flash and a thunderous clap. On and on, one after another. They never knew there could be so many so fast. The jagged shafts of yellow-white energy struck the tops of waves so close to shore they could see the individual drops of the splashes and the puffs of steam when they hit.

As the center of the storm passed over, the wind blew like a hurricane and was so cold they shivered. Waves crashed even wilder and higher up on the rocks. Each resonating boom of wave striking stone blew a huge spout of water high into the sky through a hole in the rocks the kids hadn't realized was there.

And then, as the cloud began to pull away, the wind shifted one more time, coming now from the east. That ratcheted the waves up to another level and sent them rolling over some of the rocks to the south. Now, the kids saw firsthand how the shipwreck debris ended up so high on the dune. Waves lifted the heavy boards and tossed them around in the white foam like matchsticks.

The four, with Billy wrapping his arms around the hound and Queenie holding tight to the Chief, huddled with their backs pressed against the House of Refuge wall and their eyes wide open. Witnessing Nature's power and fury firsthand, both afraid and excited at the same time.

Chapter 36. A Seminole Victory

The storm was intense, but it was also small and moving fast. As suddenly as it had come upon them, it blew out to sea. In that short time, however, it transformed their view of the ocean and their world.

The ground was clean and wet and white. A layer of ice pebbles two inches thick covered the beach and filled the nooks and crannies in the rocks. Billy and Zack picked up a few more chunks to throw at each other and danced and hopped in their bare feet through the rest as if they were hot coals. The Chief seemed mostly back to normal, although a bit subdued. He perched high on a rock and took it all in.

Some of the shipwreck had been tossed over the rocks onto the dune by the waves. The rest had simply disappeared. An area of beach south of the rocks had been scoured away, uncovering new beds of shells and possibly new treasures.

But, Zack's practical side took control. "Treasure hunting'll have to wait for another day," he said. "I'm not gonna throw away a sure thing by speculating after lost gold. It's getting late. Got to get our catch back to the inn before dinner time if we want to get paid." So they turned their back to the ocean and left the island.

Billy stood up to pole in the rear of the canoe in front of the fish. Zack took up his usual position at the bow, followed by Queenie, who held the hound. The Chief rested in the middle. The girl couldn't help babbling for all the excitement. She had never seen manatees before, never caught so many fish, never seen the ocean so crazy. Never this.

Never that. Most of all, she had never seen one lightning strike close-up before, much less so many. The hair on her arms and the back of her neck still stood on end and tingled.

"It was like Zeus himself was casting thunderbolts down from Mount Olympus!" she exclaimed, breathless with wonder at the power of Nature.

Billy nodded in agreement, but missed her mood completely. "Been thinking about that. I don't much cotton to that god Zeus. King Arthur would've handled things different at Troy—"

He stopped when Queenie did a double take and gave him a squinty sideways look that demanded, "What in the world are you talking about?"

Before Billy got a chance to right himself, Zack stole the moment. "Yes!" he exclaimed. "Zeus! That's exactly what it was like!"

Then, he started putting on a show. He jumped to his feet and struck a pose that eerily mirrored the stance the Chief had taken when spearing snook, right foot resting on the high point of the bow, right hand pointing out over the water, and left hand raised behind, with either a thunderbolt or a spear at the ready. He bellowed like the Greek god himself, "Beware Zeus, King of the Gods!"

Queenie clasped her hands under a broad smile, anticipating what Zack was up to. He started flinging make-believe thunderbolts at the water. The Chief frowned, and Billy downright glowered.

All this activity rocked the boat, but Zack was a quick study. He'd figured out his balance by then. He threw one imaginary lightning bolt after another. He even mimicked the explosions they made when they hit the surface by flailing his arms and shouting, "Shhhhsss ... Kaboom!"

The dog barked, and Queenie laughed. She even giggled.

But Zack's arm froze in mid-throw when the Chief said as if to himself, "I respect the God of the Thunderbolts."

A sheepish look crept over the older boy's features. He turned to face the Indian and said, "I'm sorry, Chief. I forgot."

"Be sorry for nothing, my friend." The Seminole dismissed the apology with a wave of his hand. "Your God is very powerful. A great teacher of lessons."

Zack tilted his head at the Chief. His arm dropped to his side.

"But, not much of a fisherman."

Queenie put her fingers to her mouth to hide her giggle. From her position near the Chief, she could see the gleam in his eye.

At first, Billy looked confused. Then he apparently figured out what his friend was up to. He stepped to the side, giving the others a good view of the fish piled up in the back of the dugout. The other three followed his gaze. Every single snook had a hole in its side where the Chief had speared it.

Zack screwed up his mouth and sat back down, his face a little pink. But he didn't stay quiet for long. In the blink of an eye, he surveyed the scene and smiled, saying, "You've got a point there, Chief. And credit where it's due. Your spear sure enough *was* fast as lightning today. You won fair and square."

He saluted the Seminole by dropping his head to the side and tipping an imaginary hat. "Hats off to you."

The Seminole accepted the salute with a nod.

But Zack didn't break eye contact. Instead, he continued with a mischievous smile. "Butcha know? This game ain't over, my friend." He paused while he settled his imaginary hat back on his head and straightened it, ending with a pat on its imaginary crown. "Other days're coming."

The Chief did not return Zack's smile. Instead, he studied the older boy's face through serious hard eyes black as coals in their dark circles. Then he pursed his lips and nodded again, only this time as if he'd figured out something important.

The Seminole tipped his head and upper body toward Zack in a gesture of respect. "I know," was all he said.

Billy thrust the push pole deep into the water until it seated firmly against the bottom and put his whole body into a mighty shove. The dugout shot toward the inn.

Chapter 37. Back at the Inn

The mood lightened considerably once the kids tied off at the inn's dock. Little Sally's big sister ran off to announce their arrival, and a small but jovial crowd gathered. A low chorus of oohs and aahs echoed as they unloaded their booty of fish and oysters.

As Zack had predicted, none of the tourist men had caught anything worth eating that day. Some of their noses were a little out of joint because the kids had succeeded where they had failed. However, most of them were fisherman optimists. They took the kids' success as a sign they could bring home similar catches the next day, if only the kids would share their secrets and tricks.

The tourist wives had been waiting eagerly for the kids' return since mid-afternoon. They asked Zack to describe the taste and texture of the species they didn't recognize, announced their choices, and bargained among themselves over who would take which. A party atmosphere circled around the four kids.

"Where were you so long?" Sally's sister asked as her mother claimed the largest snook and selected oysters one at a time for her family.

"Taking the best fish requires time … and great skill." The Chief's competitive spirits had revived, too. He answered her while raising a sideways eyebrow at Zack. The younger girl's eyes grew big when the Indian spoke to her. Zack smiled and nodded his agreement without saying a word.

As Zack and the adults sorted and haggled and discussed fishing techniques, some of the younger boy tourists played a game of chase, hiding behind tarpon-hanging stands, the corners of buildings, or their mothers' skirts. Holding a forked stick out in front of him like a gun, Sally's brother ran after another boy, shouting, "Bang... Bang, bang. You're dead."

The other boy refused to fall to the ground. Instead, he zigged aside while turning to look back and ran smack into Queenie's knees. "Whoa." She grabbed his shoulders to keep him from falling. "You playing cowboys and Indians?" She felt sure about the answer and more than a little smug about the influence she and the boys had on them.

The boy's answer, however, surprised her. "Oh, no!"

Before he could say anything else, Sally's brother slid to a stop next to them and pointed his stick at the boy. "Stick'm up!" he ordered. Raising his eyes to Queenie, he added, "You, too."

Queenie pretended fear and raised her hands.

"I'm John Ashley. Give me all your money."

"John Ashley?" No longer pretending fear, the girl lowered her hands slowly and asked cautiously, "Who's that?"

"He's the outlaw I saw today! A real outlaw. Here!"

Queenie's heart beat in her ears like a drum. Her eyes darted around the crowd, searching individual faces. "Here?"

"Naw. Not *here* here." The boy pretended to spit on the ground, acting tough. "In town." When Sally's brother lowered the stick he'd been pointing at her in his excitement at telling the story, the other boy took the opportunity to escape and ran away. Sally's brother shouted, "Bang!" and scooted after him as they both dodged imaginary bullets.

Queenie's eyes lit on Sally's sister. She walked over to the girl. "Did your family go to town today?"

The girl nodded. "Mother took us shopping."

"Did you see someone named John Ashley?"

The girl's eyes grew large and round. She nodded again. "You know him?"

"No." Queenie brushed off the idea in a casual tone. "But I've heard of him. Where'd you see him? What was he doing? Who told you about him?" Queenie stopped herself too late. She'd already pushed the child too hard.

"I don't know." The girl looked down and squirmed, struggling under the pressure. "Jeremy…" She shook her head and pointed at one of the inn employees with relief. "He's the one who talked to him. Then he told mother, 'See that man over there? That's *John Ashley*. He's a famous outlaw.'"

Queenie reached out, ran her hand over the girl's hair one time to let her know she'd answered the questions well. "Thanks."

Jeremy? Queenie looked at the employee the child had pointed at more closely. A little older than Zack, he had a similar build and coloration. Would it be safe to ask him about Ashley? Then, she recognized him. He had been the driver of the runaway wagon Billy had stopped the day before. And she also remembered seeing him that morning.

She thought it through. Jeremy worked at the inn. Must be the reliable sort. Not the kind to hang out with outlaws. It'd be safe to sound him out. She'd be careful not to raise any suspicions.

Chapter 38. Jeremy

Queenie meandered through the goings-on as if she didn't have a care in the world and finally approached the inn employee from the back. When she stood next to him, she kept her eyes on the younger boys and said, "Hi," trying to seem nonchalant. "So the kids're playing a new game now, huh?"

"Yeah," he answered. She watched him through the corner of her eye. He moved his jaw back and forth absent-mindedly. "Cops and robbers." He half-smiled as Sally's brother hid behind his mother's skirt and shot invisible bullets out of the twig. "But, it's pretty much the same rules as the cowboys and Indians they was playing yesterday."

For all her subterfuge in getting to that point, Queenie hadn't figured out a more subtle way to ask the next question. So, she turned to face him and cut to the chase. "Sally's sister says you showed them an outlaw in Stuart?"

"Uh huh." The young man returned her gaze and squinted. "John Ashley."

"I've heard of him!" Queenie tried to sound surprised. "He's a *real* outlaw!"

"Oh, John's real, all right." Jeremy looked at her warily and then turned away again. "But why do you say it like that?"

"Well..." Queenie continued looking up at the young man, trying to sound frightened and letting that statement die off into a question. "I heard he murdered somebody."

Jeremy held her eye this time. His tone cooled. "Far as I know, he's only been accused of *killing* that one Indian, and there can be a *difference* between killing and murdering."

Queenie gave her head a few small little shakes and blinked her eyes to indicate confusion.

The young man softened and explained, "What I'm trying to say is there's more than one side to that story, and I'm inclined to listen to the one John's telling. It was kill or be killed."

"Oh." Queenie knew the Chief and the other Seminoles wouldn't agree on that point. But she let that slide and kept pushing for information. "Sounds like you *know* him?"

"Yeah. Everybody knows John. He's one of us ... from just south of here." The inn worker jutted out his jaw again and rubbed his chin between thumb and fingers.

"But you said he's an outlaw. Does that mean he robbed all the trains and banks and things people say?"

Jeremy scrutinized her for a moment before answering. Queenie held her breath, hoping she hadn't pushed him too far, too. "Never asked him," he finally replied.

Before Queenie could think of what to do next, Jeremy chuckled as if he remembered some private joke and started up again on his own. "And so what if he did?" He cast Queenie a defiant smile. "There's a lot of folks around here that'd tend to look up to John, for that."

"What?" That caught the girl by surprise.

"Especially for robbing banks." Jeremy explained, exhibiting the kind of patience a parent has with an inquisitive child. "Who's the money in the banks belong to?"

Queenie stood there, puzzled and thinking he didn't really want her to try to answer that question.

Jeremy raised his palms to shoulder height, gave his head a frustrated shake, and poked himself in the chest. "Ain't *my* money. That's for sure!"

That astounded Queenie. Although he'd given her that "who-cares" look again, he sounded genuinely upset.

"It's the Yankees' and land promoters' money. There's more of them here than us, now-a-days. Raising prices so high *we* can't put two nickels together, if we try."

Jeremy swiveled his head around as if checking for eavesdroppers. "So, you see?" He checked again and bent his head close to hers. "Anyone robbing banks is doing what we ain't got the guts to do ourselves."

A light went on in Queenie's head. She clapped her hands together. "Like Robin Hood!" When she realized Jeremy didn't recognize the name, she added, "He steals from the rich and gives to the poor!"

Jeremy let out a "Yep" but quickly recalled that statement by shaking his head. After considering the idea for a moment, a sly grin broke out on his face. "But, maybe more like that outlaw out west… Name of Je … Jesse something."

"Jesse James?"

"Uh huh." His grin was broader now. "You see, I don't know about John giving his money to the poor." Chuckling now, he bobbed his head with good humor. "But far as *I'm* concerned? Taking it from rich Yankees? That's sure enough a good place to start."

"But how can he get away with it?" Genuinely curious now, Queenie added, "Isn't the sheriff hunting him?"

"The Sheriff?" Jeremy laughed and shook his head. "That citified Palm Beach fool'll never find John." Pride crept into Jeremy's voice as he said it. "John's Cracker born and bred. Shoots better than anybody. Tracks like an Indian. Knows the Glades like the back of his hand. He can live like a king out there as long as he wants to."

Live like a king? That's what Billy said about life on the prairie, too. What was it about Crackers and living off the land that made them feel so free, so rich?

Queenie shook her head, getting back on track. As much as Jeremy had revealed, he hadn't told her what she needed to know. "So, if he lives like a king in the Everglades, why was Ashley in Stuart today?"

When Jeremy responded by looking at her suspiciously, she tried to deflect his mistrust by pasting a goofy grin on her face and clasping her fingers together like a silly girl, waiting to hear exciting gossip. "Oh! Is he planning to rob the bank?"

"Naw, nothing like that." The young man hemmed and hawed. She never dropped her expectant gaze from his eyes. Eventually he continued, "All he said was he'd missed his girl out by the lake and he heard some folks he'd like to even the scales with might be here."

Queenie gulped. That was the worst of all possible answers. It took a moment to catch her breath. "Did he say what they'd done?"

"Who?"

"The folks he's looking for."

"Nope. Just said if he couldn't find them today, he'd be heading down to the hammock."

"The hammock?"

"Where his pa hides one of his stills."

"Is it close by?"

"Never been there myself. But I'm told it ain't far. A bit south and west of here ... off the Stuart-Annie Road about halfway between Indian Town and Hobe Sound. Hid pretty good back in the swamp."

Then, he studied her face for a moment and chuckled. "Why're you asking? You itching to go out there and meet a *real* outlaw face-to-face?"

"Oh, *no!*" Queenie made a show of giggling back at him and covering her mouth with her hands. "I'd be too afraid!" He seemed to buy her act. She giggled again, trying to seem embarrassed, and ran to rejoin the boys.

As she did, she replayed her conversation with Jeremy in her head and was pretty satisfied with her part in it. Playing the silly girl in awe of outlaws rather than telling the truth about why she asked the questions had been downright clever.

But one thing worried her. Based on what Jeremy had told her, any of the locals might turn out to be Ashley's secret ally. With that in mind, she decided not to tell the boys about Ashley until they were alone on the river.

Chapter 39. The Question

By the time Queenie made her way back to the boys, the fish and oysters had been divided up. They collected four shiny silver dollars, one for each of them. And, to top it all off, even after sharing what was left with the inn staff, there were still plenty of fish in the canoe for the kids' own dinners. They waved "so long" to the staff and tourist families and shoved away from the inn's dock.

Back on the water with the business of the day concluded, Billy noted how low the sun sat in the sky. "Where do you want to camp for the night. Stuart? The House of Refuge?" The way his eyes lit up when he made the second suggestion, Queenie guessed he'd vote to go back to the ocean.

"I think we should go back to the beach." That would have been her vote anyway. "John Ashley's still in Stuart."

Billy stopped poling. "How'd you know that?" He looked concerned.

"Sally's family saw him."

"John Ashley?" Zack responded to this exchange by raising noncommittal eyebrows. "Heard he was back."

Queenie and the boys exchanged glances. It shouldn't have surprised her that Zack kept up with Ashley's comings and goings the same way he kept up with everything else in town, but it did.

After considering their reaction for a second, Zack continued, "What do you care where Ashley is, anyway?"

The boys nodded their approval when Queenie started to answer the question. She told Zack the short version of everything, including what she had learned from Jeremy.

Zack whistled through his teeth and shook his head. "It's not like I know him real good or anything." He stopped himself and leaned back, giving each of the other three an eyes-wide innocent look. "But folks say Ashley's not that bad a sort. It's that short guy from Chicago he's taken up with... Name of Kid ... Kid Lowe or something like that. Now he's supposed to be real trouble."

Queenie, Billy, and the Chief exchanged worried glances. Zack had to be talking about the man who'd been smart enough not to fall for Billy's trick on the trail.

"This tall? Bandy-legged? Hard-eyed?" Billy described the man who'd captured him.

"Yep. Sounds like him."

That wasn't good news. Lowe was also the man Billy had conked on the head with his spear. And the man who had been in the car with Ashley the day before.

Zack shook his head and chewed his lower lip, then turned to the boys. "She's right, though. Best to avoid them, if you can." He didn't look too worried about it. "If you've got no appointments to be somewhere else, stay at the beach." He stopped to look at the sky. "Looks like the weather'll be fine. You can sleep on the porch of the House. Keeper won't mind. Ashley'll likely be gone by morning. *Never* stays in town for long."

Zack paused for a moment, chewing on his lower lip. "Somebody's bound to of telegraphed Sheriff Baker that he's here. He'll be hot on Ashley's tail. I'm surprised Ashley even stayed the night after driving through town big as day like he did."

Queenie breathed a sigh of relief. Zack had corroborated everything Jeremy and the Seminoles had told them and more. Ashley would be gone by morning, if he hadn't left already.

"The beach?" she asked the boys with a hopeful smile.

"The beach!" They sounded equally relieved. Billy stuck the pole in the sand and pushed, turning the boat toward the Indian River.

"Now, hold on!" Zack held his palms out as if to stop the boat. "Much as I'd love to, I can't go back to the island with you." Then he sagged his shoulders as if sorry to say it. "I've got to go home." That was when he owned up that he had been skipping school that day. If he really did intend to go to engineering college, he probably ought to show up for class on time in the morning.

So, they turned around and headed back to the dock, where they had found him that morning. As usual, they didn't make it straight there. About halfway, Zack stood up again without warning and pointed at a deserted spot on the riverbank. He directed the Chief, who had reclaimed his job poling the canoe, "Pull in over there."

Without waiting to tie off the dugout, Zack jumped out and ran through the bushes, calling back, "Over here!" A short distance from the shore, he led them into an abandoned, overgrown field. Rows of knee-high plants with dark green long pointy leaves stood out among the weeds. Zack ran into the middle and poked around those plants for a few moments before calling out, "Here we go!"

He held up something about the size of a human head. It had a rough golden skin and a spiky green topknot. "Pineapples," he explained. "One of my uncles used to run a pine plantation off this field. Made big money for a time. Isn't worth his while to work it any more, though. Not since the railroad started shipping Cuban pines raised its tariff on us. But the things still grow wild. These are about the last of the season. And when you pick them ripe like this, there's nothing sweeter!"

Soon, they all pawed through the pineapple patch, searching for their third kind of treasure in two days. Pineapple gold resting on top of fish in the back of the canoe, they headed toward Zack's dock again.

When they got there, Zack unloaded his share of the pines and fish and climbed out of the canoe. Standing on the dock above the other three, he summed up their day by flipping his silver dollar in the air and crowing out loud about how lucky he was.

"Dinner in my bag and a dollar in my pocket, just for doing what I was wanting to do anyway. Yes sir! Like I said. That's what I like about Yankee tourists. Money don't seem to mean the same to them as it does to us!" He looked down at his three new friends with a broad grin.

Before the others could respond, however, the Chief, who had been unusually quiet a lot of the afternoon, especially since the lightning strike, spoke from where he stood in the dugout. The Chief was not smiling.

"I think money may not mean the same to *me* as it does to *you*, my friend." The tone of his voice was as dark as his eyes. It caught the other three totally off guard.

Seeing the looks on their faces, the Chief took a deep breath and explained, "Much of this day we have talked of nothing but money, and that has made me think. Before my people ever heard of money, we were rich. Whatever we needed, the land provided, and we had only to thank the Creator. But we have been getting poorer ever since."

The other three were so surprised by his words, they didn't say anything when he paused to take a deep breath.

"Plume hunters killed all the great white birds and left their bodies lying in the swamp. They made much *money* selling the feathers. Now the egrets are gone from this place. But, that has not stopped the killing. The men you call *sportsmen*..." The Chief spit that word out with disdain. "They have found a new reason to kill. This morning, the great silver fish was taken from its home in the river and left hanging in the sun to rot. Why? To take a photograph? So that a *sportsman*..." He spit again as if he couldn't say the word without poisoning his mouth. "Can prove that he killed it? Such men waste the Creator's gifts! They should be banished from this land! Instead, you greet them at the train like kings."

The Chief shook his head and looked each of his friends in the eye as he struggled to get this out. Nobody took the floor from him this time either.

"Because they bring *money*?" He paused, squeezing his eyes shut for a moment. "I think this is a false thing ... like the wooden horse of the Greeks. Even if they bring *very much money*, it will prove to be a bad bargain in the end. When the silver fish are all gone, like the egrets, what will they kill next? And what will be left to buy with their money that is of value?"

After another pause for breath, the Seminole concluded, "To me, money is a bad thing to seek."

Other than telling stories and laying out plans, Billy and Queenie had never heard the Chief say so much at one time before. Nor had they ever known him to be so serious. In their surprise, they searched for some way to answer him.

But Zack didn't need to look far. He hunkered down, sat on his heels, and rested his elbows on his knees so he could take the Indian boy on eye-to-eye. "You may be right, Chief. I've had this conversation in my own head, too. And I know my uncles would agree with you. They'd like nothing better than to spend the rest of their days building sailboats and growing pines, like they always did before." Zack rocked and bounced on his heels as he thought out his next words.

"But you see what's going on in Stuart." He swept his arm around him. "Times're changing. There's new people, and new things, and new roads coming to town every day! And, it's not just happening here! Now, me?" He thumped himself on his chest. "I'm not one to go cutting off my nose to spite my own face. *I'm* gonna try as many new ideas as I can and take those new roads as far as they can take me!"

He got himself so worked up about the prospect he jumped to his feet and flipped his silver dollar even higher into the air. "And if what it takes to do that is a little money?" He grabbed the coin out of the air with a flourish and thrust it into his pocket for emphasis. "Well? Then, I'm gonna find a way to get me some!"

The Chief nodded respectfully. He had spoken his piece, and Zack had spoken his. Zack had proved himself to be a friend, and that was the way of friends.

Zack nodded back and looked around. "Sun's getting low. Got to get a move on," he said, bending down to stuff his fish and pineapples into his bag. The four said their "Thank-you's" and "See-you-later's," and flashing one more smile back over his shoulder, Zack disappeared into the scrub with a bounce in his step.

Queenie watched him go, her mind reeling. When she turned back to the Chief, his solemn eyes were still focused on the spot where Zack had vanished.

Chapter 40. The Answer

After Zack disappeared, Billy, Queenie, and the Chief reconsidered whether it really made more sense to go back to the beach. After all, Ashley would not go into the Seminole camp looking for them. They'd be safe there so long as they laid low, out of sight. Then they could leave Stuart for Tantie first thing in the morning without Ashley being any wiser.

"But..." Queenie realized she didn't want to go sneaking into the creek and hiding all night. "Last night was hot, and the mosquitoes were horrible. We'd have more we can do and be as safe and out of sight on the island." Plus the beach would be much more exciting. She knew what would tempt the boys.

They mulled it over. With Ashley out of the equation, the question boiled down to whether or not they had to leave Stuart first thing in the morning. They'd been missing for one whole day by the time they met John Tiger. With any luck, he'd sent word to their parents that they'd gone to Stuart the next day. Or sometime that day at the latest. It had taken John Tiger about half a day to pole the canoe up to his tie off spot in the Alpatiokee and walk to the camp where they found him. From there it would be maybe a short day's walk to Tantie. So, they had to plan for at least one long day, but more likely a day and a half. Would it make any difference if they got a late start in the morning? How upset would their parents be if they took another day or two getting home?

When they couldn't come up with one right answer using logic, they went ahead and decided to do what they had wanted to do all along, spend the night at the beach. Queenie beamed. The adventure continued.

They made it back to the House of Refuge right before dark. After rinsing the sand and salt off at the pump, they dried out by the driftwood fire they'd lit using Queenie's matches. "Thank you, Daddy," she whispered and blew a kiss to the west as Billy handed them back to her.

The sand between Queenie's toes was smooth and dry and still warm from the afternoon sun as she set her shoes next to the fire to dry. She luxuriated in the feel of it. The heck with not showing her ankles.

Before long, oysters popped open over coals. Later, as they licked pineapple juice sweeter than sugar from their fingers, a full moon rose from the sea, creating a golden path across the small undulating waves. Calm again after the afternoon violence, the ocean itself seemed to glow from within.

To the east and above, the moon overpowered the stars, but the low western sky still sparkled with their flickering lights. A light breeze that blew just strong enough to keep the mosquitoes at bay played with the fire. In turn, the flames sent out ripples of red and gold light that alternately revealed and hid the kids' features as they huddled around it. The crackle and pop of the burning wood accented the soothing background rumble of gentle waves that had replaced the roar of the afternoon's angry surf.

It was out of that spectacular, calm darkness that Billy finally entered the debate between Zack and the Chief.

"Chief, I've been thinking about what you and Zack had to say back at the dock."

"Yes?"

"Seems to me you could both be right."

The Seminole only grunted and shrugged in response, and Billy continued with a question, "So, you think money is a bad thing to want?"

"Money is not what my people need." The answer avoided the question.

Billy came back quickly with, "So, what *do* your people need?"

Still thoughtful. Then cautiously, as if he sensed his friend was setting up some kind of logic trap, the Chief spoke the truth. "Land." It was the most important thing they had before that they did not have now.

The fire and surf held sway for some time before Billy spoke again. "Well, I've been thinking about that, too. Zack's right. With the train coming next year and all, Tantie's likely to start changing fast like Stuart. Heck, ranches south of Kissimmee are *already* fencing off the prairie. So, if I'm going to be a cattleman, it seems to me I need to get myself some land, too. And soon."

Then he stood up and shook the buttoned-down pocket of his overalls where he held all the coins the three had collected over the past two days for safekeeping. The coins jingled over the crackle of the fire. "So, does that sound like money to you?"

The Chief nodded as if he could see the logic trap starting to close. "Yes." He let the other boy move on to his next point.

Billy sat down again. "It does sound an awful lot like five dollars and eighty-five cents," he conceded. Then, he jingled the coins again. "But, I heard that land dropped to about two dollars an acre over there between the lake and the Alpatiokee when they took the promoters to jail for not draining the swamp the way they said they would. If there's any truth to what I heard…" Jingle, jingle. "That could also be the sound of almost three acres of what you and I need the most."

The trap slammed shut. Queenie could make out the Chief's silhouette rocking back and forth ever so slightly against the moon glow on the ocean.

But Billy had more to say. "Now, you're right, too. There's bad ways of getting money, and killing off the egrets and the silver fish are two of them. But the money in this pocket? We earned that by saving little Sally from the runaway and providing a bunch of what seem to be decent folks with food to eat. Doing all that felt right. Like I was doing what I was supposed to be doing."

He turned his gaze across the fire to Queenie when he said it. She could see red and gold flames dancing in the blue crystals that were his eyes. She kept her mouth shut this time. Billy and the Chief were finding what they needed on this quest on their own. Even though her heart ached in her chest, she smiled to herself. The boys. This place. Everything made her happy.

The blue-eyed boy thought again for a while. "It seems to me, it's not the money, but what you do to get it, and what you do with it that makes the difference," he concluded in a voice that seemed intended for himself, his friends, and the universe,

They all grabbed their knees and gazed into the fire. It snapped and flickered. Small waves washed onto shore and receded back into the sea. Nobody spoke for a time.

The Chief broke that silence, speaking at first to the fire. "The Seminoles still walk this land today only because we have never surrendered to the white man. But even so, the life we know shrinks and dies and we cannot stop it. And now the train is coming."

The Indian boy turned his gaze out to the ocean and then up to the moon as he spoke. "And I have learned from this quest that while we have been trying to hold on to our old ways, the white man has been creating a new world around us. Soon, we will be swallowed up and vanish from this place forever if we do not learn to fight with the weapons of the white man's new world to protect ourselves."

That was the Chief's second long speech of the day. So he stopped to gather himself before turning to Billy. "You and Zack are right, my friend. Money is not the problem. This new life asks questions I have never considered before, and money is perhaps the answer to many of them."

He paused to take in a slow breath before continuing, "But, this day I have seen the world from the mountain and felt the wrath of the Creator. I will never again forget who I am. Yes, I need money. But I must follow the path of Abiaka and find a way to get it that does not require surrender."

Although nobody said, "Amen," heads nodded in solemn agreement all around the fire.

Queenie studied the boys' faces across the fire. How lucky they were. They knew exactly where they belonged. What they wanted. What did she want? She had no idea what she was looking for. This wasn't her quest at all.

She choked back a sob and, turning her eyes to the sky to keep them from filling with tears, was startled to find the man in the moon staring back at her, nose-to-nose. His features were so clearly defined and he seemed so close that all she had to do was reach her hand up to feel his pale cheek. Would it be cool or warm? But why was he laughing at her?

The foolishness of those thoughts brought Queenie up sharp. The man in the moon was right of course. Here she was on the most beautiful night she'd ever seen in the most amazing place she'd ever been with two friends who had just answered the most important question of their lives. And she was crying?

After all, all she'd asked for was an adventure. So what if the role she got to play in it was more Wendy than Tiger Lily? Peter and the boys needed Wendy. She took a deep breath. They needed her to tell them tales in the moonlight.

"Hey." The fire crackled as Queenie took her turn to break the silence. "I never got to tell you the beginning of the story I started on the river."

Billy looked up as he leaned over to add another log to the fire. "The Legend of King Arthur?"

194

He remembered. Queenie smiled. Of course he did. "Want to hear it?"

Both boys nodded. They scooched closer to the fire, and she began that ancient tale. The Chief especially liked the part about the wise old man who taught Arthur almost everything he needed to know to be a good king. And man. The wizard Merlin.

"Merlin could change his appearance," Queenie told him breathlessly, "from white to black. Be big and then small. Even invisible if he wanted to."

"Huh," the Chief grunted and grinned across the coals at her. "We have stories of shape changers and people you cannot see, but his magic must have been very strong to do so many different things. I will have to ask the elders if they have heard of such a one."

Billy pictured himself reaching down, grasping a magic sword by its hilt. He swung it above his head in great sweeping arcs that ended with its blade pointing triumphantly at the moon. Queenie could see it in her mind's eye. The boy and the sword glowed.

And so it was that the last thoughts in the three kids' heads as they drifted off to sleep that night were about how magic, luck, and fate can change a poor young boy into a great hero if his heart is pure.

Chapter 41. War Cries

The next morning, when Queenie woke up on the porch of the House of Refuge, the dawn reflecting off the ocean was so brilliant she could hardly force her eyes to open. She promised herself if she ever stayed the night at the beach again, she'd sleep on the river side of the dune. For now, however, it was time to start back to Tantie.

Queenie laced her shoes up over her ankles. Then the boys and she started making their way from the ocean back to Stuart. Like their journey from that city to the ocean, it took longer than they expected.

No sooner had they begun than they heard a loud and strange commotion coming from the other side of a small island in the Indian River. Some of the ruckus was obviously shouting and splashing, but they didn't recognize what was creating a mixture of outlandish high-pitched squeaks and rough low grunts. It sounded like a major battle between mythological creatures was under way.

Not wanting to barge into a situation unprepared, they grounded the dugout and ran though the underbrush with Billy in the lead. After he gave the "Stop" signal, they sneaked forward on their hands and knees and peered between the big round leaves of a sea grape bush.

When the Chief saw what was happening, he stood up. Billy pulled him back down before he could do anything. Two Yankee tourist boys older than Queenie and both bigger than Billy, one of them a lot bigger, were doing all the shouting. The splashing, squealing, and grunting were coming from the manatee cow the kids had seen the day before.

Somehow, the Yankees had looped a rope around her tail, and they were dragging her backwards toward the beach where she would be helpless.

The manatee grunted and screamed rough angry squeals. She rolled and fought in the water, thrashing her tail and digging into the sandy river bottom with her flippers, trying to crawl back to her baby. But the boys only yipped and whooped and pulled harder. They dragged her slowly backward through the shallows toward the beach, laughing like it was all great fun. The manatee calf swam anxiously back and forth a short distance out, in water barely deep enough to keep it afloat. It called for its mother in long shrill panicky squeaks.

"We must stop them," the Chief said in a deep, steely voice.

Queenie nodded solemnly and rose to a half-crouch. This was so wrong. She wrapped her fingers around the stone in her sling, ready to race into battle with the Seminole.

Billy pulled them back again. "These're probably the same two Zack said took the bull," he whispered. "Judging from what he told us, they're not likely to pay us much mind if we just walk down there all nice and friendly like and ask them to stop. So…"

He looked at Queenie. "You remember that story you told us about the Trojan horse?"

"What?" Queenie and the Chief both asked.

Billy scrambled away on his hands and knees, gesturing for them to follow him out of the tourist boys' hearing. They crouched, heads together, and he explained in a low voice, "The Greeks used the horse to make the Trojans think the war was over. They pretended they'd gone away."

Queenie couldn't see how that helped with anything.

"Like the *Indians* that used to be on this river."

The Chief frowned.

"Wait. Hear me out." Billy extended his hand palm first and started to lay out his plan. "We can get rid of those two by doing the opposite …

197

making them think a new war is starting." Having captured their attention, he laid out the details, concluding minutes later. "So, you'll need the spears." As his two friends took off for the dugout to get them, Billy snuck back to his spot overlooking the two tourists.

When Queenie and the Chief were in position, Billy gave the "OK" signal and burst out of the sea grape trees, running at top speed, straight for the Yankee boys. He thrashed his arms frantically and screamed, "Help!" at the top of his lungs. "Help! Indians! They almost got me! Indians! Run for your life!"

The two tourist boys turned to face him.

Billy didn't slow down when he got close. Instead, he barreled directly into the bigger of the two at full speed. He hit the Yankee's stomach with his shoulder so hard the air burst out of the tourist's lungs with an "Oomph," and he let go of the rope. The two of them tumbled to the sand and rolled to the water's edge.

"Wha...?" The boy sputtered and grunted, trying to untangle himself. "Huh?"

"Hey!" Not strong enough to keep the manatee from getting away by himself, the smaller tourist boy tried planting his heels. "Heyyyy!" His heels plowed ruts through the sand as the sea cow dragged him slowly toward the shallows.

"Indians!" Billy took exaggeratedly deep breaths and kept his eyes wide as he jumped up, pulling at the boy he'd knocked over to get up, too.

The bigger boy scrambled to his feet, ready to fight. He tried to shake Billy loose and swung at him at the same time. Billy ducked. "Help me," he whined. He looked up at the sea grapes, and the boy checked his second swing.

Holding on to the boy's belt, Billy bent his knees and swung the bigger boy around so that he stood between Billy and the center of the island. He crouched low behind the Yankee as if trying to hide from something in the sea grapes. The boy looked from Billy to the trees. Billy picked nervously at the boy's shirtsleeve, yanked on his arm, and begged breathlessly as if in a panic.

"Help me … please? They're on the warpath!" He panted and pulled his hair out away from his head with one hand. "They say they're taking back the river. Planning to scalp any white man they catch on it!"

It wasn't working. The tourist boys didn't buy Billy's story. They looked back and forth from him to each other. "Come on," the smaller one, still unfazed by Billy's performance, half-shouted to his friend, beckoning with his head that he should come help with the sea cow.

The bigger one raised an eyebrow and shrugged, fist still drawn back. He cockily blew out some breath. "Shuh. There ain't no Indians here anymore." He brushed Billy's hands off his arm and shirt. Puffing up his chest, he loomed menacingly over Billy as if getting ready to fight. Billy cowered at his feet, and his friend called for help again. The manatee pulled even farther away.

The big boy spit into the water next to Billy and took hold of the rope again, muttering, "Crazy local son of—"

Billy gave another signal and it started. Beating that sounded like drums on the other side of the island. Rustling in the bushes, as if a large number of people moved swiftly through the trees. Voices calling out from all directions in a strange language the tourist boys would never be able to recognize. A dog barked, and savage calls that sounded like war cries echoed through the trees.

Out of sight in the sea grapes, the Chief and Queenie ran back and forth, beating on John Tiger's wooden firebox and thrashing at tree trunks and bushes with the spears. They called nonsense words to each other in Muscogee using different voices and yodeled at the top of their lungs.

The eyes of the tourist boys grew wide. They looked at each other and then at Billy.

"Quick! Before they see us!" Billy grabbed the bigger boy again, this time by the arm, and tried to pull him toward his rented tourist canoe. "Oh, my God! It's too late!"

That was the next signal. The Chief ran to the edge of the sea grapes and stopped so the tourists could barely make him out among the branches. Billy pointed at him. "They've found us!" He pulled harder on the tourist boy.

The Chief yelled what sounded like a curse in a deep Muscogee voice. He jumped up and down and pointed at the Yankees. He shook his spear threateningly and motioned for the rest of his band to follow him. Then he faded away into the bushes again. Queenie appeared in another location and disappeared just as quickly. Then the two started running around, making more noise, and yelling even louder than before.

"It's really Indians." The tourist boys looked frantically at each other, their mouths hanging open. "But they told us—"

"Come on!" Billy tugged urgently at the smaller boy's shirt. "Or we're done for! They're calling their friends!"

At that very moment, a spear came flying over the sea grapes and landed with its point in the sand about twenty feet short of them. Only then did the bigger boy's courage break. He dropped his end of the rope and started the race to their canoe.

Billy herded them along, yelling, "Hurry! Hurry! They're almost here!" He helped shove the canoe off and jumped into it with them, fleeing with the two Yankee boys to the mainland and pleading with them to paddle faster and faster all the way.

Chapter 42. Freedom

Now that the manatee cow was loose, she grunted and chirped as loud as she could, flapped her tail, wiggled, and crawled on her belly and flippers to deeper water until she could slide below the surface. She and her calf nuzzled each other for a moment and then headed across the grass flats as fast as the little one could follow. Luckily, it wasn't very fast. The Chief and Queenie rushed back to the dugout and soon caught up with them.

The water was so shallow the sea cow's back skimmed along the surface. Her tail splashed with each powerful push. The full length of the tourist boys' rope trailed out behind her.

The Indian pointed at it and shook his head. "As I feared. We cannot leave her this way. The rope will catch on something and hold her. They will both still die."

He handed the push pole to Queenie and moved to the front of the canoe. After opening his pocketknife, he leaned over the bow, fished the end of the rope out of the river, and pulled it in without putting any tension on it. Queenie poled the canoe so silently the manatee still didn't know the Chief was there. When he got close enough, the boy wrapped the rope around one hand and leaned over the side with his knife in the other, waiting for the sea cow's broad tail to break the surface again.

When it did, Queenie could see the problem. The struggle with tourist boys had pulled the loop so tight it dug deep into the manatee's thick skin. Plus, the flapping of her tail made it a moving target. The

Chief couldn't cut the loop off without hurting her unless he slipped his fingers underneath.

After glancing back over his shoulder at Queenie, he reached down and squeezed his fingers between the Manatee's skin and the loop. The already frightened creature squealed in shock at his touch. It bucked and changed directions suddenly, trying to get away. The Chief went over the side with a splash.

The manatee labored across the shallows toward the deeper water of the nearby channel, taking the boy with her. Lying across her massive flat tail, the Chief's whole body bounced crazily up and down through the water like a rodeo rider on an undersea, bucking bronco.

As the manatee fled over the grass flats, the Chief plowed up a wake, his head and shoulders breaking water on each of the tail's upswings. Then, time ran out. The sea cow crossed into the darker blue-green of the channel and dove. She, her calf, and the Chief simply disappeared.

Queenie suddenly stood surrounded by water so smooth and silent that all the splashing, chirping, and yelling of moments before seemed to have happened on another day in history. She shoved the pole against the bottom one more time and then stood as tall as she could, shading her eyes against the sun, trying to see which direction they had gone.

Time seemed to stand still. The dugout bobbed lazily in the channel. An osprey glided overhead, hovering like a kite on the ocean breeze. It searched the water, too. Its lonely "Cree," the soft buffeting wind in her ears, and the gentle lapping of ripples against the dugout's sides made up the sum total of all sounds in the girl's universe.

"Chief," she said aloud to herself. "You did all you could do. Let her go." She turned to look in another direction, shook her head, and stamped her foot with a loud klunk. "Where are you?"

Something klunked back.

The girl whirled so quickly she almost lost her balance and fell into the river, too. Had she run him over? She searched the nearby water for a sign. Then she noticed the pocketknife lying in the bottom of the canoe and the brown fingers grasping the side. Another hand appeared, dropping the knotted end of the rope into the dugout next to the knife.

It made a softer klunk.

She didn't see the boy's bright smile till she knelt down to help him roll himself into the boat. At first, he leaned forward on hands and knees, trying to catch his breath with saltwater dripping off the tip of his nose. Then he held the rope up over his head as if displaying a prize he had won. Queenie could see where he had cut the loop, setting the manatee free.

"Whooo-eee!" he laughed, and took another deep breath. This time, he winced and stopped short to rub his chest and shoulder. "Ouch." He flexed his neck slowly as if to get kinks out of it. "I must warn our cow hunter friend that branding sea cows may not be as easy as he thinks." He let out another deep breath and a longer, but more subdued, "Whoooo." It stopped with both a wince and a grin.

When they picked Billy up a short time later at the Salerno dock, the blue-eyed boy could hardly contain himself.

"You should've seen it! Those two're so scared..." He hooted and slapped his knee. "It ought to keep them off the river for a week!" He slapped his knee another time. "Shuh! They may *never* come back!"

He laughed again and leaned forward, grinning like a conspirator. "You see, I warned them that the locals'll likely make a show of laughing at them when they tell the story ... and trying to convince the other tourists it couldn't possibly have happened the way they know it did."

He paused, looked from one of his friends to the other, and sat back again, full of himself. "And then, I told them they shouldn't take personal offense at that. It's just that the locals're trying to keep the Indian trouble on the hush. They're afraid Yankee tourists like them'd stop coming down and spending their money if they knew two or three of them get taken by the Seminoles every year, et by gators, or just up and disappear in the jungle for some other reason."

Queenie's heart almost broke as she looked at her two Billies. How brave they were. How hard they'd fight for their lives. But the odds sure seemed against them.

"They're going to keep coming, you know."

"Who? Those two?" Billy tilted his head in the direction of where he had left the tourist boys. "I don't think so."

She shook her head. "Other Yankees." Then she shrugged at the Chief. "White people. You can't stop them. There's too many."

Zack was right. Trains rolled in from the north like waves at the beach. Each brought something new and took something old away. Almost all the faces that peered out through of the train windows were white. Mostly not tourists. New people. Adventurers, businessmen, lost souls come to make new money and new lives and a new Florida. She gave the Chief a wan smile.

The Indian nodded without expression.

Chapter 43. Anna

Even after they started laughing and feeling good again about what they'd accomplished to buoy their spirits, it seemed like it took forever to pole the rest of the way to Stuart. This time they were working against both the river and the tide.

When they finally reached the Seminole camp, the sun was well past its highest point in the sky. Anna told them she hadn't seen John Ashley in town when she met the morning train. They whooped at their good fortune. Relieved of that fear, they set about convincing themselves it was already too late to continue up the St. Lucie toward the lake that afternoon. That didn't take long. The truth was they wanted to watch another train unload and possibly taste another soda.

The kids walked into town with Anna and her two little hogs. That day, she wore a beaded headband and even more necklaces than the camp's elder. Her skirt and shawl were downright flashy, dominated by intricate geometric designs created out of small colorful snippets of cloth even brighter than the shirt John Tiger's wife had sewn.

While they walked, she explained that dressing up in her most colorful Seminole clothing was a trading trick she had figured out. Her unusual outfit and the two tamed hogs captured the attention of tourists and other Yankees when they got off the train.

"They laugh at hogs, but pay whatever I ask for my sewing." Winking as if she was sharing a secret, Anna pulled a patchwork shirt out of her leather purse and showed them her handiwork. "It is the little pieces of color they like."

She held it up against the Chief's plain shirt to demonstrate the design improvements she had made. Before the comparison could embarrass the boy, however, she continued, "But, they do not know that the pattern tells a story. Our story. She pointed to a series of bright squares turned on their sides to make a string of diamonds. "This is the path to the great city in the sky." She pointed to thin strips of dark cloth that radiated outward from each other like spokes on a wheel. "And this shows how we leave messages in the fire."

As she explained other symbols, the Chief fingered the designs and looked at her with new eyes. He nodded his approval.

Then with a sly grin, the woman continued, "And sometimes they pay extra to take my picture." She pulled her hogs in close and struck a pose. "Like this." She narrowed her eyes, transforming her winning smile into a frightening glare that was so exaggerated the kids laughed out loud.

"Some days I make much money." Anna shrugged. "Others…" She pursed her lips and eyebrows, held both hands out palm up, and lifted her shoulders.

When they got to town, she said, "I must go," and walked directly to the station to claim her favorite spot to greet the tourists.

"I'll go with you." The Chief's statement was actually a request for permission. "Maybe more of us will attract more buyers," he suggested.

"Could be." Anna gestured with her chin for him to come along.

Billy and Queenie made "suit-yourself" faces, and the Chief scampered off with the Seminole woman toward her favorite spot, tossing back over his shoulder, "I'll be at the station."

Chapter 44. Two Hogs

Queenie and Billy watched the crowd and hubbub build in anticipation of the train's arrival from the shade of a building across the street. Within minutes, the first whistle put the town on alert that the engine was approaching the trestle that crossed the river and would pull in soon.

A few minutes after the unloading and loading and milling about started in earnest, loud barking and screeching erupted behind the cars and wagons that separated the road from the tracks. Female voices wailed as if in grief, and Anna's two hogs burst out from under a buckboard, squealing loudly and heading across the street towards Queenie and Billy. Then the Chief flew after the hogs through the gap between a horse-drawn wagon and a motor car.

A moment later, they knew why the hogs had fled the area as fast as their little legs could carry them. The biggest dog Queenie had ever seen was trying to drag its owner, a tourist lady in a fancy blue traveling dress, after the hogs through the same narrow gap the Chief had used.

Black-and-white and as big as a small pony, the dog's bark rattled the store windows and started the horse snorting and prancing. After a short struggle to hold it back, its owner tripped and fell on her face in the dusty road. She let go of the leash, and the dog was free. It burst past the horse as the hogs skidded around Queenie and squealed their way along the side of the building toward the river.

The Chief gave Queenie and Billy a quick "here-we-go-again" look as he raced past in pursuit of the hogs. Queenie and the hound took off after him as Billy stepped forward to face the oncoming canine.

With no weapons, the only thing Billy could do was stand his ground between the two buildings. He spread his arms and legs to make himself seem as big as he could. At first, it worked. The dog stopped. It looked at him. They shadow-danced for an instant.

With his knees bent at the ready and his hands out, Billy tried to keep himself between the beast and the river. It didn't take long for the dog to size up the situation. It lunged, though not at Billy. It bounded through the space between him and the wall. The boy dove for its leash as it bolted by, but missed by inches. By the time he picked himself up off the ground, the giant canine had disappeared after the hogs, his friends, and his hound.

Fearing the worst, Billy sped toward the river. When he got there, he almost fell down laughing. Queenie and the Chief stood a hundred feet off shore in waist deep water, holding muddy and wet hoglets up to their chests. The big black-and-white dog shuffled uncertainly back and forth on the high edge of the riverbank like he didn't know what to do next.

Less than one-quarter his size, Billy's hound dog stood below him at the water's edge. When the big dog took a few tentative steps in one direction, the hound moved with him, growled and showed his teeth, and the giant dog stopped. When he tried going the other direction, the hound cut him off again. Billy's hound was herding the big dog like a black-and-white cow.

After giving the problem a little thought, Billy figured if that big dog had traveled successfully on the train all the way from some northern city, it probably wasn't as dangerous as it looked. So he snuck up behind the creature, grabbed the end of its leash, and started talking to it. Before long, the dog stood panting at Billy's side. When Billy called the hound over to introduce the two, the hound acted cocky about it, and the big dog was so petrified at first that it shook all over.

With both dogs on their leashes, Billy led the way back to the station, followed at a safe distance by his two wet friends carrying the two muddy hogs. The tourist lady who had lost her dog was being tended to by her family members. Anna was nearly in tears.

No wonder everyone in town came out to meet the train. It couldn't possibly be this exciting every day, but they sure could get used to being the center of all this attention if it was.

Chapter 45. A Surprise

What happened next was the biggest surprise of all. As Queenie handed over the second hog, a familiar voice called her name and commanded her, "Come here, right this instant, young lady!"

Her mother? The girl whirled and searched the crowd. "Mother!" She ran toward the woman. Right before she reached her, Queenie's father appeared from the back of the train. He dropped the bags he carried, swept his daughter up in his arms, and swung her around.

When her feet touched the ground again, Queenie spun to face her mother. And stopped. Her mother grabbed her shoulders and held her at arm's length. Then, the woman pulled the girl to her with such force that it drove the air out of her lungs. She squeezed Queenie longer and harder than she ever remembered being squeezed before.

When her mother finally released her grip a little, the girl blurted, "What are *you* doing here?" That was a mistake.

Her mother pushed away, looked down at the front of her own dress, and began to brush the mud Queenie had left there off with her hands. "What are *we* ... doing here?" The woman stumbled over the words. She looked first at the girl and then up at her husband. "What ... are... *we*...?" Her mouth kept moving, but no sound came out. She looked up at her husband again.

Queenie had never seen such a lost look on her mother's face before. Right then she knew she'd miscalculated back in John Tiger's camp when she convinced herself that her parents wouldn't be all that upset if she went to Stuart instead of returning straight to Tantie. She was in trouble. Big trouble.

Her father took over, using a softer, calmer tone. "We were worried."

The girl looked from her father to her mother and back again. She could explain. "About what? Didn't John Tiger—"

"Yes, the Indian you met got word to Tantie right away," her father interrupted. Even he turned stern. "But not that first day. Not before we had searched and nobody could find any sign of you. Not before a run boat found the boy's empty skiff far down the lake near the Ft. Lauderdale canal."

As her father made his point, Queenie started to see how badly this might go. She'd put her parents through a lot. Of course, losing the boat wasn't her fault, but…

Her father continued, "Most folks thought you had all likely been lost to the lake. Or to the alligators."

"But, when did you—" she tried again.

"Late on the second day."

"Oh." Queenie felt better. That was pretty fast under the circumstances.

"The Indian… Tiger was it? Met a man traveling to Tantie on horseback almost immediately after you three started for here." Her father swung his arm out to indicate Stuart. "He carried the news."

"What were you *thinking*?" Now her mother interrupted, her face darker, almost crimson. "Running off like this. You should have been home days ago!"

"I'm sorry, Mother. But it didn't start out…" The girl didn't think she'd done that much wrong. "I mean, I told you I was going out on the lake. And then the storm blew up." She thought she was entitled to at least a little sympathy, given everything she'd been through. "And we did start straight back for Tantie. But after we ran into the outlaws, we didn't know what else to do."

"Outlaws?" The word exploded out of her mother's mouth.

Uh oh. John Tiger's messenger apparently hadn't told them about the outlaws. No wonder...

The boys had worked their way to the edge of this happy-angry parent-child reunion. They nodded their heads in unison. Seeing Billy's eyes light up, Queenie rushed her forefinger to her upper lip and gave him the "silence" signal. Too late.

"John Ashley and his gang," said Billy, stepping even closer. Queenie rubbed her finger across her upper lip two more times. The Chief's eyes widened, but Billy was totally focused on Queenie's mother. He missed the signal again and continued with more than a little pride, "We had to fight them." Still basking in the glow of that victory, he looked downright cocky when he said it.

The woman breathed in a startled open-mouthed gasp. Her hand flew up to her face, too.

"When?" Queenie's father asked.

The boy still didn't see it coming. He closed his eyes and worked his fingers, trying to count backward. "The first morning after the storm." He held up one finger like he intended to hold up a second finger and tell the rest of the story, too. He did. "And then, he came here looking for us, and—"

In a panic, Queenie reached out to stop the boy. Before she got to him, her mother did it for her by letting out a moan. Turning on her heels, the woman hid her face on her husband's broad chest with her fists bunched next to her cheeks. The big man put one arm around his wife and took hold of his daughter with the other. He pulled both of them tight to his body.

With one eye smashed shut against her father's shirt, Queenie glared at Billy with her other eye and gave him the "silence" signal again. Seeing it this time, the boy took a giant step backwards.

Queenie's father held his wife and daughter close to him until the older woman's breathing calmed down. When he released them back into the world, he said calmly, "You two stay put." His hand lingered on his wife's arm as he turned back toward the station. "I've got to go tend to the rest of our baggage, but I'll be right back."

Shooting a withering glance at Billy, Queenie tried to smooth things over by showing her mother she had not forgotten her manners. She started to introduce the boys. That didn't go well, either.

Even though her mother's eyes were damp and red, she could still shoot daggers with them. "You!" She aimed them at Billy.

The boy stepped back again and bumped into the Chief who had slid behind him as if trying to become invisible. Queenie's mother locked on him next, anyway. She shook her head, took deep breaths, and started making frustrated hand gestures. Before she could choose the words she wanted, her husband strode back down the platform and picked up their bags.

"Station master says Ashley's left town."

The Chief bounced on the balls of his feet and grinned at Billy triumphantly. Billy ignored him, using his blue eyes to count his toes. Queenie let out a whole lung-full of air with a "woosh." At least they didn't have Ashley to worry about any more.

"And he says our goods'll be safe here at the station for the night," the big man continued. "We can find lodging in Colored Town just down this road."

Queenie's father pointed with his chin at the crushed rock road that ran south along the west side of the railroad tracks. "This way. It's not far." He nudged his women in the right direction with the suitcases. "Best get a move on."

"Hold on… I need to—" Queenie started toward the boys.

"No." Her mother intervened.

"You don't understand. I have to—"

213

"No!" Her mother gripped her arm so tightly it hurt. They stood eye-to-eye, and Queenie noticed for the first time she had grown to be the taller of the two.

"*You* don't understand! We searched everywhere," her mother went on. "Then they found the boat..." Her gaze momentarily lost its focus. She gathered herself. "The minute we heard you were safe, we started packing. We found a ride to Fort Pierce the next day. And we caught the first train here. And... And..." Her voice petered off.

"*And!*" The woman fought to regain control, stepping back and looking her daughter up and down as if seeing her for the first time. Her eyes flew wide. Her hand flew to her mouth again. "Oh, my God!"

Queenie followed her mother's startled gaze down ... to her knees.

Her mother's hands flew to the knot holding Queenie's skirt up in pantaloons, but she couldn't control her fingers. They plucked and fluttered uselessly. She couldn't get the knot untied.

Queenie gently took her mother's hands in hers, moved them aside, and undid the knot herself. Her skirt fell free, torn and tattered, yet covering her legs all the way down to her ankles.

"What could you possibly have been thinking?" Queenie's mother pulled herself back together.

Queenie shook her head and shrugged as if she didn't have an answer. That wasn't the time to try to explain.

"You know you were raised better than that."

"Yes, ma'am." The girl dropped her chin to her chest and stared at the ground.

The woman's expression softened and she reached one hand up as if to touch Queenie's cheek. Then her glance fell on the girl's wild hair and the petticoat strip that didn't quite hold it in place.

"And what is *this* supposed to be?" She ripped the headband off her daughter's brow, threw it to the ground in disgust, and grabbed the girl by the arm again. "We have to get you cleaned up right away!" She tugged the girl toward the path her husband had indicated.

"But—"

"Don't you '*but*' me, young lady! *And* don't make me take you by the ear!"

That was it. Queenie shook her head, gave the boys a "what-can-I-can-do-about-it" look, and followed her mother single file down the tracks to Colored Town.

Chapter 46. Colored Town

Colored Town came as a surprise. Within minutes, downtown Stuart quickly fell away behind Queenie and her parents, and the hardened road dwindled into a soft rutted trail. Gnarly oaks with small, shiny, dark leaves and short-needled sand pines that all leaned in one direction as if blown by the wind lined the way. Scrub jays with bright blue heads and gray breasts flitted around the three human intruders, gliding from one low branch to another, tracking them with big black eyes as they strode by. Small creatures made rustling sounds in the underbrush. The fine white sugar sand smelled hot and dry.

The station master had told Queenie's father they'd find Stuart's colored community about half a mile down the road. What they found was an area of mostly empty land that had recently been carved out of the scrub. It lay on both sides of the railroad, which cut diagonally through it.

On the east side of the tracks, newly grubbed streets and wooden stakes marked the sides and corners of small white rectangles of recently cleared ground. Here and there, small tree branches, bushes, and palmetto roots that couldn't be used for anything else had been gathered into burn piles to be lit as soon as they were dry enough. Three dark-skinned men raising the roof of a larger building near the cleared area's northern edge and a few isolated houses along its southern border were the only signs that people of any color might actually live there.

A little farther down, both sides of the tracks were slightly more built up. Several structures scattered over even smaller lots. Unlike the plots to the east, the parcels to the west squared off to face the diagonal of the tracks rather than the points of the compass.

Just like in Stuart, all the buildings on both sides of the tracks looked brand new. But the houses in Colored Town didn't have the porches, railings, and dormer windows that made the larger white people's houses pretty to look at and more functional. Simple, one-story Cracker cottages, spare rectangles of rough-planed wood with tin roofs, their wooden shutters designed to keep out the elements hung open. Cheesecloth had been nailed over the glassless windows in an effort to keep out the bugs. Some had covered porches. Few had been painted. The bare, raw wood of the unadorned walls still looked fresh, and all of the houses sat a foot or two off the ground on blocks of fat lighter pine.

The tiny yards of the lots with homes on them were crammed to capacity. Giant cast-iron cauldrons bubbled over laundry fires. Clotheslines, small garden plots, hand pumps, and newly planted citrus trees filled the rest of the space, with outhouses in the corners farthest from the wells. A few dark children, too young to work but old enough to run about unattended while their mothers cooked or boiled the laundry, twittered and called to each other on the vacant lots like robins in the spring. The soft smell of wood smoke floated on the air.

Following the station master's directions to the church, Queenie's father led them to a small building and knocked. A round, very dark-skinned church matron came to the door and greeted them in a slow, sing-song accent, the likes of which Queenie had never heard before. From some Caribbean island, she guessed. Or possibly Africa itself.

When Queenie's father told the matron they were looking for Colored Town, she flashed a bright, good-natured smile and explained with equally good humor, "Oh, you made it here, just fine! But..." She lowered her voice as if speaking confidentially, "As you can see, it's not much of a *town* just yet."

To emphasize her point, she gestured toward the vacant lots with her hand. "Only a few handfuls of colored folks be living in Stuart proper at this time. But, times be changing. And for the better!"

Seeing the questioning looks on their faces, she kept going. "Used to be they was no place here we was allowed to stay. We had to stay out whey we be working."

She pointed at the houses dotting lots that were obviously a little older. "Last year, though, some white folks set aside land down here near the track so's they can rent us some houses. They built a few and plan to build some more. Today these houses be whey we most be staying."

Queenie felt her mother stiffen beside her. Then her mother shuddered, the skin between her eyes gathering into a strange wide-eyed frown as the matron went on.

Queenie didn't know what to make of what the church woman was telling them or the way her mother was reacting to it. The colored houses in Stuart weren't much. Still, they were a whole lot better than their dirt-floored cabin in the Cypress Quarters. She glanced up to see what her dad was thinking.

He took in the matron's words with narrowed eyes and a slight frown, too. His head shifted slightly from side to side as she spoke. When he had the chance, he did what he usually did. He asked a question. "What's going on over there?" He gestured toward the newly cleared lots and the larger buildings they had passed where the men were working.

"Oh! That be the good news!" The matron puffed up a little and answered proudly. "This year, after they made the city, the council done voted to divide up some more land on this side the tracks and passed a law saying we be allowed to buy those lots for ourselves if we can raise the money."

Queenie's jaw dropped and hung there slightly open. The city had to pass a *law*? To *allow* colored people to buy their own houses? Her mind reeled.

She hadn't given a thought about how or where the few colored men she had seen loading goods and picking up tourists at the station in Stuart lived. Until her family started its trek down the Kissimmee, she had spent her whole life surrounded by colored people in comfortable, colored communities. Her grandfather had owned a house and a store back in Baltimore even before her mother was born. Eatonville and Rosewood had been the same, only smaller. Even the colored cowman up on the Kissimmee owned his own land and cattle.

But her father always said those places were "too dependent." Was this what he meant? Were all those colored people comfortable in all those other places only because Whites *allowed* them to be?

Of course. That was what Frederick Douglass was talking about. Her father had made her memorize it.

"No man can be truly free whose liberty is dependent upon the thought, feeling, and action of others."

Queenie's mind raced. She rubbed her forehead with her fingers. She'd heard her father's words a thousand times, yet this was the first time they made sense. He didn't want to live in a place where colored people could only have and only do the things white people *allowed* them to have and do.

The white councilmen of Stuart probably meant well. But, if Whites had the power to give something, they had the power to take it away. And you couldn't count on them. After all, they'd done it once before. Back on the day her father was born. The day the president pulled the troops out of Carolina. They could do it again.

Queenie searched her father's face with new understanding. He was on a quest to find a place where they could be free rather than comfortable. Or maybe just safe.

Queenie's mother's face contorted in inner turmoil. She shook her head and halfway turned her back to the church matron. Queenie's father still met that woman's dark eyes and nodded his understanding.

Thus encouraged, the church matron continued brightly, "More and more folks be coming now. Taking advantage of both sides the tracks. That building you pointing to? They be opening a barber shop and a dining place in that one. And soon, they be building a pressing business, too."

In her enthusiasm, the matron stepped forward and pointed at an open triangle of land bordered by the railroad and two sand trails. "And you see over there? That be a park. The church be saving up to buy that corner right on the other side … across from it."

She turned back to catch Queenie's father's eye again. "And now there's even talk of building a school. Won't be long, we be having everything we need. This is going to be a *fine* place to be!" She bobbed her chin up and down, worked her hands together excitedly at her waist, and emphasized that conclusion with her toothy smile. "A fine place."

Queenie's father nodded thoughtfully as his fingers closed gently around his wife's upper arm. She had turned to stare across the tiny sandy park at the vacant lot where Stuart's Colored-owned church would one day stand. Her eyes vacant, her chest and shoulders rose and fell slowly in a silent sigh.

Still smiling, the church matron patted her other arm. "Come along, chile," she said giving the younger woman a gentle push away from the tracks. "They's a lady with extra rooms down this way. Let me show you. You looks like you need you rest."

Chapter 47. The Message

The church matron was wrong. The last thing Queenie's mother wanted was rest. The minute they settled into their rooms, she stripped the tattered dress off her daughter and threw it into the trash. Then she heated water out on the wood fire, stood the girl up in a cast-iron laundry kettle, and went over her from head-to-toe, scrubbing and scraping, trimming and combing.

When Queenie finally appeared before her mother, once again in a clean dress and dry shoes, she looked almost exactly like she'd looked before she met the two boys. Her mother stepped back, and after scrutinizing her daughter from top to bottom, pronounced her verdict. "That's better."

The girl endured all this by retreating into her head to work out a winning argument for going to see her friends. She sprung it when she saw the opportunity.

"But, *Mother*," she said in her best gentrified tone, "the Seminoles fed me and gave me a place to stay when I needed one. I *must* thank them in person for their hospitality. It really wouldn't be proper not to."

She knew it would work. Partly, she could tell her mother's shock at finding her alive and well had started to wear off. But mostly, the woman had to agree because Queenie was invoking one of *her* rules of etiquette. Her mother gave in, though not until she had made the girl promise she'd behave like a proper young lady. Even with that, she still made it clear she wouldn't be taking her eye off the girl, not for one instant.

Queenie's father had stayed out of it. While the two women in his life found their own way to mutual agreement, he talked with the church matron and the lady who had taken them in. Once informed of his wife's concession, though, he acted as if he had known all along how it would come out.

He crooked his elbow out to her. "Okay!" Reaching his other hand toward his daughter, he asked, "Can you show us the way to the Seminole camp, so we can pay our respects?"

Queenie nodded.

"Well, lead on, then. Oh… And do you think the boys will be there?" He winked at Queenie. "We have a message to deliver."

"A message?" She had things to tell them, too.

"From their families."

When they got to the camp, Queenie introduced her mother and father to the elder woman first, mixing a few phrases of Muscogee she had mastered with simple English she knew the woman understood.

Her mother told the elder, "Thank you for taking care of our little girl," as she reached out to shake the woman's hand.

The elder smiled and tipped her forehead downward in response, but kept her hands clasped at her waist and her distance proper. "No thank me. Queen take care of self." Tipping her head toward Queenie, the old Seminole continued, "Strong *woman*."

Heat crept up the girl's neck. That was high praise from the usually reserved elder who had held her family together for thirty hard years.

Before anyone had a chance to say anything else, Anna walked up. She and the elder spoke for a moment in Muscogee, and the elder stepped aside. Anna greeted Queenie in English, thanking her over and over.

Queenie's mother offered her hand again when introduced, saying, "I saw you at the train. You were the one with the … uh … the…"

"The hogs. Yes! That is me." The Seminole beamed at the colored woman, taking the offered hand in hers. "Your daughter is very brave. You must be proud. I could doubt the other stories because I have only heard them. But today I saw with my own eyes."

"Other stories?"

Queenie saw that look creeping back into her mother's face. She distracted her by running over to Billy and the Chief who had kept their distance this time. She dragged the boys into the group. Her father helped by announcing that he had a message for them.

"My pa?" Billy asked nervously.

"Took me a while to find him." The big man gave his daughter a look that let her know she should have left her parents more information about who she'd be with before traipsing off, then continued, "He took it okay. Was a bit worried at first, though. Like the rest of us."

The boy fidgeted and looked away.

"But he never really fell into it. Told me from the beginning, 'That boy's not stupid enough to get himself killed out on the lake,' and left it at that."

The Chief snickered and gave Billy an elbow. Billy pushed back with both hands.

"Your family…" Queenie's father stopped the horseplay by turning his focus on the Chief.

The Indian boy stood up straight. Wide-eyed and still, holding his breath.

"Said pretty much the same thing."

This time, Billy elbowed the Chief. The Indian boy stood there grinning.

"The message I have for you boys," Queenie's father continued, still looking at the Chief, "is some members of your clan will be coming into town soon to do some trading. You can wait and return to Tantie with them or make your way home the way you got here. Just leave a message here at the camp if you leave."

The boys gave a happy start and almost "whooped" with relief.

When her father couldn't hold his stern frown any longer and broke out in a grin that matched the Chief's, Queenie almost screamed. It wasn't fair. She was older. Had much more schooling. She'd made it through the same storm, made the same decision to come to Stuart, and everybody acted like that was some kind of tragedy, or, worse, like something she wasn't *allowed* to do, like she'd broken some sacred rule.

But the *boys*? For *them,* it was a grand adventure? Something they were expected to do in the natural course of things? And everybody whooping and hollering to celebrate the fact that they finally did it?

"Ugh!" The girl shook herself in disgust. She'd done everything they'd done. As good as they did. Sometimes better, but did anybody pat her on the back and say "Good job?" No. She was a girl. She got, "How could you?"

She could handle being Colored. All she needed to do was find the right place. But being a girl? They'd still treat her like this, no matter where she was.

"Ugh!" She stomped her foot.

Before Queenie could explode, Anna stepped up and announced that the elder welcomed Queenie's family for dinner.

"Please tell the elder we'd be delighted!" Queenie's father didn't even look at his wife before accepting.

Queenie couldn't wait to see the look on her mother's face when the elder handed her the big eating spoon right out of the pot. To her surprise, however, Anna fumbled around on one of the platforms and produced a stack of tin bowls. Queenie rolled her eyes. Nothing was going right.

After a hearty meal of stew, sofkee, and flat bread, followed by pineapple Queenie had probably picked for dessert, everyone gathered around the campfire under mosquito bars telling stories. That was when Billy, Queenie, and the Chief finally told Queenie's mother and father most of the story of the past five days the way they saw it.

Later, as Queenie and her parents made their way through the scrub back to Colored Town, Queenie's mother didn't say a word. She wrapped her arm around her daughter's waist and held her close. Queenie slipped her arm over her mother's shoulders and hugged her back. They walked like that almost the whole distance.

Queenie had no way of knowing they would stay in Stuart only that night and one more. And those would be her last real nights in Florida.

Chapter 48. A Change of Direction

Queenie had a difficult time falling asleep even though she lay in a soft, comfortable bed for the first time in five nights. For one thing, too much was going on in her head. For another, her parents were discussing something on the other side of the wall in low, serious voices, and she couldn't make out what they were saying.

The next morning, her mother announced, "We've..." Her eyes darted to her husband's. "We've had enough of wandering the Florida wilderness. We're going back to Baltimore."

"Baltimore?" It caught Queenie by surprise. She wasn't ready to leave the jungle. That would be bad enough. But all the way back to Maryland? City streets, cars, dresses, regular school. No more spending time with her father looking for the right place. She didn't want to go. She *really* didn't want to go. "What will we—"

"I can teach." Her mother didn't let her finish. "Your father can work in my father's store. This will give you a chance to get a proper education—"

"But—"

"No 'buts', young lady." Her mother had her mind made up. "No more gallivanting around the countryside with your father ... and God knows who else ... picking up things willy-nilly on the fly. You will graduate from a proper high school. That's what you need to enroll in Morgan College."

Queenie lifted her eyes to the heavens and stopped listening. This *wasn't* about her education. Her mother was the best teacher in the world. Good enough to get her into any college. Plus, with her father's schooling, too, she was already way ahead.

No. Her mother wasn't *comfortable* here anymore. That's what it was. Not since she saw Colored Town. If she stayed, she'd have to face the truth. *She'd* have to admit Queenie's father was right. She wasn't free or safe. Not here and maybe not anywhere.

And another thing. And this galled the girl even more. Her mother was taking her back because she didn't want Queenie going off and having adventures. She wanted *her* daughter to be like all the other *good* little girls. To stay where proper young colored girls were *allowed* to stay and do what proper young colored girls were *allowed* to do. She actually thought Queenie'd go back to being the way she was before, if she could only get her out of the jungle.

Queenie's whole body quivered with frustration at the unfairness of it all as she shifted her attention back to her mother's words. What she heard was, "Far far away from all this backwoods, frontier nonsense."

"But Mother—" Queenie tried to keep the anger out of her voice. She'd never started a fight with the woman before, and starting one now wouldn't help.

"No!" Her mother cut her off before she could argue back. "There's nothing you can say to change *our* minds!"

The girl tried another approach and got the same result. They would *not* be staying until the members of the Chief's clan got to Stuart so that she could spend some more time with her friends. Now that the woman had decided what she wanted to do, she had turned herself into stone.

"We're getting on that train as soon as everything can be arranged." It was her final word on the subject.

Later that morning, however, Queenie's mother relented a little. She let Queenie go into Stuart with her father to arrange for their train tickets and to do some shopping. If they had time when they finished, the two of them could spend it with the boys.

Queenie took advantage of her first chance to get her father alone. As they walked through the scrub toward town, she tried to convince him to change his mind, but he had only one thing to say.

"She needs to go back. It's her home."

"But I—"

He shook his head, his eyes begging his daughter to understand.

Queenie's anger finally got the best of her. *He* was the one who didn't understand. He should be standing up for himself, for *her*, not blindly doing what her mother foolishly demanded!

"But what about me?" She spit out the question. "What about *you*?"

Her father looked as if she had struck him. "She needs to go—"

"Home. I know! But you and me, where's *our* home?"

The words dripped venom. Queenie didn't care if she hit him when he was down. Let him see how angry she was. *He* was the one surrendering. Abandoning her and everything he always wanted and believed in, everything *she* wanted and believed in too, without a fight.

The man took a long time answering. His eyes searched Queenie's face and then the ground and the trees before he spoke. Finally, he said, "*My* home ... is with her."

His words were only a whisper in the woods, but the truth they proclaimed ricocheted through Queenie's head. It bounced off the scrub oaks and got lost in the sky. Who knew where it would land? Her father was sacrificing everything, including her, for the woman he loved. For the first time in Queenie's life, he looked helpless. Tears gleamed in his eyes.

It was that simple. Queenie was going back to Baltimore. There was nothing she could do about it. And as of this day, she was on her own.

When tears flooded her eyes, too, the big man crumpled heavily down on a stump and pulled her onto his lap. Queenie went reluctantly and sat there stiffly, resisting as he patted her back. But it was too much. She laid her head on his shoulder, like she used to when she was a child, and hid her face in his chest. He wrapped his arms around her and held her tight.

Uncontrollable sobs wracked both their bodies as they mourned their separate losses.

Chapter 49. Promises

Eventually, Queenie and her father ran out of tears. It was settled. Queenie was going back to Baltimore. The only thing left was to put a face on it.

After they finished their shopping and said their "Thank-yous" and "Good-byes" in the Seminole camp, they found the boys fishing a short ways up the creek. They stopped and stood side-by-side as Queenie and her father approached.

Billy whistled. "I see what you were talking about. That is one fancy dress." Then, he elbowed the Chief. "She cleans up right good, don't she?"

Instead of ignoring him like she normally did when he said things like that, Queenie used it as an opportunity to break the news all at once. "Well, I have to get used to dressing like this again. I'm going back to Baltimore in the morning."

Both boys' mouths dropped open. They looked at each other and then back at her, before Billy shrugged and said more formally than usual, "Well, if that's what you want, then—"

"It's not what I want." Queenie tried to keep her composure. "But it's what's going to happen." She looked to her father for help one more time. Hoping he'd change his mind.

He didn't. "It's my wife." He sighed. "It's too hard on her down here."

"But you haven't found what you came for, yet. Don't you want to keep looking?" It sounded as if Billy was trying to help the man come up with an excuse to stay. With a tilt of his head toward Queenie, the boy continued, "I mean … she's real sharp when it comes to figuring out things. And she's good on the trail."

The first straight-forward compliment the blue-eyed boy had ever given Queenie almost made her start bawling all over again.

"I have to take her mother home." Her father didn't budge.

The boy's shoulders sagged when he heard the man's answer, but he regained his composure quickly. "Well, then, I guess that's that." After making a point of wiggling his shoulders as if stretching them out, he stood up straight and smiled a half smile at Queenie. "So, you're taking another train ride, eh?"

She silently thanked him for changing the subject. "Yep," she answered, "catching it in the morning."

The Chief had stood there listening. She noticed that the dark circles the lightning had left around his eyes had faded somewhat over night. Without saying a word, he took a step toward her and placed his hand on her arm. She covered it with hers and squeezed. That almost broke her resolve, too. Luckily, she'd worked out a strategy for deflecting this situation.

"Here…" She shook herself loose. "I have something for you." She handed each boy a folded piece of paper. Billy took a quick look and put his in his pocket. The Chief unfolded the note she had given him and studied it for a moment. Then, he folded it back up again and stood there, looking awkward.

Queenie explained. "We can write. Letters and things. That's the address in Baltimore where I'll be staying. It's my grandfather's house."

The Chief's look escalated from awkward to embarrassed. After a few instants under her confused scrutiny, he admitted in a flat voice, "I do not know how to write … or read."

"Oh!" Queenie's hand flew up to her mouth. She should have known that and wished she'd given his feelings more thought. Then the answer hit her. "You can learn!" Always an optimist *and* very encouraging. "Your English is really good! It can't be hard with your English already so good."

The Chief looked her in the eye for the first time, dropped both of his shoulders, and blew out an exaggerated breath of defeat. "We have no schools."

Queenie almost fell for it. Then she caught herself. "Don't give me that, Chief. I know you. You've already figured out reading and writing are things you need to know." She flashed the boy a dazzling smile. "And, like my daddy always tells *me*..." She turned the smile on her father, giving him a taste of his own medicine. "Anything you really *want* to do, you can find a *way* to do."

That was true in this instance. But she wasn't quite sure she still fully believed it in general.

When the Indian boy only grunted in response, she knew she'd read him right. "And you can practice by writing *to me*." She flounced to put a period on that sentence. The Chief gave in with another grunt.

Then, she turned an even brighter smile on Billy. "You already know how to read." When the boy nodded warily, she cut to the chase. "If you write, I'll write back."

He hemmed and hawed, resisting. After a bit, he gave in. "Okay." Then he hedged his bet. "Not likely too much, though. Seeing as I'm not real good at it."

After everything that had happened in the past twenty-four hours, Queenie was hanging on by her fingertips. She wasn't in the mood for arguing about one more thing. "Then you'll just have to stay in school till you *get* good at it!" She sounded as final as her mother.

Billy countered, "Tantie don't have a high school like they're building here in Stuart."

Queenie stamped her foot. "Okay!" She glared at the boy. "If you don't want to go to school, don't." She took in a long deep breath. "And if you don't want to write?" She threw her hands up in the air. "Just do whatever it is you *want* to do. But, don't expect me to waste my time writing *you*, if *that's* what you decide."

Throughout her demonstration, Billy's eyes kept dropping to the ground, where he drew circles in the sand with his toes, and coming back up again. He didn't say anything. All he did was grunt, too.

That's when Queenie's father finally came to her aid. He changed the mood by asking the boys what new things they had seen and done during their adventures. With only one sideways glance at Queenie, they told him about the tourists and about Zack. That led to their talk on the beach and their dreams for the future.

"So, when we get home," Billy ended, "we need to find a good way to make some money because we need to buy some land."

Now, making money on the Florida frontier was a subject near and dear to Queenie's father's heart. He'd been studying that question ever since he stepped off that first train outside of Eatonville. "I have a few ideas about that," he offered. "But first, what have you learned about that since you've been in Stuart?"

It turned out they had learned a lot. Soon the four of them were deep in a conversation about the possibilities that lasted until the Chief pointed at the sun.

Standing up, he announced, "The train will be here soon." Turning to Queenie's father, he added, "Come. You should see the way Anna sells to the tourists."

Queenie looked up at the man. "Can we go, Daddy? Please."

He nodded, and the kids took off running. They caught up with the Seminole woman as she approached the station with her hogs.

"Come," the Chief beckoned Queenie's father when he trotted up behind them. "We can help with the shirts. I think you will like them."

Queenie's father grinned, his enthusiasm matching the Seminole boy's. The kids had told him about Anna's handmade souvenirs and the clever way she attracted the tourists' attention. "Maybe I'll pick up a few tricks of the trade," he laughed as he followed the woman and boy to the other side of the station.

Chapter 50. Face-to-Face

Queenie stopped her father before he took two steps toward the station, by laying her hand on his arm. "I'd sure love a soda, Daddy." Pointing to the drug store across the street, she added, "If you give us the money, Billy and I can bring some back for everybody."

"Sure, Sweetie," the big man answered absentmindedly, stretching his neck to keep his eyes on the two Seminoles as he withdrew his hand from his pocket and handed her several coins. Saying, "I'll be right over there," he hurried to help the Chief spread Anna's colorful creations out on the bushes that lined the tracks so the tourists could get a good look at them.

Billy, Queenie, and the hound crossed to the far side of the dusty street. Free for the first time all day, and knowing her father would be occupied with Anna and the tourists for a while, Queenie stopped in the shade near the drug store window. She couldn't think of anything to say.

Equally silent, Billy made a show of scrutinizing the items on display in the shop window. Before long, however, he was studying the goods and sundries through the glass with the same intense curiosity he and the Chief had given the cow hunters' gear the first day she had seen them in Tantie.

Bent at the waist with his hands on his knees to get a better look at some small item, he whistled, then said in a low voice, "There's stuff in there I never heard of." Turning his head up to face her, he asked, "What do you suppose they *do* with it all?"

Queenie had to smile. That boy was so cute sometimes. There was so much he didn't know. She slipped the money her father had given her into his hand and shoved him toward the drugstore entrance. "Go on in and buy the sodas. Take your time poking around some if you like. The hound and I'll be over there." She pointed to a shady grassy area between two buildings a short distance farther away from the station.

When he hesitated, she pushed him again. "Go on. Maybe you'll *learn* something."

Billy made an indignant face, then winked and went inside.

Queenie walked the dog to the corner of the building. With all of the town's attention focused on the train's arrival, she saw no one near her on the streets. After all the tension of dealing with her mother and the confrontation with her father, she relished having a moment of peace and quiet to herself. The sunny warm afternoon air made her drowsy. While the dog sniffed around, she leaned against the wall and her mind wandered.

She'd miss the boys. How was she going to survive in Baltimore? No, she didn't want to think about that. The shirts Anna was selling. That was it. Those shirts were sure something to look at. On the other hand, they wouldn't be much use in an emergency where you needed strips of sturdy cotton. Queenie's fingers fluttered over the curved shape of the stone inside the new bag she'd bought at the dry goods store to replace her sling for carrying things. Still Anna was selling a fair amount of those shirts. They seemed to be the kind of thing tourists liked, all bright and different. She'd talk to her father about that. He could help the boys.

A growl and a yank brought her back. The hound was trying to come to her, but he'd snagged his leash on a small bush. He growled more deeply as she knelt to untangle him. The hair on his back stood on end the way it had when he had sensed the panther.

Before Queenie had time to think about what might have upset him, a gruff male voice hissed behind her, "Get up slow and natural like."

She did as the voice commanded, then turned around and stood face-to-face with the short, bandy-legged outlaw who had captured Billy on the Old Wire Road. Kid Lowe, the one Zack said was the most dangerous of the lot, held a gun up tight next to his body where only she could see it. Its barrel pointed at her stomach, so close she almost felt the steely cold of it.

A thousand thoughts raced through Queenie's head all at once. Zack and Jeremy had been wrong? Or betrayed her? No. Not Zack. Jeremy! She had underestimated him. He played her along then sold her out to Ashley. What was she going to do?

Her eyes searched the streets for help and didn't find any. The only visible people were blocks away, backs to her, at the station with her father, Anna, and the Chief.

Billy? He couldn't see what was going on from inside the drugstore. Probably couldn't hear her if she screamed.

Should she run for it? Yes.

No. Lowe was too close, his finger on the trigger. The hole at the end of the barrel grew wider the more she looked at it. She had to think of something.

As if responding to her silent plea, the hound launched itself at the man. The outlaw didn't even blink. He clubbed the dog between the eyes with the butt of his pistol and it fell to the ground. Taking advantage of the distraction, Queenie turned to run. The man was quicker. He grabbed her upper arm before she got two strides away.

The dog staggered and turned back to the outlaw growling again. Without letting go of Queenie's arm, Lowe kicked the hound in the ribs. He fell to the ground with a yelp, then whimpered and struggled to rise once again. Queenie swung her free fist at the outlaw's face, but even though he was small for a man, he was bigger and stronger. He blocked her blow with his gun hand, and yanked her almost to the ground with his other. Fierce fingers dug into the flesh of her upper arm.

"Tie him up, or I'll shoot you both now."

Queenie tied the leash to a small tree, running her hand down the hound's back as she did so. She didn't see any blood or obvious broken bones. Maybe he'd be all right.

Lowe had released her to secure the hound. As soon as she finished, he pulled her up by the hair on the top of her head and ripped the new cloth bag off her shoulder. Finding only the stone inside, he breathed out, "Sheesh," and threw it to the ground next to the dog.

Taking hold of Queenie again, he ordered, "Now walk to the river. Nice and quiet like."

This time, she did feel the gun. Its cold, hard muzzle pressed between her shoulder blades. The man trailed slightly behind her and to the right, pushing her forward with the pistol in his left hand, and controlling her direction with his other hand on her right arm. Out of sight of the street and stores, he took small purposeful steps, holding her upright when she stumbled, until they reached an isolated boathouse that sat out over the river.

Keeping the gun against her back, Lowe released Queenie's arm and rapped on the door, calling out in a hoarse whisper, "It's me. I got one."

A voice answered, "Come in," followed by the sound of the latch lifting.

The door opened, and Lowe shoved the girl inside. When she regained her balance, she stood face-to-face with John Ashley. The far end of the boathouse opened directly to the river. Sunlight reflecting off the water illuminated the shadowy interior with ripples of light. She could see the outlaw clearly.

Ashley's eyes bored into hers, the hard dark blue of cold steel, almost black. He wore a green-and-white plaid shirt, khaki pants, and scuffed brown brogans. The bulge in the right pocket of his khakis halfway down the outside of his thigh looked like a gun.

Queenie gulped in short shallow breaths. She couldn't let herself panic the way she had with the Indigo. She had to maintain control. Even though Ashley didn't have his gun in his hand, now that she was here, he could kill her and get away without anybody knowing about it if that was what he wanted.

Chapter 51. The King of the Everglades

To Queenie's surprise, Ashley took a step back. His eyes widened and he turned to Lowe, frowning. "You sure she's the one?" he asked.

"Uh huh." The smaller man nodded his head vigorously. "Never was no Indian. She's colored like Jeremy told us. The right age and size. She's cleaned up a bit since he saw her, but … but she had the dog." The man fumbled to defend his reasoning. "It's her, all right."

When Lowe mentioned the hound, Ashley made a guttural noise that sounded like a disgusted growl. "She's just a kid."

Queenie nodded, wild-eyed.

"So?" The shorter outlaw scowled and spit into the water. "She knocked you out cold on the trail. You ain't gonna let her get away with that, are you?"

Ashley walked around in tight circles for a while before telling Lowe, "Go back out. If she and the hound're here, that fish boy's likely nearby, too. Find him and whoever else's with him. I'll take care of her."

Lowe muttered, pocketing his pistol. He closed the door with a thud as he left.

Ashley latched it behind him. Then he turned to Queenie. After scrutinizing her head-to-toe with an expression on his face she couldn't read, he said, "Didn't get much of a look at you out on the Wire Road." He paused before continuing, "All of you kids?"

As Queenie started to nod her affirmation, the outlaw read it on her face. "I spent all this time chasing a passel of kids?"

He rolled his eyes and head up and to the right, revealing the bruise her stone had left on his left jaw. He raised his right hand as if to slap his forehead in frustration, but didn't. Instead, he ran his palm over the top of his head all the way to the back.

Queenie noticed a grimy bandage wrapped around his hand. It had to be several days old. Maybe Jeremy was right. Maybe Ashley wasn't as bad as they thought. Maybe he'd cut his hand trying to push the car and it was *his* blood Billy saw on the car's seat.

Queenie started breathing again. She had an idea. Nodding and forcing a gleam into her eye, she asked as casually as she could muster, "You tell the folks in town you've been trying to settle a score with a bunch of *kids*?"

Ashley's eyes widened.

Before he could silence her, she added, "And did you tell them what the kids *did* that you have to get even for?"

His expression shifted to confused and from there to embarrassed. Then, the color of his eyes shaded more to the far blue of the ocean's horizon as he looked out the open end of the boathouse at the river and a gleam of amusement crept into them.

"Huuu." Ashley blew out a breath and looked at her again. "You're a feisty one, ain't you?"

Queenie nodded again, holding his eyes with hers. That characterization played right into her plan. She continued, "Well, you see, folks like Jeremy say there's no reason for *kids* … like me and my friends … to be afraid of you. They say you're not the bad man they paint you out to be. That you're a Florida hero like Jesse James … or Robin Hood." She tried both names, hoping he'd know at least one of them and feel flattered.

"How do you mean?" Ashley hesitated, looking interested.

"They're outlaws, both of them. Like you. And they're famous like you." She paused to let that sink in as a compliment. "They stand up for poor folks. Only rob from the rich."

Ashley rubbed the sore spot on his jaw while he contemplated the idea. "Uh huh," he finally agreed, showing her a lopsided grin and seeming to enjoy the comparison.

"And you know?" Queenie paused to let his attention shift back and then pressed her advantage. "Jeremy says folks look up to you. Says you're the best ... the *King* of the Everglades."

Ashley silently mouthed the words "King of the Everglades." A satisfied smile broke out on his face.

When his focus shifted back to Queenie, she continued, "So, I was thinking. A hero like the *King* of the *Everglades* wouldn't hurt poor helpless kids. What would folks say?"

Ashley squinted out at the river with his lips pursed for a while, then turned to face her. His shoulders shook slightly in a chuckle as he rubbed the bruise on his jaw again and drawled, "From what I saw of 'em, I wouldn't exactly call 'em helpless."

Queenie felt pretty good about the way the conversation had gone so far, and she wanted to keep him talking. But that was the last line of the script she'd composed in her head on the spur of the moment. Not knowing what her next line should be, she winged it.

"So, why do you do it?"

"What?" Ashley looked startled at this change of direction, the hint of humor gone from his voice.

Queenie gulped. Had she gotten too personal? "I asked why you do it. Why are you an outlaw? I mean..." She stammered, trying to recover.

"Nobody ever asked me that before." The look on Ashley's face shifted from confusion to suspicion. "What do you want to know for?"

Startled by the intensity of the outlaw's reaction, Queenie shook her head and shrugged her shoulders, looking for a way to excuse the mistake she'd made. "I don't know. Never talked to an outlaw before. I'm curious. I..." Then she stopped herself. "No. That's not it." She stood up straight and told him flat out, "The truth is I'm the kind of person who likes to understand things." She took a deep breath. "And folks say you're smart. The best at hunting and stuff like that. I just don't understand." *That* was the truth.

Ashley reacted as if she had hit him. He stared at her with his mouth open. Then, his features tightened up, distorting his face as if in pain. He took several deep breaths, trying to compose himself. Finally, he squeezed the words out through tensed lips.

"What else am I s'posed to do?"

"But robbing banks and things like that?" Queenie actually cared about the answer. "Doesn't that hurt your family, your friends—"

"No!" He cut her off, shaking his head, his eyes cold again and his voice pure anger.

But Queenie could tell it wasn't aimed at her.

"Only Yankees and fancy sons of Yankees got money to put in a bank! That's the *problem*!" He spit out the words defiantly and looked at her as if challenging, "So what do you think about that?"

Queenie didn't speak. What he said jibed with what Jeremy had told her and with the way her father described financial dealings on the frontier. He said that Crackers out in the jungle didn't need banks. Most of them couldn't put more than a few silver dollars together at a time and kept what little money they had hidden away in coffee cans and sacks.

"Money they been taking from *us*!" Ashley went on, striking his chest with the knuckles of his bandaged hand. Then, he walked back and forth a few steps, thinking about it, even turning his back to her at one point. His face darkened from pink to blood red. His voice shook.

"Flocking down here like carrion birds in the winter, waiting for us to die off. More of *them* now than us. Taking everything. Changing everything." He shifted his weight from foot to foot. His eyes no longer focused on the girl. "Folks like my pa ... and Jeremy's? Tended their land most all their lives? Shuh!" He spit in the water.

"State sells it out from under them. And then they have to pay off some fat Yankee promoter or the tax man just to keep the same land they had for years? And only, *then,* if some Yankee newcomer's not offering to pay more?"

It all came together. A knot tightened in Queenie's stomach. She watched the outlaw pace as he fumbled for the next words.

"And what are we supposed to pay them with? They're outlawing 'shine. Logged all the trees. Killed off most of the deer and gators. Can't take enough hides this side the Glades to live on anymore."

Ashley blew out a little breath and shook his head from side to side. Then he gave Queenie a narrow-eyed smile that didn't make him look happy.

"Wouldn't hire the likes of *me* to weigh nails!" After a pause, he shrugged, "Anyway ... living cooped up in a store like that all day? That'd kill me just as fast." He sucked air into his lungs again. "Maybe, faster."

Queenie had stood still as a statue, mouth shut throughout the outburst she had provoked. Now Ashley leaned his upper body so close that their faces were inches apart. *"That's* why I do it. That's why I *rob* banks!" His voice rasped and his eyes almost begged for the understanding she had said she wanted, or her approval.

To Queenie's horror, she did understand. And she sympathized. She'd seen the same painful shadow that haunted Ashley's gaze the day before in the Chief's eyes. They were alike. All of them. This outlaw, the Chief, and Billy. Her. Even the alligators. Their worlds were crumbling and washing away like the sand on the beach in the storm.

And Ashley was lost. He couldn't see a way through, couldn't find a new place, a new path to follow. All he could see was how badly he was outnumbered and outmanned and how unfair it all was.

"You won't win, you know." The words slipped out between Queenie's lips in a tone so low she almost looked around to see who had said them. She held her breath, hoping with all her heart Ashley understood how sorry knowing that made her.

Ashley's head twitched back as if she'd hit him again with her stone.

"Not fighting them this way. The Seminoles. They tried..."

Queenie wanted to explain about Osceola and Billy Bowlegs. How they were lied to, murdered. Sent west. But she couldn't put together a coherent sentence.

At a loss, she touched the sleeve on Ashley's forearm with her fingertips. "There's got to be another way." She'd scrounged through her head and couldn't come up with a better answer. All she could offer was hope. "Maybe they'll let you go if you stop—"

The slight true smile that flicked across Ashley's lips brought her to a halt. His eyes softened and met hers for an instant as if thanking her for the kind words. Then, he stood straighter and dropped his eyelids. When he raised them again, his eyes had turned back to steel.

"And what would stopping get me?" His voice flat and cold.

That was the part she hadn't figured out yet, either. Abiaka's people had stopped making war, but they were still fighting for their lives.

Ashley didn't wait for an answer. His voice rose again. "This is *my* home!" He breathed in and out loudly through his nose. "*Mine!*" He almost shouted, hitting his chest even harder with his fist.

"If I can't keep them from taking it..." He breathed out, his tone lower, resolved. "The only thing left is to make them pay the highest price I can."

In that instant, Queenie realized that nothing would save John Ashley. He had made his decision. He would die a glorious, but useless, death on the battlefield like the heroes at Troy. The problem was this wasn't a story in one of her mother's books. This was real life, and it hurt her heart.

Chapter 52. The Standoff

Queenie searched franticly for the next words that could possibly make any sense. Before she found them, Ashley jerked to attention and looked over her shoulder. Queenie heard scruffs and scrapes on the decking outside the boathouse through the door. Someone knocked.

"It's me … Kid," the voice a low growl.

Even Queenie could tell it wasn't Lowe. Who? Of course. Her father disguising his voice. He had come to save her.

Ashley wasn't fooled either. He tilted his head, suspicion spreading over his face. Slipping his right hand into his pocket he called back, "Be right there, Lowe."

He was setting a trap. Her father didn't own a gun. She had to save him. Yelling, "No! Don't!" as a warning, Queenie tried to get between Ashley and the door.

To no avail. The outlaw shoved her out of the way as easily as a fly and lifted the latch. The door burst inward so hard it hit the wall.

Then, it bounced back with equal force and almost knocked Billy off his feet. Billy?

With a look of surprise, the boy took a little jump backward as the door came crashing in his direction. He barely got a forearm up in time to keep it from hitting him on the nose. After fending it off, he crouched low in the doorway, shifting his weight from side to side and pointing a pistol into the cool dark interior of the boathouse.

A gun? Where'd Billy get a gun? Queenie looked from the boy to Ashley. Billy had obviously intended to surprise Ashley and get the upper hand by knocking him down with the door or at least off balance.

His plan might have worked, if the outlaw had been standing close enough. But Ashley was no dummy. He'd anticipated the move. After lifting the latch he leaped aside as nimble as a panther, pulling his pistol out of his pocket as he did. He'd have had the clear advantage if the gun sight at the end of the barrel hadn't snagged on the cloth in his pocket making him lose a second to work it free.

It all might have been truly comical, except that Ashley succeeded in freeing his pistol at the same time Billy regained his balance. Now the two stood eight feet apart in the reflected shadow light of the boathouse, gun barrels pointed directly at each other, with Queenie a little behind the outlaw and to his left.

It looked like a standoff, but that didn't tell the truth of the situation. At any moment either one of them could pull the trigger and the other one would die.

For possibly the first time in her life Queenie didn't think. She acted. Shouting, "No!" she surprised the outlaw. Using his left shoulder for leverage, she flung herself between the two and swung around to face Ashley, feet apart, palms extended toward him.

The move pulled Ashley's gun to the side, away from Billy for an instant. He quickly regained his balance. Now it pointed directly at Queenie's stomach. "Get out of the way," he demanded. "Don't make me shoot you."

Queenie's heart pounded in her chest. She had to stay calm. Sucking in a deep breath, she forced herself to believe he wouldn't pull the trigger. "No!" All of her efforts to keep her voice steady failed. The word came out high and thin.

Ashley's eyes softened, letting her know he didn't want to shoot her. Tilting her head without looking away from the outlaw, she lowered her voice an octave and issued a command, "Listen to me … *both of you!*"

Both of them froze, looking at her rather than at each other. The muzzle of Billy's pistol slid down and slightly to the side so that it no longer threatened the girl.

He stood on tiptoes to keep tabs on Ashley over her shoulder. "Get out of the way," he hissed the same command Ashley had given.

"Be quiet," Queenie hissed back at him out of the side of her mouth without turning around. Leaving her back to Billy, she spoke softly to the outlaw. "You don't want to do this."

Ashley raised his eyebrows in response.

She swung one shoulder back so she could point at Billy with her thumb while keeping her eyes on Ashley. "He was born on the frontier. Just like you."

The outlaw's eyes darted to Billy and then back to Queenie.

"The train's going to get there soon, and everything's going to change. Just like here." She stopped long enough to let that sink in. "And he's going to have to fight for his home … for his life. Just like you."

Queenie took a deep breath, praying Billy'd keep his mouth shut.

He did.

"But one thing's different." She paused. "If he gets the chance, *he'll* find a way to win!"

Ashley's head tilted back slightly. Then he craned his neck to scrutinize the sandy-haired boy standing there in old rolled-up overalls and bare feet holding a pistol that pointed at the boathouse floor. After looking him up and down the way Horace the tourist had that first day, the outlaw rubbed his jaw with his free hand and let out his breath.

Queenie almost cried for joy when she saw the tension leave his body.

"Hey, fish boy," Ashley called out after a moment, making eye contact with Billy over Queenie's shoulder. "I should of expected you'd show some guts and come busting through the door with a gun. Or some such tomfoolery. So what do you say?"

Ashley let out a smaller, ironic little breath and held his pistol up so that Billy could see that he had taken his finger off the trigger. "I'll put my weapon away if you do the same."

Still holding his gun high, Ashley turned his eyes back to Queenie and added, "If that's all right with *you*, I mean."

Queenie ignored the glint in his eye and the sarcasm in his voice. She'd pretended to be a princess her whole life. She knew how to play the part. In a haughty voice, she gave them both permission. "You may."

Ashley's eyebrows shot up again. He nodded and lowered his pistol slowly, keeping his eyes on Billy as he did.

Queenie half-turned and ordered Billy to do the same with a little jerk of her head and body.

He responded with a questioning look. "Okay."

"Thank you." The girl looked from him to Ashley and sighed in relief as the guns slowly disappeared into pockets.

Chapter 53. Kid Lowe

"That Lowe's gun?" Ashley asked Billy, still speaking over Queenie's shoulder.

The boy nodded.

"So where's Lowe?"

"Out cold," Billy answered and then grinned. "Again."

Ashley stifled a chuckle, but said seriously, "We'd best tend to him, then. He's a mean one. You don't want to have him trailing after you." Ashley stepped around Queenie. "Where is he?"

With a dumbfounded look on his face, Billy slid one foot back to stand sideways under the doorjamb and pointed toward the ground outside. "Down there." Then, he stepped out of the way so Ashley could walk past him.

Left alone with Queenie, he mouthed the word, "What— "

"Come on." Ashley interrupted. He knelt next to Kid Lowe, who lay on the ground, out cold. Billy had used half of the petticoat leash to hogtie the little man's hands and feet behind his back like a calf set for branding. A four-foot piece of framing lumber lay by his side.

Seeing the leash, Queenie asked, "How's the pup?"

"Left him tied up near the street. Didn't want him giving me away," Billy whispered to Queenie, not taking his eyes off Ashley.

"I mean is he *okay*?" Queenie didn't feel the need to whisper.

Billy's face let her know he didn't understand why she had asked.

"Lowe kicked him."

"Shuh." Billy let out an angry breath. "Seemed all right when I left him." He turned back to the little outlaw. "If I'd of known, though, I'd of hit *him* a little harder."

Lowe groaned, starting to come around. Billy grabbed Queenie's arm and pulled her toward the street.

Ashley took his gun out of his pocket and said, "Hold on."

Confused, Queenie froze. Billy dropped to a crouch. That pulled the cloth of his overalls so tight over his legs he couldn't get his hand into his pocket to grab the gun.

Before he could stand straight and retrieve his weapon, though, Ashley asked, "Lowe kicked your dog?"

"*And* hit him on the head with his gun," a relieved Queenie answered angrily.

Ashley let out a sigh and turned his pistol around, holding it by the barrel. "Like this?" He conked the tied-up outlaw on the side of the head with the handle of his pistol. The smaller outlaw lay quiet again as Ashley stood up and dusted himself off. "Ain't right to kick another man's dog."

Billy's jaw dropped open. Queenie held her hand to her mouth to suppress a giggle.

"Been wanting to do something like that for a while. Shouldn't of took up with the son of a gun in the first place." Ashley looked down at the man shaking his head. "Yankee..." He made the word sound like a curse. "Mean as a snake and you can't trust him. One day he's going to shoot somebody and it's as likely to be me as anyone else."

Ashley motioned for the kids to stay put as he repocketed his pistol. "Give me a minute to think of something." After walking back and forth chewing on his knuckle for a few moments, he squinted at Billy. "Did he see you?"

251

Billy shook his head, mouth still open. "No. I caught him from behind." He winked at Queenie. "Been *schooled* in sneaking around unseen and unheard by the best of them."

Queenie smiled openly at the boy. The Chief was going to love that part of the story.

Not in on the joke, Ashley ignored it and responded flatly, "Good." Then, looking at Queenie, he added, "Guess I'm going to have to save him from your family, then."

When the kids' jaws gaped wide in confusion, he shook his head as if he couldn't believe how dense they were. "I mean, I've got to get him out of town and make sure he don't come back looking for you."

Ashley bent down, picked up the piece of lumber, and handed it to Queenie. "Here. If he wakes up, hit him again. I'll go get the car." Turning to Billy, he added, "*You* stay out of sight."

Within minutes, Ashley drove up to the boathouse in the stolen car. Lowe hadn't moved. He'd been so still Queenie had started to get concerned he'd never wake up.

"Did you have to hit him?"Ashley asked. He shrugged when she said she hadn't and said to Billy. "Help me load him up."

After they rolled Lowe onto the backseat like a sack of potatoes, Ashley turned to Billy again and said, "Now hit me."

Queenie gasped, "What?"

Ashley made a face at her. "You didn't think I'd let *you* hit me again, did you?"

He pointed at the piece of lumber and directed her back to the car with his eyebrows. She moved to a position where she could deal with Lowe if he showed signs of waking up.

Nodding at Queenie, Ashley turned back to Billy. "Not my jaw. She's done enough damage there already." He pointed to his nose and leaned forward. "Here. Only once. But, make it a good one."

Billy hesitated.

"Come on. He'll be coming out of it soon." Ashley pointed at Queenie. "And if I'm going to convince him I saved him from *her* five half-Indian brothers, each of them bigger and meaner than a she bear with cubs, I need to look like I've been in a fight." He tapped his nose again.

Billy rolled his eyes, but reared back and hit the outlaw as hard as he could. Then, he howled, "Ouch!" And turned around in a circle, biting his lower lip and clenching and unclenching his hand.

Ashley stood there, shaking his head in disgust, the tip and side of his nose turning a pretty rosy pink. "Shuh." The outlaw rubbed his nose. "That's another kind of *schooling* you might ought to look into. Guess I have to do it myself."

Without wasting another second, Ashley butted the rough wooden wall of the boathouse once with his forehead. Then, he punched the wall twice with his fists as if the building had started the fight. After pulling his shirttail out of his pants and messing up his short hair, he looked sufficiently scratched, bruised, and in disarray to claim he'd been in a brawl.

"That ought to do it," he concluded and strode to the car.

Lowe snored softly in the back. Ashley untied him and gave Billy a strange look as he handed over the petticoat leash. Sitting in the driver's seat, he stuck his arm and head through the window, holding his palm out toward the boy. "Almost forgot the gun."

"Oh, yes, sir." Billy fumbled in his haste to get it out of his pocket. "Never learned to use the danged things, anyway." He handed it over.

Ashley looked to the heavens and shook his head.

"Wait!" Another question had been bothering Queenie. "I forgot to ask. How'd you know we were here?"

The outlaw checked to make sure his henchman was still out cold before answering. "When we got to town, Jeremy told us some fool story about a crazy Cracker fish boy and his friends who stopped his runaway and then put on a show for the crowd."

A smug look spread across his face. "Wasn't that hard to put two and two together. That get up you was wearing weren't exactly normal, you know."

Ashley shook his head then laughed a hollow laugh. "Now if you'll want to go bragging that you had a run in with the *King of the Everglades*..." He tilted his head, puffed up a little, and flashed Queenie a grin as he savored the sound of that phrase. "That's fine by me. Just do me a favor and don't tell 'em the details."

Then, he shrugged and dismissed the thought with a wave of his hand. "Nah. Tell 'em whatever you want. Nobody'll believe it anyway." Winking at the two, he gunned the engine and pulled away, leaving a puff of dark exhaust fumes behind.

Chapter 54. Lost

Queenie and Billy watched Ashley turn the corner and disappear.

"Want to tell me how that all came about?" Shaking his head slowly, the boy sounded more than a little confused.

"Later." Queenie started toward the street. She didn't want to talk about it.

What to make of Ashley. Was he good or evil? Was there someplace in between? After everything that had happened, she had a difficult time believing he'd murdered anybody. On the other hand, the Chief and his family believed with all their hearts that he had gunned Desoto Tiger down in cold blood. The scary thing was that for one small instant she hadn't cared if he did. All she'd wanted was for Ashley to somehow survive.

She saw herself in him. That's what it was. Who's to say she wouldn't do exactly what he was doing if she was in his situation. And how far off was she? Her mother was trying to change her. Her father had abandoned her. Once she boarded the train in the morning, she'd be alone, outnumbered and outmanned, like the rest of them.

What were they all going to do? It was too complicated. Queenie needed to sort it out.

"This is not the time to talk about it." She escaped by racing toward the hound, wiping the tears that had started forming out of her eyes with her knuckles.

She felt better when the dog wagged his tail, bounced, and strained against his tether as if nothing unusual had happened. He had only a slight limp to show for his mistreatment, and Billy let him run free while he reconnected the two parts of the leash.

Whooooo-oooooo! Whooo!

The train whistle? Queenie jerked upright and squeezed her eyes shut trying to comprehend. The episode with Ashley had seemed to last a lifetime, but in reality it had all taken place in the blink of an eye, the time it took to unload and load the train.

"We've got to get back!" She shouted, grabbing her bag and the sodas from the shady spot where Billy had left them. She handed the boy his drink and moved quickly toward the station where the crowd had started drifting away. Billy and the hound followed close behind.

He caught up with her as the engine roared back to life, belching black smoke out of its smokestack. Queenie decided to preempt any further questions about her encounter with Ashley by asking, "So, how'd you get the upper hand on Lowe?"

To her great relief, the boy's chest puffed up and he took the bait. He was eager to tell *that* story. He swaggered more than a little as he started, "I knew something was wrong when I found your stone."

He was swaggering mightily by the time he finished explaining how he'd knocked Kid Lowe out and tied him up. Then he described how he'd come up with the idea to burst through the door. "Thought I'd catch Ashley by surprise, though."

Bursting through that door was the bravest and the dumbest thing Queenie had ever seen. She couldn't decide whether to hug the boy or cuff him on the ear for being so stupid. So she took pity on him and didn't let him know how ridiculous it had looked.

The truth was she was a bit impressed. After all, he had come to her rescue, and he was lucky he didn't get killed.

"Sure surprised *me* when you came in with the pistol like that! Would you have shot him?"

"If I had to." Billy flexed his shoulders and stood even taller. "And..." He stopped walking. "If I figured out correctly how to use the danged thing." He ducked his head and hid a grin. "Guess we'll never know for sure."

"You've never shot a gun before?" That astounded her even more.

"Oh, I've shot my pa's rifle once or twice. But where am I supposed to get a hand gun to practice with?" His head dropped again, this time as if the subject embarrassed him.

Then, he winked. "Didn't even have a dog last week, though. Guess I might ought to try putting a pistol on my list and see what happens."

Blindsided once again by both how brave he had been and the way his brain held on to details and put everything together, Queenie reached over and touched his arm. Instead of saying, "Thank you," which is what they both knew she meant, she said, "Well, you sure had me fooled."

Then, she smiled ironically. "But Ashley's right. Nobody'll believe a word of it."

The prospect of recounting his heroics perked Billy up. "The Chief'll believe it," he said, moving eagerly toward the station. "If you back me up."

"No!" Queenie turned on him, leaned close. "You can't tell him! Not now! Not here!"

"Why not?"

"My father." She was adamant. "If he finds out what happened..."

She didn't know exactly where she was going with that. She simply didn't want her father to know. Not, yet, anyway. So she took the easy way out and blamed it on her mother.

"He'll tell my mother and she'll place me under lock and key and keep me there till I'm back in my grandfather's house in Baltimore."

Queenie paused to draw in a deep breath. "And, then, I won't be able to meet you and the Chief at the drug store in the morning while we're waiting for the train."

At first Billy shook his head and narrowed skeptical eyes at her. Then he arched his eyebrows and shrugged his acquiescence. They hurried the last few yards to the station.

To Queenie's surprise, her father didn't even ask what had taken them so long. He'd been so caught up helping Anna sell shirts and other trinkets to the tourists that he hadn't even noticed they'd been missing. Relieved, but also disappointed, the girl handed Anna and the Chief their bottles of soda.

Her father waved his off. Holding the last of Anna's shirts up under his chin with two hands, he stretched it as wide as he could across his chest. When it didn't reach either of his shoulders, he burst into laughter, saying, "Shoots, Anna. You make these shirts too small."

Taking the shirt from him and shaking her head, Anna folded it and slipped it into her bag, also laughing. "No. No. It is you. You are too big."

"Guess you'll have to make me one up special, then."

"Ahh, but that will cost you extra." Anna's black eyes flashed with sly good humor.

"Very good!" The big man slapped the Chief's back and chuckled with the Seminoles like old friends or co-conspirators.

When Queenie's father finally accepted the bottle she still held out to him, he lifted it high and posed a toast. "To Anna and the Chief."

They went on to toast the success they had that day and the bright future the Seminoles would have selling crafts like Anna's shirts to tourists at the station. The Chief beamed under the man's praise as the three of them took ceremonial swigs from their sodas, enthralled by the money-making possibilities of Anna's new enterprise and totally ignorant of the life-and-death drama Queenie and Billy had played out a few blocks away and a few minutes earlier. Queenie sipped her drink silently.

Chapter 55. Lucy

The next morning, when the Chief didn't mention John Ashley, Queenie figured Billy had already told him his version of the story five times and had warned him not to say a word about Ashley to her. That was a good thing because she still wasn't up to talking about it. What was she going to do? It was her last day.

Billy bought treats at the drug store with money Queenie's father had given her. Even with hard candy to suck on, their mood stayed somber. Having little to say and with no destination in mind, they ended up walking east along the river beach, away from the ferry dock, as far away from the hustle and bustle of downtown Stuart as they could get and still be close enough to hear the northbound train pull in.

That was where they met Lucy. She had short scraggly brown hair, blue-eyes, and looked to be about eight or nine years old. Barefooted, she had rolled her overalls up above her knees, so she could work a small seine net through the river's shallows. As they approached, Lucy dragged her net to shore and dumped a small passel of mullet onto the sand. When the fish started flopping around her bare feet in an effort to work their way back into the water, Billy and the Chief helped her collect and throw them into her basket. Lucy explained that she caught mullet every morning to sell to the alligator farm.

"Alligator farm?" How had they missed hearing about an alligator farm?

Lucy said it was a bit off the river and not easy to find. "But they pay me a quarter every day for fish. I'm saving up money to buy an airplane."

"An airplane?" That was even more bizarre. Even Queenie had never seen an airplane.

"Sure." The girl stuck out her jaw. "Why not? I can fly if I want to!"

Then she spun around and said, with the same no-nonsense attitude, "I don't have time to stand around talking if I'm going to earn my quarter before lunch."

The Chief followed her back into the river and started helping her work the seine. Maybe they'd earn two quarters.

Left alone with nowhere else to go and nothing else to do, Queenie and Billy sat down on the sloping riverbank and watched. The morning air was cool. The sky was blue. The sun, sparkling like diamonds on the water, turned Lucy and the Chief into shimmering silhouettes with unintelligible voices that floated in to shore like the calls of sea birds on the breeze.

Billy alternately tossed pebbles into the ripples and sighed long deep sighs. It went on that way for a while before he unbuttoned his pocket and handed Queenie two silver dollars.

"Your earnings," was all he said.

Queenie didn't say anything back. She looked at the two silver pieces long and hard before putting them in her new cloth bag with the stone.

When Billy spoke again, he asked, "What do they do when it's over?"

She turned to him. "When what's over?"

He still faced the water. "The quest. What do heroes do when they get back home?"

A short intake of breath. The question hit Queenie so suddenly it almost stopped her heart. Meaningless sounds roared in her ears. She quickly turned her face back to the river as tears welled up in her eyes. He had asked her question. And she didn't have the answer.

It was over. The boys were going home. But not her. She didn't have a home to go to. She'd end up selling nails in her grandfather's store, dying a long, slow death. She turned to Billy for help, but he still stared at the distant shore.

At that point, a commotion out on the river drew their attention. Lucy had thrown down her seine sticks in what appeared to be a huff. She stomped straight toward them with the Chief not far behind. She planted both feet directly in front of Queenie and stood with her hands on her hips.

Indicating the Chief with a toss of her head, she asked defiantly, "Is he really the Chief?"

The Indian, who had stopped out in ankle-deep water a safe distance behind the girl, made a "what-am-I-supposed-to-do" face at Queenie and shrugged.

Having wiped her eyes as they approached, Queenie struggled with the question at first. Then, she looked down at Lucy, standing there in wet overalls and bare feet, tan and dirty knees sticking out for the whole world to see, feeding alligators so that she could buy an airplane and demanding to know what she wanted to know. The answer came to Queenie with total clarity.

This was *her* life, *her* picture puzzle. And like her father always said, it was up to her to decide what it would look like.

Her parents might be able to drag her all the way to Baltimore, but nothing they could do would ever turn her back into the girl she used to be. She was heir to the throne of the Amazon Queen. And they couldn't keep her locked up reading other people's stories forever. She'd bide her time with her eyes open. When she had gathered enough of the right puzzle pieces, was strong enough, she'd set out on *her* quest … and find *her* place in the world.

Maybe it would be an actual place like it was for Ashley and the boys. Or maybe it would be someone she loved, like in her father's case.

One thing she knew, though. She'd be free to do the things she wanted to do. She wanted it all, and she wouldn't stop until she found all the pieces.

Queenie pulled herself to her full height and spoke with the most mature and formal tone she could muster. Her Indian Billy had become the Chief on his quest, and so she told the girl the truth.

"Chief is not a word in the Seminole language. But it is what we call him. He is brave and also wise. And he will be a leader of his people one day, because he understands the pattern of the things that make up the world and he can always find the way."

Queenie caught the Chief's eye. He puffed up a bit and stood a little taller in the background as Lucy mentally chewed on Queenie's answer. After an instant, the younger girl relaxed a little and grunted, "Okay," back over her shoulder.

But she didn't take her gaze off Queenie. Instead, she stepped closer and stared the older girl straight in the eye.

Lucy said in a lower voice, "He says you are the Amazon Queen. But you don't look much like an Amazon, whatever that is, or like the queen of anything for that matter."

Queenie treated it as a question. She leaned even closer, so close it appeared the two girls were sharing a secret. Yes. The truth. Now that she knew what it was.

"You cannot always trust the way things look, Lucy. Long ago, the Amazon Queen was a great warrior who was defeated only through treachery. Her blood flows in my veins. I am growing strong, and now I possess an ancient stone with which I have done things that are amazing even to me. But there is much I have yet to learn. And more I have to prove."

She caught the Chief's eyes for an instant before returning her focus to Lucy. The Seminole understood. He had understood long before she did. He returned her look with a nod, and she continued, "The throne of the Amazon Queen sits empty now, but one day when I am ready, I may claim it."

As she spoke, Queenie reached into her new bag and took out the black stone. She handed it to the girl. Lucy pursed her lips and nodded absentmindedly as she scrutinized the thing, turning it over in her hands so that its many dark faces caught and reflected the sunlight.

Then she abruptly handed the stone back and stepped in front of Billy. Although she stared straight at him, she aimed her question at Queenie. "So, if that one's the Chief and you're the Queen, what's he?"

Chapter 56. The Hero

The suddenness and intensity of Lucy's question startled Billy so much he jumped to his feet, his mouth open. "I'm..." he stammered. "I don't ... I ... uh."

Lucy tilted her head and watched the boy struggle. But now that Queenie knew where she was going, it didn't take her long to come to his rescue.

"His story has not yet been written," she told both of them as she stepped in front of the boy with the black stone grasped tightly against her chest.

She looked at him and continued in a voice meant for Lucy to hear, too, "But we have learned a few things on this quest." As she said this, she solemnly held her stone out in front of her at arm's length and touched his left shoulder with a stately air of formality. "He has the courage of a hero." She touched the stone to his right shoulder.

Billy followed the stone from shoulder to shoulder, mouth open, eyes wide.

"And like the knights of old, his heart is true." Queenie touched his chest over his heart.

Taking half a step closer, Queenie raised her eyes to meet his. Holding his gaze without blinking, she spoke softly this time, as if she and he were the only two present. "But, this I have also learned, my blue-eyed Billy. In this changing world, *you* don't need to find a magic sword."

She paused to brush his hair out of his eyes before continuing. "The true source of *your* power lies here." She tapped his forehead lightly with the first two fingers of her right hand. "Like my stone, its final shape has not yet been determined, and its secrets have not yet been revealed. But it will take the form you need when the time comes." Her hand slid downward, her palm brushing first his cheek and then his jaw.

The four young people stood frozen in that tableau, when Queenie's father broke the spell by calling out for her. "I have to go," she almost whispered.

Lucy reanimated first, saying she had to get back to work anyway. Queenie took her hand, gave her a slight curtsey, and whispered, "Fly, Lucy..."

"I *will*, you know. And I'll be the first," the younger girl called back over her shoulder and ran into the river.

"Yes." Queenie said it softly, as much for herself as for the younger girl. "Yes."

Queenie turned her back to the river and scrambled up the riverbank. As the Chief jogged after her, he called out to Lucy that he'd be back to help if she'd promise to show him the alligator farm.

Only Billy hadn't moved. He still stood rooted to the same spot when Queenie suddenly whirled around and ran back to him. "It isn't over!" she exclaimed as she threw her arms around his neck.

Once again, Billy stood there with his hands by his side. "What?"

Queenie let him go and stepped away to a more proper distance before continuing excitedly, "The quest! I should have thought of this before! Just because the heroes go home, it doesn't mean their adventure is over. A quest is always part of a much bigger story! And..." she took a deep, excited breath, "And you and the Chief already have a new treasure to look for when you get back!"

For the slightest moment, Billy stared at her with narrowed eyes and half-open mouth. Queenie chewed on her lower lip and studied him while he processed her words. Then, his head popped up straight with a start and his eyes sprung wide as he said in the most serious tone she'd ever heard him use, "You meant it. What you told Ashley. Didn't you?"

Queenie took an involuntarily step back, trying to get a better look at this ever surprising boy. When he hadn't asked her about what she'd said about him, she'd assumed he'd missed that exchange in all the excitement. She nodded slowly and waited to hear his next words.

"It may take us a while to sort things out. But we're gonna find a way to win." He sounded so confident that Queenie's heart skipped a beat. "Because…"

The boy stood taller. Shoulders back at attention, he tapped his chest twice with the knuckles of his right hand, the way the Chief had when he announced that he had taken his American name to honor two great Seminole leaders, the two who had followed different paths trying to save their people and their way of life.

"We're never gonna surrender."

Queenie fist flew to her chest, too. That was the answer. The only answer. She pressed her knuckles against her heart and repeated his vow.

"Never."

Holding her eyes, the boy said it one more time.

"Never."

Chapter 57. The Gifts

Queenie's father called her name again, this time more insistently. As she and the boys trotted across the crushed rock road toward the train station, one of those odd coincidences that happen sometimes happened. They stopped to let a bicycle go by in almost exactly the same spot they had met Horace the tourist. Billy stood in the middle, with the Chief to his right. The Seminole was the one who noticed.

"Seems like a long time ago," he said.

When Billy squinted at him, trying to figure out his meaning, the Indian closed one eye, tapped his lips with his forefinger, and mimicked the tourist's way of talking. "You sure do look like a Florida cow hunter to me, young man."

It only took a second. Billy struck his cow hunter pose and responded nonchalantly. "Well then, son, I'm guessing that means *you* must be a Seminole Indian." He pointed his finger at the Chief.

The Seminole stuck out his chest and assumed his warrior stance with a glint in his eye. "I am."

Queenie looked at the boys with her mouth open. It had been little more than three days since they had met Horace the tourist at the station, yet they seemed so ... so different ... bigger somehow.

Something dropped with a bang by the station's door. She glanced toward the sound and caught a proper, well-dressed, young colored girl staring at her in the station window.

"Who?" The girl seemed startled to see her, too. And she looked familiar. Queenie smiled at the girl fondly and mouthed the words, "Goodbye, Wendy."

Widening her stance and crossing her arms over her chest, Queenie lifted her chin proudly. Then she gave the girl in the window a little final wave and turned back to face the boys. They were waiting for her.

Billy pointed his finger and said, "And you. You are...?"

Ready to get started, her voice as strong and deep as the Chief's, Queenie responded to her cue, "I am an Amazon."

All three of them whooped and laughed and danced a little. When Queenie looked back at the station window, the girl in the glass was laughing, too.

Her father called her name more loudly as the train pulled up to the landing. During her family's years of roaming the Florida frontier, they had slowly surrendered most of the belongings they had brought with them from Baltimore to the wilderness. They were traveling light, with just a few trunks to load once the northbound train rumbled and wheezed to a stop.

While the unloading and loading went on, Queenie took a gift for each boy out of her new cloth bag. She handed the Chief a snow white feather. Then she told him its story.

In the early morning the day before, Anna had walked right under an eagle in a pine tree. She hadn't even known it was there until its wings rattled the tree branches as it took flight.

"But instead of soaring away, the eagle glided down to the ground and stood in front of her. It walked back and forth for a while ... all the time keeping one eye focused on her face ... to tell her something. After making sure Anna understood, the eagle tilted its head sideways twice and flew away, leaving behind this one tail feather as a gift for you. She asked me to give it to you."

Although the Chief acknowledged the feather by tipping his forehead toward it, he did not reach his hand out to accept it. He tried to explain, "I will not always be a member of the Bird Clan."

"It is the eagle's gift. Not mine." Queenie wasn't about to let him turn it down. That stopped his retreat cold. When his fingers finally touched the feather, she told him the eagle's message, "So that you may always see where things belong in the world."

The Chief took several open-mouthed breaths as he blinked back tears. Then, he bowed his head. "Thank you."

Queenie nodded back and turned to face Billy as she pulled out a red bandana she had bought at the dry goods store. She said loud enough for bystanders to hear that a bandana was something every cow hunter needed. With a grinning nod to her mother, she added, "So, I guess you can scratch 'bandana' off your list, too."

But when Billy bent his head down so she could tie it around his neck, Queenie made a silent wish and whispered in his ear, "Please do me the honor of wearing my colors, oh knight, and..." She slipped the two silver dollars he had given her into the button down chest pocket of his overalls with the rest of the money they had earned on their quest, saying, "I need a place to come home to."

He pulled his head back and tilted it to the side, scrutinizing her through narrowed eyes.

She whispered quickly, "It's on *my* list."

A glint sprang into his eye. He leaned close again and took her hand into both of his as if to thank her. He pressed something hard and smooth against her palm. It felt warm, as if he had been holding it tight for some time.

Then, as part of the same gesture, he gave her one of his goofy grins, bowed his head even closer, and whispered back in perfect English, "As you command, my queen."

"All aboard!"

Queenie's head jerked away at the sound. She took a deep breath, determined to stay strong. It was time.

Dropping quickly to her knees, she took the hound's ears in her hands. He wagged his tail as she pulled his nose to hers, moved her head side to side, and whispered, "I'm going to miss you." Then, her mother pulled her by the arm, and she stepped up into the train.

As she took her seat by a window in the back of the last car, trying to catch one more glimpse of Stuart and the boys, Queenie wasn't sure what to make of Billy's last words. She'd never been able to tell whether that boy was pulling her leg or not when he did things like that. And this time was no different.

So as much as she still wanted to believe in heroes and magic and happy endings, when the train lurched forward and she waved goodbye, she knew one thing for sure. She was setting out on a new adventure. What she didn't know was whether Billy and the Chief were going to be a part of it.

Until she uncurled her fingers and saw the piece of sea glass.

She squeezed it tight as the train crossed the river. Some time later, she placed it in the cloth bag with her stone and started waiting for the first letter.

Epilogue

When the old cowboy reached the end of the Queen's tale, it was so late that dew had started settling out of the air onto the surfaces of things, making the night feel even cooler than it was. He stretched his arms wide, arched his back, and looked around. A couple of the Boy Scouts and one of the old timers had dozed off in the warmth of the coals.

As the kids from the high school audio-visual class packed up their equipment, the tall thin black girl who had been running the sound recorder stopped by to thank him. He could have been mistaken, but as she held his hand a little longer than necessary, he noticed that her eyes looked red around the edges.

After telling her she was welcome to come by any time, he called out his "Good nights" to the others who walked to their cars, preferring to sleep in their warm beds at home rather than under the stars. Then, he watched the last few campers straggle off to their tents.

Finally, alone with the fire, the old cowboy looked deep into the embers till he could count the small, individual tongues of orange and yellow flame that licked them slowly but surely into ash.

Only when he relaxed did the cowboy realize his shirt was damp and he was shivering. He shrugged his arms into his long leather jacket, put his wide-brimmed hat back on his head, added a few small logs to the fire, and propped his feet up next to it. That was better.

Then he breathed in a deep, deep lung-full of the cool, damp air, leaned back in his chair, and took in his surroundings one more time. Not bad. Not bad at all. Over in the east, the full moon had finally broken free of the pine trees. Now, it dangled like a giant Christmas tree ornament in the sky, and it did have a rainbow around it.

It had been a good story. A true story. He sighed and then chuckled to himself. Those kids sure had grown into themselves pretty well. Done what they set out to do. Traveled far and wide, some of them. But in the end, they always came back home, back to this remnant of the jungle between the lake and the ocean where it all began.

The fire hissed. It was struggling. He adjusted the logs to give it more air. The flames jumped back to life.

The old cowboy took in another slow, deep breath as he leaned back into his chair. There were so many more stories to tell. But those were stories for another day.

"...the present was an egg laid by the past that had the future inside its shell."

Zora Neale Hurston,
Moses, Man of the Mountain (1939)

"Josie Billie and Frank Brown - Immokalee," 1908. It was not uncommon in early Florida for Seminole and white boys to be friends. Such a relationship is described in the best-selling children's book series by Harvey Oyer, III, which is historical fiction recounting *The Adventures of Charlie Pierce*. Charles W. Pierce grew up in the Palm Beach County area and kept a detailed journal of his life which was published under the title *Pioneer Life in Southeast Florida*. Photo Credit: State Archives of Florida, Florida Memory, http://floridamemory.com/items/show/30787

Telling Their Tales

*The places, faces, and lives that
Inspire this story*

"Billy Bowlegs III and Willson Tiger," c. 1915. Billy Bowlegs III, who is shown here in traditional dress, was a Muscogee speaking Seminole who lived north of Lake Okeechobee in the early Twentieth Century. He was active in developing viable commercial enterprises for the tribe. During that time period, Seminoles started wearing white men's clothing such as shoes and long pants. Photo Credit:
State Archives of Florida, Florida Memory,
http://floridamemory.com/items/show/141555

The Chief

This story and the character of the Chief were inspired in part by the Seminole warrior, Coacoochee, whose American name was Wildcat. One of the Seminole heroes who outfought future President of the United States, Colonel Zachary Taylor, in the Battle of Okeechobee on Christmas Day 1837, Cooacoochee laid down his weapons a little over three years later.

He made the statement quoted at the front of this book when he met with United States Army Lieutenant William T. Sherman on the banks of the Indian River thirty miles east of the Okeechobee Battlefield to discuss peace.

The Army "removed" Coacoochee and his band of Seminoles to Arkansas along with a band of Black Seminoles led by John Horse. Threatened with war and slavery even there, John Horse and Coacoochee then led their people to Mexico where some of them became the fabled "Buffalo Soldiers" and all of them lived free at last.

Sherman went down in history as the Union general who marched through Georgia during America's Civil War, slashing and burning everything in his path including the City of Atlanta.

"A Dahomey Amazon," c. 189-. The last surviving Amazon of Dahomey is thought to have been a woman named Nawi who died in 1979. Photo Credit: http://diasporicroots.tumblr.com/post/3207950998/the-dahomey-amazons-the-dahomey-amazons-were-a

The Amazon Queen

The myth of the Amazon Queen and her daughter portrayed in this novel is fictional. However, tales about Amazon Queens leading fearsome bands of female warriors into battle go all the way back to Greek mythology and classical antiquity.

Queenie's family legend that she is the descendant of the Queen of the Amazons was inspired by an article published by Zora Neale Hurston in 1927 in which she interviewed a former slave named Cudjo Lewis. The last known survivor of the last United States ship known to bring slaves from Africa, the *Clotilde*, Lewis told Hurston he had been captured by Amazons from the Kingdom of Dahomey, which is now the Republic of Benin.

Further research revealed that Dahomean Amazons played a key role in West Africa during the second half of the nineteenth century. Fighting as an elite regiment of the Dahomean Army called "Mino," which meant "Our Mothers," they defeated the French in several battles. Eventually though, their outdated Winchester rifles, spears, and knives were no match for the machine guns and cavalry of the French Foreign Legion. Dahomey became a French Colony in 1894.

The photograph to the left inspired the author's vision of the powerful woman Queenie wants to be.

Portrait of Zora Neale Hurston - Eatonville, Florida, c. 19—. Photo credit: State Archives of Florida, Florida Memory, http://floridamemory.com/items/show/33048

Queenie

The character of Queenie was inspired in part by Zora Neale Hurston. Growing up in America's first African-American owned and run city, Eatonville, Florida, in the early 1900's, Hurston began her schooling at her father's knee. She later attended Morgan Academy in Baltimore, Maryland, and Howard University in Washington D.C., and ultimately received a degree from Barnard College in New York.

Hurston challenged every American stereotype of femininity and race. She smoked, laughed out loud, and wore slacks and fedora hats. In 1928, she published an essay in *The World Tomorrow* titled "How It Feels to Be Colored Me" that rankled both segregationists and members of the Harlem Renaissance of which she was soon to become a dominant force. In it, she declared that she was "not tragically colored." She explained that she had "seen that the world is to the strong regardless of a little pigmentation more or less."

Hurston returned to Florida as an anthropologist in the 1930's working to document and preserve the rural black culture of the state as part of the Federal Government's Works Progress Administration program. While there, she helped Mary McLeod Bethune start a school of dramatic arts "based on pure Negro expression" at Bethune-Cookman College in Daytona Beach.

Two years later, she published her acclaimed novel, *Their Eyes Were Watching God*, key portions of which take place near Lake Okeechobee.

In 1952-53, Hurston braved retaliation by the Ku Klux Klan by going to rural north Florida to cover the trial of Ruby McCollum, a black woman accused of killing her prominent white lover. She published the story in *The Pittsburgh Courier*.

In 1955, she wrote an editorial criticizing *Brown v. Board of Education*, the United States Supreme Court decision that began the dismantling of segregation in America by holding that a separate education is not an equal education. Hurston argued that its conclusion that African-American students were incapable of getting a good education unless they went to white schools was wrong, harmful, and demeaning.

Hurston traveled frequently, but the place she said felt like "home" was a small cottage a few blocks from the Indian River in Eau Gallie, Florida. She first rented the cottage in 1929 while she was writing a collection of black folk tales and voodoo titled *Mules and Men* that was published in 1935.

By the time she rented the cottage again and attempted to buy it in 1951, a white neighborhood had grown up around it. Unable to complete the purchase, she was evicted in 1956, but continued to live and work in other communities along the river.

Hurston's last home and grave are located in Fort Pierce, Florida, where she died in 1960. They are just a few miles inland from the spot where Coacoochee had tried to make peace with Lieutenant Sherman on the banks of the Indian River a hundred and nineteen years earlier.

Glimpse of Indian River, c. 19--. This graphic shows a view of the Indian River north of Fort Pierce not far from Zora Neale Hurston's cottage. Photo Credit: State Archives of Florida, Florida Memory, http://floridamemory.com/items/show/160819

"The notorious Ashley gang," c. 191-. These photos show the Ashley gang after Kid Lowe left it. Called the King and Queen of the Everglades, John Ashley and Laura Upthegrove were Florida's version of Bonnie and Clyde, star-crossed lovers who were either folk heroes or cold-blooded killers, depending on your point of view. Photo Credit: Thomas A. Markham, www.Tommymarkham.com.

John Ashley

John Ashley and Kid Lowe were real outlaws, although the events involving them described in this story are fictional. In 1914, Ashley turned himself in to face trial for the murder of a Seminole named Desoto Tiger. Later, fearing he would not be judged fairly because the trial had been moved to south Dade County, he escaped from the Palm Beach Jail.

In 1915, Ashley and his gang robbed the Bank of Stuart. While trying to get away, Kid Lowe shot Ashley in the face. Lowe claimed it was an accident. As a result of the shooting, Ashley lost his left eye and was captured.

A jury in Miami convicted him for the murder of Desoto Tiger, but that verdict was overturned on appeal. Although rumors of his violent nature abounded, it was the only murder he was ever charged with.

Then Ashley went to prison in central Florida for the Stuart Bank robbery. He arrived at the prison wearing a white suit and a black eye patch and was so famous and popular that prison officials had their photo taken with him, as if he were an honored guest.

Ashley soon disappeared from his cell and spent the next several years as a pirate, running whisky and rum between the Bahamas and Stuart, which was one of the main entry points for illegal liquor on the east coast of the United States during Prohibition. In 1923, he robbed the Stuart Bank again. But in 1924, the Sheriff of Palm Beach County ordered an ambush set for him on the Sebastian Bridge about an hour and a half north of the St. Lucie River.

The legend of the King of the Everglades came to an end in a hail of gunfire on that dark night. It is disputed to this day whether he and his men were handcuffed and shot in cold blood or resisted arrest.

Alto "Bud" Adams, Jr., sitting on a cow pen fence on the Adams Ranch c. 1937. Bud was eleven years old in 1937 when his father, Alto Adams, Sr., purchased 15,000 acres of unfenced grassland northeast of Lake Okeechobee between the Kissimmee River and Fort Pierce. He fenced the land to keep out the Cracker scrub cows and stocked it with a higher-quality breeding herd. Ten years later, Bud became a full partner in the cattle operation known as Alto Adams & Son. With 1,600 head of cattle valued at $40 a head, Bud began instituting the innovative pasture management and breeding programs that make him a legend in the industry. Seeking to develop cattle that thrive in Florida's hot and wet climate while producing the highest quality meat, he bred Herford bulls with Brahman cows. The resultant Braford breed is recognized worldwide. Bud has never stopped innovating. Today, the Adams Ranch comprises 50,000 acres in three counties and uses modern techniques such as DNA testing to determine which cattle to breed for more and better beef. Photo credit: www.adamsranch.com

Billy and the Old Cowboy

The characters of the old cowboy and his father, blue-eyed Billy, were both inspired in part by renowned Florida Rancher, Alto "Bud" Adams, Jr.

After John Ashley was shot to death, his family members were so sure he had been gunned down in cold blood that they immediately hired Adams' father, Alto Adams, Sr., as their attorney to pursue a coroner's inquest. Their efforts to have the killing declared a murder failed in the face of staunch resistance by local authorities. Adams, Sr., later went on to serve as Chief Justice of the Florida Supreme Court.

In 1937, Adams, Sr., established the Adams Ranch on 15,000 acres of prairie land northeast of Lake Okeechobee. Two years later, after being appointed to the Florida Supreme Court, he sold his cattle, but not his land, to Irlo Bronson, one of the most prominent cattlemen on the Kissimmee Prairie. Adams' teenage son, Bud, went to work for the Bronson operation and began mastering the skills that make him the legendary cattleman he is today.

Bud served in the Navy during World War II, but returned to ranching as soon as he could. In 1947, when he was 21, a Philadelphia businessman purchased the 20,000-acre Allapattah Ranch, a portion of which lay within the Alpatiokee Swamp west of Stuart, for $22 an acre. Bud was given the job of informing the local cow hunters whose open-range cattle still roamed that wilderness that he'd be fencing the property.

The cowmen were unsaddling their horses when he approached their cow camp at the end of the day. Realizing that closing the open range would change their lives forever, Bud expected trouble. But when he explained the situation, they agreed not to cut the new fence, not out of deference to the property owner or the law, but because they knew and respected him. Bud told them he was "most appreciative." They kept their word, and the fence stood. Thus ended the historical open-range, cow-hunting era east of the big lake.

After the fences were in place, Bud drove 300 high-quality cattle out the Martin Grade to graze on the rich grasses of the Allapattah. It was his first time in charge of a cattle drive, and he didn't lose a single cow. By 1948, Bud was running the entire Adams Ranch.

Named "Ranch of the Century" by the National Cattlemen's Beef Association in 1999, the Adams Ranch is still managed by Bud with the help of two new generations of Adams cowboys. It is the fifteenth-largest cow-calf ranch in America and is world renowned for the quality of its beef and dedication to environmental stewardship.

Alto Adams, Sr., using bull whip to control cattle in cow pens on the Adams Ranch c. 1937. Photo credit: www.adamsranch.com

"Cowboy at an open range roundup," c. 1910. Florida's cattle industry was begun by cow hunters who rounded up open-range scrub cows and drove them to market. By 1910 when this photo was taken, however, many Florida ranchers had started fencing their properties because they were breeding a higher quality of beef cattle and wanted to keep their blood lines pure. Fences also helped control disease and pests such as ticks that were carried by untended livestock. The fences reduced the range of both the scrub cows and the Seminoles who had also wandered the wilderness at will until this time. The land between Lake Okeechobee and the Atlantic Ocean, however, remained open range until 1948. Every winter, the Florida Cracker Trail Association honors Florida's historic cattlemen by hosting the Florida Cracker Trail ride. Horseback riders gather in Bradenton near Florida's west coast and head east across the Kissimmee Prairie, ending up six days and one hundred twenty miles later in Fort Pierce on the Indian River. Photo Credit: State Archives of Florida, Florida Memory, http://floridamemory.com/items/show/153003

"Florida State Normal and Industrial School class of 1904 - Tallahassee, Florida." Although there were few state-supported schools for them in frontier Florida, African Americans eagerly sought and achieved higher education. This image of a class that graduated the year before the Florida State Normal and Industrial School for Colored Youth became an official institution of higher learning demonstrates how educated young African-American ladies and gentlemen were expected to comport themselves. [Shown: Robert William Butler, John Adams Cromartie, Arthur Rudolph Grant, Walter Carolus Smith (front row at left), Rufus Jason Hawkins, Walter Theodore Young, Rosa Belle Lee, Marguerite Guinervere Wilkins [Smith] (3rd from left, top row), Sara Grace Moore, Winifred Leone Perry, Margaret Adelle Yellowhair (2nd from right, front row).] Photo Credit: State Archives of Florida, Florida Memory, http://floridamemory.com/items/show/26289

Queenie's Mother

Mary McLeod Bethune was one inspiration for the portrayal of Queenie's mother as a female college graduate in the early 1900's dedicated to improving the lot of individual African Americans through education. In 1904, Bethune, the child of former slaves, founded the Literary and Industrial Training School for Negro Girls in Daytona, Florida, with one dollar and fifty cents in her pocket and five young students. She later explained, "I believe that the greatest hope for the development of my race lies in training our women thoroughly and practically."

Although it had been illegal to educate African Americans in many states before the Civil War ended in 1865, schools operated by a variety of church groups began springing up as soon as the war was over. Bethune began her education in a one-room schoolhouse run by the Presbyterian Board of Missions of Freedmen in South Carolina. In 1894, she graduated from Scotia Seminary in North Carolina, the mission of which was to prepare the daughters of former slaves for careers as social workers and teachers.

In 1899, when Bethune moved to Palatka, Florida, to run a Presbyterian mission school, higher education was not the norm in Florida for Whites, and public education opportunities for African Americans were non-existent in many places and lagged far behind in others. By 1923 when Bethune merged her school with the Cookman Institute for Men from Jacksonville, it boasted hundreds of students and offered a curriculum equal to that of the white high schools.

That is not to say there were no public education opportunities for African Americans in Florida in the early 1900's. Starting in 1887, those who were able to complete high school were eligible to attend the State Normal College for Colored Students in Tallahassee. It became an official institution of higher learning in 1905 and was later renamed Florida

Agricultural and Mechanical University. There were eleven graduates in its class of 1904, six of whom were men and five of whom were women.

The inspiration for Queenie's mother being a graduate of Morgan College in Baltimore, Maryland, came from Zora Neale Hurston. In 1917, the twenty-six-year-old Hurston wanted to go to college, but she had never graduated from high school. Claiming to be ten years younger, she enrolled in Morgan Academy, the high school division of Morgan College and graduated the next year.

Morgan College was a college for African Americans that had been founded in 1867 as the Centenary Biblical Institute by the Baltimore Conference of the Methodist Episcopal Church. In 1890, it been renamed Morgan College, and it awarded its first baccalaureate degree in 1895. It is now known as Morgan State University.

Mary McLeod Bethune and students, c. 1905. Photo credit: State Archives of Florida, Florida Memory, http://floridamemory.com/items/show/149519

"Live Manatee," c. 19--. Manatees are aquatic mammals that have a lifespan of about 60 years. They have no known natural enemies except for man, for whom the slow moving, gentle herbivores were easy prey and a good source of food on the frontier. Once widespread, their numbers had been so decimated by the eighteenth century that the English declared Florida a manatee sanctuary and made manatee hunting illegal. Under Spanish and later United States governance in the nineteenth century, however, their numbers continued to decrease. In 1893, manatees first received protection under Florida law, and in 1907 this law was revised to impose a fine and/or jail time for molesting or killing them. As this photo demonstrates, however, enforcement was not uniformly strict, and manatees remain threatened. This picture was the inspiration for the chapter titled "War Cries." Photo Credit: The Thurlow/Ruhnke Collection.

"Dr. Cyrus R. Teed stands beside a tarpon," c. 19--. This photo captures the attire and attitude of tourists who came to Florida to fish for Tarpon and other trophy fish. Fortunately, tarpon are hardy and are not endangered. However, commercial fishing is not allowed and sport fishing for them is regulated to encourage fishermen to release them alive. Only two may be possessed at a time and a fifty-dollar tag must be purchased to kill and keep one. The taking of Stuart's more popular fishing trophy, sailfish, is governed by state law within three miles of the Atlantic Coast and by federal law between three and nine miles out. There is a per-person limit, a length limit, and a fee that must be paid. But now most sail fishermen catch and release the fish and document their success in other ways. *Photo Credit: State Archives of Florida, Florida Memory, http://floridamemory.com/items/show/9018*

Zack

The character of Zack was inspired by Stuart residents, Curt Whiticar and Hugh Willoughby.

Coming from a family of boat builders and commercial fishermen, Whiticar's visionary boat designs and promotion of the first catch-and-release programs for sailfish helped transform Stuart from a sleepy little stop on Flagler's Florida East Coast Railway into "The Sailfish Capital of the World."

Whiticar built his first boat when he was fourteen. By the time he was twenty-three, he was designing boats that met the specialized needs of fishermen and the challenges presented by the Indian River and the changeable St. Lucie Inlet. Whiticar Boat Works continues to build and service some of the best fishing boats and yachts in the world to this day.

Hugh Willoughby, an aviation pioneer, adventurer, inventor, photographer, race car driver, and naturalist, had an estate on Sewall's Point, the long, narrow peninsula that separates the St. Lucie and Indian Rivers. Having worked with the Wright Brothers, Willoughby designed and built his own airplanes near Stuart. In January 1914, he took the first aerial photographs of Stuart from one of his own planes. A replica of one of his planes is exhibited in the Elliott Museum.

In the late 1800s, Willoughby was one of the earliest, if not the first, white man to cross the Everglades. His detailed report of that adventure, *Across the Everglades*, published in 1898, remains one of the premier sources of information about the "River of Grass" before the state started draining it. He also published a Seminole-English dictionary.

Willoughby Creek, which bears his name, enters the St. Lucie River between Stuart and Port Salerno. Whiticar Boat Works is located along its shore.

"Seminole woman with two hogs in downtown Stuart," c. 19--. It was not uncommon to see Seminoles on the streets of early Stuart. They routinely came to trade and conducted a thriving hog business. The logo of Stuart Heritage, Inc., a not-for-profit organization dedicated to preserving local history, is based on this photograph. Photo Credit: The Thurlow/Ruhnke Collection.

Anna

The character of Anna was inspired by one of the most popular symbols of the City of Stuart, a photograph of a Seminole woman walking two small hogs on a leash in downtown Stuart in the early 1900s. According to one newspaper article, her name may actually have been Anna.

"Seminole woman and child in canoe," c. 191-. The wide areas of the Indian and St. Lucie Rivers were too shallow close to shore for the larger boats utilized by the white settlers. To accommodate them, the settlers built docks that jutted out to deeper water. Photo Credit: State Archives of Florida, Florida Memory, http://floridamemory.com/items/show/141632

Just Fishing," c. "19--. This photo was the inspiration for the character of Little Sally. It and the photo of Dr. Teed also demonstrate the construction of fishing camps and the stands used to display a prized catch.   Photo Credit: The Florida Center for Instructional Technology, University of South Florida, Florida Trails, http://fcit.usf.edu/florida/docs/f/ft13.htm

Lucy

The character of Lucy was inspired by a story told at a Stuart Heritage meeting about the speaker's aunt. In the early 1900's, when she was about eight years old, she started seining for mullet in the St. Lucie River. She sold the mullet to an alligator farm for twenty-five cents a day. Her goal was to save up her quarters and buy an airplane, which she did. She was one of the first women to earn a pilot's license in Florida.

"Stuart Train Station," c. 191-. The Florida East Coast Railway replaced the existing Stuart station with this one in 1913. It used an almost identical design when it constructed the first station in Okeechobee City, which welcomed its first train in January 1915. The Thurlow Collection (Lawton Geiger).

"Longhorn cattle with extremely long horns," c. 19--. Florida scrub cattle were the descendants of Andalusian cattle brought to Florida in 1521 by Ponce de Leon and released to assure a food source for future Spanish settlers. By the mid 1800's after more than three hundred years of adaptation, they were a self-sustaining, hardy breed, but they did not produce the best beef for modern tastes and economical mass production. As the frontier was settled and fenced off, their numbers diminished. In the Twentieth Century, as real estate enterprises spread across the remaining undeveloped lands they still inhabited, scrub cattle intruded into residential areas, wreaking havoc on golf courses and well-groomed lawns. Considered a nuisance, like the hogs the Spanish also introduced, which have overrun much of the southern United States, most of Florida's scrub cows were rounded up by Florida's few remaining cow hunters and hauled away. Both the cattle and the men who hunted them almost disappeared. Photo Credit: State Archives of Florida, Florida Memory, http://floridamemory.com/items/show/26847

Florida Crackers

Nobody knows for sure how Florida Crackers got their name. Two things are certain, however. The term applies to descendents of white pioneers who came to the Florida frontier in the Nineteenth and early Twentieth Centuries, and Florida Crackers take pride in it today. The theory as to its source they tend to support is that the nickname refers to the loud cracking sounds made by the bull whips of Florida cow hunters when they were herding cattle.

The characters of Queenie and Billy were both inspired in part by Iris Wall, a strong independent woman who grew up hunting cows near Indiantown, a small community about half way between Lake Okeechobee and the Atlantic Ocean. A Florida Cracker and proud of it, Wall runs the 1,200-acre High Horse Ranch outside Indiantown. In 2006, she was named Florida's "Woman of the Year in Agriculture."

One of her passions is preserving the best of "old Florida." She serves on the board of the Florida Cracker Cattle Association and the Florida Cracker Horse Association, and is dedicated to conserving these rare old breeds as living links to Florida's history. Wall keeps a herd of Cracker cattle on her ranch and still rides a Cracker horse.

A member of the Florida Cracker Hall of Fame and the Florida Cracker Trail Association, stories about Wall's youth in the Florida jungle have been retold in *Cracker Tales* by Iris Wall, and more recently in the children's book *Iris Wall, Cracker Cowgirl* by Carol Rey and Eldon Lux, published by Pelican Press in 2012.

Seminole Indian Cowboys

"Seminole Cowboys," c. 19--. Although this photo was taken after the Seminoles acquired the Brighton Reservation in the late 1930's, it gives a sense of the vast open cattle lands north of Lake Okeechobee and west of the Kissimmee River. Photo Credit: Thomas A. Markham, www.Tommymarkham.com.

African-American Cow Hunters

The story Queenie tells about the African-American cattleman on the Kissimmee Prairie who invited her family to stay with him so that her mother could educate his children was inspired by a rancher named Tom Silas. In 1942, *The Saturday Evening Post* published an article by Zora Neale Hurston profiling his son, an African-American Cracker Cowboy named Lawrence Silas. Hurston reported that Lawrence owned thousands of acres on the Kissimmee Prairie, more than fifty miles of fence, and thousands of cattle at the time.

Born in 1891, Lawrence was a second-generation Florida cow hunter. His father, Tom, was a former slave who moved from Georgia to the Kissimmee Prairie soon after the end of the Civil War. Tom Silas got his start cow hunting by working for a white rancher named Readding Parker, who allowed him to take some of his pay in cows. From that beginning, he built a 2,000-acre ranch on which he ran thousands of head of cattle. When he died in 1909, leaving thirteen children and no will, however, his ranch was split up.

Although Tom Silas never learned to read, he acquired tutors for his children and sent five of his oldest boys to study at Booker T. Washington's Tuskegee Normal School in Alabama. He even brought a teacher to start an African-American school in what is now Osceola County.

Lawrence Silas learned cattle ranching from his father and told Hurston that cow hunters live like kings out on the prairie. He built his own cattle kingdom after the loss of his father's. Throughout his life, Silas maintained good relationships with white cattle ranchers on the Kissimmee Prairie, such as Irlo Bronson on whose ranch Disney World now sits. There are roads in the City of Kissimmee named after both Silas and Bronson.

"Stuart's Business District," c. 1910. According to Ernest E. Lyons in *The Last Cracker Barrel*, early Stuart looked like a western mining town. By 1912, the center of downtown was moving east on Flagler Avenue which ran along the railroad tracks with the construction of more modern buildings made of locally produced cement blocks. Photo Credit: Thurlow Collection (Robert Gladwin).

The City of Stuart

When the City of Stuart was first incorporated on May 7, 1914, the community was growing rapidly and had high hopes for the future. By 1917, it was still a very small town, but its expectations were buoyed by plans for a bridge across the St. Lucie River, notably the last missing link in the Montreal to Miami Highway. At that time, it boasted the following businesses and organizations:

"1 bank, 2 cafes, 5 drays, 5 hotels, 4 lodges, 2 doctors, 1 theatre, 1 bakery, 2 lawyers, 2 dentists, 2 garages, No saloons, 2 churches, 1 saw mill, 1 newsstand, 3 boat shops, 1 shoe shop, 3 land offices, 2 fish houses, 1 brass band, 2 drug stores, 3 mails daily, 1 ice factory, 3 newspapers, 3 paint shops, 1 lumber yard, 1 public school, 2 barber shops, 1 planing mill, 1 camera shop, 1 hand laundry, 1 woman's club, 1 public library, 2 meat markets, 1 sanitary dairy, 2 pressing clubs, 1 millinery shop, 1 furniture store, 5 grocery stores, 2 baseball teams, 1 hardware store, 2 plumbing shops, 1 blacksmith shop, 1 Chinese laundry, 3 dry goods stores, 1 photographic studio, 4 real estate agencies, 2 watch repairing shops, 1 Boy Scouts' organization, 1 dress-making establishment and 1 girls' Camp-Fire organization."[2]

---

[2] *The Stuart Messenger*, 1917, as reprinted in "Historical Vignettes" by Alice L. and Greg E. Luckhardt in www.TCPalm.com's *Your News* on February 13, 2013.

Historic Ferry over St. Lucie River, Stuart, F
connecting Palm Beach and St. Lucie Countie

"Historic Ferry over St. Lucie River," c. 191-. By 1914, the automobile had begun revolutionizing tourism in the United States, having already led to the creation of automobile clubs that demanded a system of interstate highways. One of the most exotic and popular with auto tourists was the Montreal to Miami Highway, which ran along Florida's east coast and eventually became US Highway #1 in Florida. The ferry over the St. Lucie River is historic, because it was the last ferry on the Montreal to Miami Highway. The part of the highway between Ft. Pierce and West Palm Beach had been the bane of auto travelers not only because of the wait for the ferry, but also because the highway leading to and away from Stuart was a poorly maintained frontier road more suitable for ox carts than automobiles. All that changed when the last bridge on the Montreal to Miami Highway, the bridge across the St. Lucie River, was finally constructed in 1918, followed by the creation of Martin County in 1925. Photo Credit: Thurlow Collection (Bp Walton).

Stuart continued to grow during the Florida real-estate boom that escalated following the end of World War I. In 1925 when Martin County was created out of portions of Palm Beach and St. Lucie Counties, Stuart was reincorporated and became Martin County's provisional county seat.

The other challenger for county seat was the newly-platted community of Indiantown, which was located in western Martin County near the site of a historic Seminole settlement the Whites had labeled Indian Town on their maps.

By 1925, a navigable waterway from the Gulf of Mexico to the Atlantic Ocean had been created by dredging canals that connected Lake Okeechobee to the Caloosahatchee and St. Lucie Rivers. The Seaboard Air Line Railway had also laid tracks east of the lake to connect Tampa and West Palm Beach.

In keeping with standard railroad land-development practices that helped drive the real-estate boom, the president of Seaboard, S. Davies Warfield, planned and promoted the new city of Indiantown at the intersection of the railroad tracks and the canal. He envisioned it as a modern metropolis that would become the center of rail and water commerce in Florida.

The question of which community would be Martin County's first county seat fell to the Florida Legislature. Warfield pushed hard for Indiantown. The story goes that he had the advantage because a lot of members of the legislature were on his payroll.

But the people of Stuart were charming and enterprising and had a secret weapon. It was the Prohibition era and Stuart was one of the bootlegging capitals of the entire east coast of the United States. It won the hearts and votes of the legislators by supplying them with smuggled liquor and sending flowers to their wives.

"Workers harvesting pineapples in the Indian River region," 19--. Beginning about 1879, Pineapples were one of the first commercial cash crops grown in the Indian River Region. At first they were shipped by schooner to Baltimore. Once the Florida East Coast Railroad reached the region in 1894, they were shipped by rail. By 1895, the Jensen area along the Indian River was known as the "Pineapple Capital of the World." However, after the FEC rail line reached Key West in 1912, it entered into an agreement to import pineapples from Cuba and began charging Florida pineapple growers a premium price to carry their products. That, followed by pests and the scarcity of fertilizer during World War I, effectively ended the commercial pineapple industry along the Indian River. Photo Credit: State Archives of Florida, Florida Memory, http://floridamemory.com/items/show/99

But Warfield's grand dream for Indiantown began to die like so many others when a massive hurricane hit Miami in 1926. By the time it hit, some of the later boom projects, such as Picture City which was being promoted near Hobe Sound by the Olympic Holding Company, were already having trouble due to changes in the nationwide economy. Nonetheless, that Miami hurricane is generally touted as the beginning of the end for the Florida real-estate boom.

Then Warfield died suddenly in 1927, and the railway withdrew its support for the Indiantown project. That was followed by the hurricane that devastated the Lake Okeechobee area in 1928, which dealt the Florida real-estate boom and Davies' dreams for Indiantown a final knockout blow. Its beautifully designed streets and neighborhoods lay largely empty.

By the time the end came, however, the community of Stuart, which had laid its foundation before the railroad got there, was firmly established. It survived the Great Depression of the 1930's and has served as county seat through thick and thin to this day.

Stuart is still a small town by Florida standards, though. Initially that was due to circumstances beyond its residents' control, but more recently, it's because Stuart's residents prefer it that way.

"Gilbert's Bar House of Refuge - Stuart, Florida," c. 192-. In 1876, the U.S. Life-Saving Service constructed ten houses of refuge along the east coast of Florida. These houses were staffed by "keepers," and their families who provided food and shelter for shipwrecked sailors. The Gilbert's Bar House of Refuge is the last of the ten remaining. After the United States Coast Guard was created in January 1915, it assumed operation of the House and added the second story windows in this photo in 1918. In 1942, when German U-Boats torpedoed freighters along this part of Florida's coast, a lookout tower and additional buildings were constructed on the property. Decommissioned after the war, the house sat empty until it was taken over in the mid 1950's by Martin County to be operated by the newly-formed Martin County Historical Society. From 1963 to 1987, it served as a refuge for sea turtles under the guidance of Ross Witham and the Florida Department of Natural Resources. Since then, it has been a museum that is open to the public. Also the oldest building in Martin County, the House of Refuge is listed on the National Register of Historic Places. Photo Credit: State Archives of Florida, Florida Memory, http://floridamemory.com/items/show/31647

"A couple stands next to the wreck near Hutchinson Island's Gilbert's Bar House of Refuge - Stuart, Florida," 189-.   Shipwrecks along the Florida coast were not uncommon during frontier days, and the maritime laws governing salvage turned them into financial opportunities as well as objects of curiosity. The rocks on which this couple are standing are one of the most distinctive and dramatic features of Florida's Atlantic shore. Photo Credit: State Archives of Florida, Florida Memory, http://floridamemory.com/items/show/31646

"Seminole village in Sabal palmetto hammock," c. 1922. A Seminole camp consisted of open-sided palmetto thatch chickees centered around a cooking chickee and fire. The logs in the fire radiated out from the center in a star pattern. As they burned, they were pushed toward the middle to continue fueling the fire. During the Seminole wars, when the Seminoles were being hunted by United States Army and would have to abandon their camps in a hurry to avoid a battle, they used the fire logs as a code to tell other members of their family or clan which direction they had gone. Photo Credit: Photographer - John Kunkel Small, 1869-1938. State Archives of Florida, Florida Memory, http://floridamemory.com/items/show/49996

The Seminole Camp near Stuart

The description of the Seminole camp in this story was derived from first-hand accounts of Seminole camps and life on the frontier. Seminoles regularly camped outside of town when they came to the Stuart area to trade with the white settlers who began arriving in the 1880's.

Reverend Henry Harjo was a Muscogee-speaking member of the Creek tribe who had been born on a reservation in Oklahoma. He had homesteaded land in Oklahoma and had the good fortune to discover oil on it. Around 1901, he started coming to the Lake Okeechobee area as a Baptist Missionary. His goal was to establish schools and jobs for the Seminoles and to convert them to Christianity.

By 1914, he had chosen Stuart as his home base in Florida. He purchased twenty-five acres on Poppleton Creek, about a mile south of the Stuart railroad station in 1916. That was one place the Seminoles had camped when they came to town. In 1925, Harjo's land was surveyed and given the name it has today, Indian Grove.

"Three generations of Seminole Indians," c. 1912. The Seminoles have a tightly-knit, matrilineal descent system, according to which the husband belongs to his wife's clan. A daughter is a member of her mother's clan for life, and a son is a member of his mother's clan until he marries. As a result, children born to non-Seminole women were born outside of Seminole society and were members of no clan. Another result is that females in a clan tend to be close blood relatives. Photo Credit: State Archives of Florida, Florida Memory,
http://floridamemory.com/items/show/4308

The Seminole Tribe of Florida

The Seminoles were among the first Floridians to recognize the economic power of the tourism industry. One of the ways they found to survive in early Twentieth-Century Florida was by selling Seminole crafts, such as the unique patchwork clothing for which they are famous, to tourists.

In March of 1916, the Seminoles also became the main attraction in an annual weeklong festival sponsored by the West Palm Beach Chamber of Commerce called the Sun Dance. Led in part by Billy Bowlegs III, a Muscogee-speaking Seminole who lived north of Lake Okeechobee and who later also became a member of the Kissimmee Chamber of Commerce, up to two hundred Seminoles imported a complete Seminole village into downtown West Palm Beach.

Everything in town came to a halt for the festival, as locals and tourists dressed in Indian costumes and danced in the middle of Clematis Avenue. Another attraction at the Sun Dance was the combined Ringling Brothers and Barnum and Bailey Circus.

Even before 1916, the Seminoles had realized that they needed to acquire their own land to survive as a culture and a people. With the support of Whites such as James Mallory Willson of Kissimmee and his wife, Minnie Moore-Willson, whose flawed but effective book *The Seminoles of Florida* (1896) brought their plight to the public eye, the Seminoles lobbied state and federal politicians and tried to raise enough money to establish a reservation.

"Seminole man and boy in dugout canoe," c. 191-. Because roads on the frontier were few and unreliable, water was the most efficient mode of transportation. Long before white settlers arrived, the Seminoles had mastered the art of building dugout canoes from giant bald cypress trees. They were perfect for the swamp environment. The long, thin shape allowed them to carry people and goods through narrow waterways, while the natural buoyancy of the wood and the flat design made it possible to navigate in the shallows using a pole that doubled as a paddle. Photo Credit: State Archives of Florida, Florida Memory, http://floridamemory.com/items/show/27333

Two thousand acres in what is now western Martin County was proposed as a home for the Muscogee-speaking Seminoles. But the Seminoles couldn't agree that it was the best land for them, and it was sold to white settlers before they could raise the money to buy it. Over the next several years, other proposed land acquisitions similarly fell through. Many of the Seminoles who had lived in Indian Town east of Lake Okeechobee were forced to move to a reservation in Davie near Ft. Lauderdale.

The Seminoles finally established a much larger reservation near Lake Okeechobee's northwestern shore in the late 1930s. There, they slowly grew a herd of cattle by combining traditional cow-hunting skills, which had been passed down by word-of-mouth since before white Americans took over the industry, with modern techniques learned working with and for white cowmen.

The cattle industry helped sustain both their people and their culture. In 1957, the United States Government recognized the Muscogee-speaking Seminoles as the Seminole Tribe of Florida, giving them the sovereign right to govern their own lives they enjoy today.

"Captured alligator," 1882. During the late 1800's and early 1900's, the Lake Okeechobee region, which arguably had more exotic flora and fauna per square mile than any other place in North America, was a prime destination for adventurers and sportsmen. Numerous journals and magazine articles popularized the area by recounting the tourists' adventures. Almost every article described at least one confrontation with alligators. They were everywhere and presented a continuous danger and source of excitement to visitors and new residents. Before long, however, hunters harvesting their hides and teeth, which were used to make jewelry, decimated the population to the point where Alligators were placed on the list of endangered species. Now that it is illegal to kill them, they've made a comeback and once again are a source of danger and excitement to those who encroach on their territory. Photo Credit: State Archives of Florida, Florida Memory, http://floridamemory.com/items/show/31258

The Alpatiokee Swamp

When Spain ceded the Florida Peninsula to the United States in 1819, the federal government took title to all vacant land in the new Territory. It transferred the "submerged" lands to the State of Florida when it was created in 1845 with the intent that they would be drained and developed.

Those holdings included the swamps, rivers, and sloughs that moved water from the vast Kissimmee River basin in central Florida down the peninsula, through Lake Okeechobee to the Everglades and the Florida Straits. Although those lands constituted Florida's largest asset, they had very little value so long as they were under water.

The new state desperately needed two things: better transportation and more settlers. At the time, creating a system of canals to make travel easier and drain the submerged lands appeared to be the long-term solution to both problems.

Politicians, land speculators, and community builders immediately laid plans to dredge them. From the beginning, those plans included a canal through the Alpatiokee Swamp that lay between Lake Okeechobee and the high sand ridge that runs along Florida's east coast.

Most of the development plans for central and southern Florida were put on hold, however, until after the period of "Reconstruction" that followed the Civil War. As a result, the State of Florida was still largely undeveloped and almost bankrupt by 1881. Hamilton Disston, a Pennsylvania industrialist turned real-estate developer, provided the cash it needed to survive the financial crisis by purchasing four million acres of mostly submerged lands for twenty-five cents an acre. Disston immediately began dredging the long-awaited canals. He started by connecting a series of lakes in central Florida to the Kissimmee River.

Disston failed to complete the entire plan. However, the state eventually took it over, and by 1912, settlers, business people, and tourists could travel by steamboat from Kissimmee in central Florida, down to Lake Okeechobee, and across it to canals that connected to Fort Lauderdale on the Atlantic Ocean and Fort Meyers on the Gulf of Mexico. Settlement of Florida's internal frontier was finally possible.

It wasn't until 1928, about a hundred years after it was first proposed, that a navigable canal linking Lake Okeechobee to the Atlantic Ocean through the South Fork of the St. Lucie River was completed. Yet, due to the area's unique topography, that canal did not drain the Alpatiokee. Although it cut off the water's route to the south, the Alpatiokee's wetlands still stood four-feet deep during the rainy season.

In the mid-Twentieth Century, following a series of devastating floods, the state and the Army Corps of Engineers developed a plan to provide drainage for the prairie north and east of Lake Okeechobee. That plan added a canal through the northern part of the Alpatiokee. When its plug was removed in 1961, water cascaded out of the swamp, through the wide St. Lucie River to the Atlantic Ocean for days. The Alpatiokee finally succumbed to man's designs.

In 2002, state and local agencies purchased the 20,000-acre Allapattah Ranch in northwestern Martin County, Florida, between Lake Okeechobee and the St. Lucie River, much of which had been part of the Alpatiokee Swamp. The South Florida Water Management District is using the land to cleanse water flowing into the St. Lucie River as part of Everglades restoration.

Today the ranch is open to the public as the Allapattah Flats Wildlife Conservation Area, which is managed by the Florida Fish and Wildlife Conservation Commission. Hardy souls can still get a taste of Florida's early environment and history on its hiking and equestrian trails, primitive campsites, and hunting areas.

"Florida Panther - The state animal of Florida," 188-. In Seminole lore, the Florida Panther was the Creator's choice to enter the world first because it combined beauty, power, and patience. A favorite subject of journals and magazine articles in the late 1800's, by the end of the Twentieth Century the Florida Panther was almost extinct with as few as thirty big cats living in the wild. According to the United States Fish and Wildlife Service, federal protection, habitat preservation, and a breeding program that introduced female cougars from other parts of the United States had grown the population to between one hundred and a hundred and sixty panthers by 2011. Photo Credit: State Archives of Florida, Florida Memory, http://floridamemory.com/items/show/18767

Tantie's First Store
1905

Lewis M. Raulerson's Store
Est. 1905

"Lewis M. Raulerson's Store in Tantie," C. 19--. Lewis Raulerson opened his store in Tantie near Taylor Creek in 1905. After the Florida East Coast Railway reached Okeechobee City in January 1915, he moved it to a new location in the city. Photo Credit: Thomas A Markham, www.tommymarkham.com

Tantie / Okeechobee City

The first white settlers in the wilderness near Taylor Creek on the north shore of Lake Okeechobee arrived in the late 1800's. They were mostly male adventurers—cattlemen, hunters, trappers, and fishermen who lived off the land, sleeping in tents or palmetto thatch huts.

The area originally went by the name "The Bend," and one of the first families to call it home were the Peter Raulersons, who moved there from Fort Bassinger, about forty miles to the north. The first building Raulerson constructed was a barn-like structure, in which his family resided until they could build a log cabin. By 1889, the growing settlement claimed to have six young children in residence—enough to qualify for a school.

Newcomers started arriving in larger numbers during the 1890's after Hamilton Disston dredged the Kissimmee and Caloosahatchee Rivers. That opened Lake Okeechobee up to steamboat traffic from Kissimmee in the north and Fort Myers on the Gulf of Mexico.

In 1902, residents decided they needed their own post office. They named it Tantie in honor of Tantie Huckaby, a well-educated woman from South Carolina who was the third teacher at the school.

By 1905, Tantie was finally big enough to support a store, and Peter Raulerson's son Lewis opened one. The store, like most of Tantie, was located near Taylor Creek because there were no real roads. Goods were more easily transported to and from the area by boat.

When Captain T.A. Bass helped start the first commercial catfish industry on Lake Okeechobee in 1906, fishing camps began springing up along the lake's shore. In the beginning, the catfish were shipped across the lake and down the Caloosahatchee River to Fort Myers for transport to the north.

"Fishing on Lake Okeechobee," c. 1915. Even after the Florida East Coast Railway reached Okeechobee City, making it the catfish shipping center of the lake, fishing was still labor intensive, hard work. Photo Credit: Thomas A Markham, www.tommymarkham.com

In 1910, the Florida East Coast Railroad changed everything by announcing plans to build a spur line down the east side of the Kissimmee Prairie to connect Lake Okeechobee's north shore to Florida's east coast. The railroad's land company had acquired land near Taylor Creek and immediately began planning a new modern metropolis called Okeechobee City on it. The surveyors and workmen who came to lay out the city were the beginning of a boom that started slowly but lasted fifteen years.

When the canal connecting Ft. Lauderdale to the south shore of the lake opened in 1912, Ft. Lauderdale became the main distribution center for Okeechobee catfish to the north, a title it held until the railroad reached Okeechobee City in 1915. By then, the railroad's new city even had a hotel. It was incorporated by the Florida Legislature later that same year.

With the arrival of the railroad, Okeechobee City became the dominant player in the lucrative Lake Okeechobee fishing industry. Businesses like Raulerson's Store that used to depend on the waterways for transportation moved onto newly-platted city lots laid out by the railroad. Fish houses and an ice house took their places on Taylor Creek, and a cypress company began logging the old first growth cypress forests that had they had been unable to log before due to lack of transportation.

Two years later, the county of Okeechobee was created, and Okeechobee City became its county seat.

Meanwhile, the cattle industry thrived on the Kissimmee Prairie north of the lake. Both fishermen and cowboys had the weekend off, and both groups tended to congregate in the little settlement along Taylor Creek where they could find, goods, whiskey, and girls.

Cowboys would come to Okeechobee on Saturday Night, drink whisky and fight with the fishermen. They would fight all night in Flagler Park across from Okeechobee Hardware.

"Okeechobee Cow hunters," c. 191-. Tantie and Okeechobee City were both wild and wooly frontier towns. Cow Hunters and fishermen tended not to get along, and it wasn't a good thing that they both had Saturday off. When both were in town, someone was usually drinking, and fights were common. Photo Credit: Thomas A Markham, www.tommymarkham.com

Both groups were comprised of bold adventuresome men who chose a hard life on the frontier over the civilized city life available on the coasts and in the north. And, for some reason they did not get along. The mix of testosterone and whiskey often led to weekend fights which became legendary in the growing town.

By the mid-1920's, S. Davies Warfield's Seaboard Air Line Railway had constructed tracks from Tampa to West Palm Beach through Okeechobee. But, it was W. J. (Fingey) Conner, a paving contractor and tycoon from Buffalo, New York, who brought Okeechobee City fully into the Twentieth Century.

In 1924, he built Florida's first toll road, Connor's Highway, to connect Okeechobee to West Palm Beach. Then Connor also constructed a bridge across the Kissimmee River making it possible for automobiles to take his highway across the state from Tampa to West Palm Beach. Every automobile that did had to pass through the toll booth in Okeechobee City.

In a short ten-year span, Tantie had changed from a tiny, isolated frontier community with no modern amenities into a bustling commercial center that boasted thousands of residents and all of the newest conveniences, including a movie theater and a Ford dealership. Connor had bought up land along his highway and made Okeechobee City the focal point of a nationwide land promotion campaign. Billed as the Chicago of the South, it seemed destined to become the preeminent city in central Florida.

Then the bubble burst. The bottom fell out of the real-estate market and then the stock market. Both Connor and Warfield, the tycoons with a vested interest in the region, had died by the end of 1929, but their legacy lives on in the carefully planned community with parks and boulevards on Taylor Creek just three miles north of the big lake's shore.

Capt. Bass Boat Success Operating out of Okeechobee, Fl 1915 At Mouth of Taylor Creek

"Capt. Bass boat Success," c. 1915. Before the Florida East Coast Railway reached Okeechobee City, the best way to travel was on the water. Boats such as the Success carried passengers and freight, but they had to be small to navigate the creeks and dredged rivers and canals that connected Lake Okeechobee to places like Kissimmee, Ft. Lauderdale, and Florida's west coast. Photo Credit: Thomas A Markham, www.tommymarkham.com

"Ehrhart & Raulerson Sawmill, Tantie, Fl.," c. 1915. Almost every new settlement on the frontier had its own sawmills to provide lumber for local houses and businesses. When the Florida East Coast Railway reached Okeechobee City in 1915, however, a cypress company started logging the first growth cypress trees that had escaped large-scale commercial logging up till that point. The logs were not processed in this sawmill. Instead, they were loaded on the train and carried north to the cypress company's mill for processing. Photo Credit: Thomas A Markham, www.tommymarkham.com

"Ol' FEC #6 Coming Into Opal Curve
Okeechobee Co., Florida. C. 1915"

"Ol' FEC #6 coming into Opal Curve," 1915. The first trains to Okeechobee and Stuart were steam locomotives. By 1915, the Florida East Coast Railway operated several locomotives of the same design as Number 6 seen in this photo. Each had its number displayed on its nose. Those that served Okeechobee traveled through an encroaching wilderness. Okeechobee City was the end of the line. On the early schedules, the train arrived there one day and left the next. Having no continuing schedule to meet down the line, gave the engineer discretion to vary his arrival time, and the train would often stop along the way to Okeechobee to let passengers hunt or conduct other activities. As a result, the arrival times in Okeechobee were not entirely reliable. Photo Credit: Thomas A Markham, www.tommymarkham.com

The Rosewood Massacre

Queenie's father's quest to find a place where African Americans could live free and safe from interference by Whites was inspired by the Rosewood Massacre. Rosewood was an independent African-American community northwest of Gainesville, Florida, that had been established in 1845. In January 1923, Rosewood was wiped off the face of the earth when members of the Ku Klux Klan burned it to the ground, killing a number of its more than 300 residents, none of whom ever returned to their homes.

The men, women, and children of Rosewood fled into the surrounding woods and swamps. Train conductors from Cedar Key heroically stopped to pick up women and children who had escaped and carried them to safety in Gainesville. They didn't pick up men, however, because it was too dangerous.

The Rosewood massacre was part of the escalating racial violence that spread across the nation following the reorganization of the Ku Klux Klan in 1915 and the return of African-American soldiers from fighting in World War I with a new sense of freedom and a need to compete for jobs during harsh economic times.

Prior to the massacre, on election day in November, 1920, Whites had rioted in Ocoee, a small mixed-race community near Orlando and about ten miles from Eatonville, when African-American men insisted they had the right to vote. One black man was lynched, and several others died when Whites burned the colored section of town.

The Ocoee riot overshadowed the historical significance of that election as the first time women of any color were allowed to vote in the United States.

"Florida East Coast Railway steam engine #30 - Fort Pierce, Florida," c. 19---. The terrain followed by the Florida East Coast Railway between Fort Pierce and Stuart was much different from the terrain down the Kissimmee Plain to Okeechobee. Initially boats and trains were both powered by steam engines fired by wood harvested along the waterways and tracks. They were noisy and belched black smoke from their stacks. Over time, however, wood got scarce, and both trains and boats shifted to internal combustion engines.   Photo Credit: State Archives of Florida, Florida Memory, http://floridamemory.com/items/show/31148

1914, the Last Innocent Year

The end of 1914 marked the end of innocence on Florida's last frontier. As soon as the Florida East Coast Railway line reached Okeechobee City in January 1915, there was new money to be made harvesting catfish and logging cypress, but also subdividing and selling the land. Newcomers flooded in to claim their pieces of all those pies. No longer isolated, the frontier was also no longer insulated from the troubles that plagued the rest of the world.

World War I had already begun in Europe. The United States was not involved, but in February 1915, Germany imposed a barricade around Great Britain. When that led to the sinking of the Lusitania with the loss of one hundred thirty-eight American lives a few months later, America was on its way to battle.

That same year, filmmaker D. W. Griffith set back the nation's chances of racial harmony by releasing a movie titled "The Clansman" (now known as "The Birth of a Nation"). Its heroes were white men who formed the first Ku Klux Klan after the end of the Civil War to defend white culture and virtue. Its villains were northerners and African Americans portrayed by white actors in black-face as stupid and aggressive.

The Klan had died off by 1900, but "The Clansman" helped resurrect it. The second Ku Klux Klan, which formed in Georgia in 1915 with additional new anti-immigrant, anti-Catholic, anti-Semitic, and prohibitionist agendas, used the film to recruit new members to its cause.

But, even with the challenges faced by the rest of the world, the boom on Florida's last frontier seemed here to stay. It survived the war, the deadly Spanish flu epidemic American soldiers brought home in 1918, and the increased racial tensions created when major companies started importing lower-paid African-American laborers to work in the fields and to build railroad tracks and highways.

Then Mother Nature intervened. In 1926, a hurricane destroyed much of Miami. Two years later, a second hurricane killed thousands of the newcomers who had moved onto the recently drained swamps around Lake Okeechobee. The burst of the Florida real-estate bubble was followed by the Stock Market Crash of 1929 and the Great Depression of the 1930's. Without the railroads and land speculators promoting them, the newly-established modern cities of Okeechobee and Indiantown languished, while Stuart muddled through.

Left to fend for themselves, many newcomers went back to where they came from. Those who stayed became the next generation of old timers. Many of them survived the Depression the same way the old timers before them had survived, by making do with what the land provided: fish from the lakes and rivers, vegetables and fruit from the fields and groves, and cattle from the prairies.

The boom never came back for a lot of different reasons. That's likely why the land between the big lake and the river where Coacoochee said his last farewell hasn't changed as much as you might expect in almost a hundred years.

Some folks think that's a good thing.

"Man trying to find the bottom of a wet spot," c. 1912. At the beginning of the Twentieth Century, roads on the Florida frontier were little more than game trails that had been widened first by foot traffic and later by ox carts and other wagons. Over time, they were grubbed and stumped (cleared), like the road in this picture, making them wider and smoother. However, most of them still followed the natural grade of the land through sand and swamp, making it crucial to check the depth of water before driving into it. Photo Credit: State Archives of Florida, Florida Memory, http://floridamemory.com/items/show/3942

Live your dreams. Follow the River.

4/2014

4/2014

CPSIA information can be obtained at www.ICGtesting.com
Printed in the USA
LVOW12s1311300314

379537LV00002B/779/P